Praise for

JILL SORENSON

"Sorenson makes her characters realistic, flawed,
and appealing. Deftly handled violent action and red
herrings rush this thriller to a believable ending."
—*Publishers Weekly* on *The Edge of Night*

"Taut with emotion, suspense and danger.
Sorenson expertly weaves the two stories
into a heart-wrenching conclusion."
—*RT Book Reviews* on *The Edge of Night*

"One of the best books of the year…
nonstop, heart-pounding excitement."
—*RT Book Reviews* on *Stranded with Her Ex*,
Top Pick! 4.5 stars

"(A) high tension romantic thriller...culminating
in a page-turning climax. Despite the mystery,
the real tension comes from the emotional relationships,
full of explosive sex and terrible secrets."
—*Publishers Weekly* on *Crash into Me*

"It was definitely hot. Sooo hot. Jill Sorenson
is my new favorite romantic-suspense author!"
—*USA TODAY* bestselling author Victoria Dahl
on *Crash into Me*

**Also available from Jill Sorenson
and Harlequin HQN**

FREEFALL
AFTERSHOCK

JILL SORENSON

BADLANDS

HARLEQUIN® HQN™

Recycling programs
for this product may
not exist in your area.

ISBN-13: 978-0-373-77834-8

BADLANDS

Copyright © 2014 by Jill Sorenson

HARLEQUIN®
™ www.Harlequin.com

Printed in U.S.A.

BADLANDS

CHAPTER ONE

PENNY STILL HAD NIGHTMARES about the earthquake. Whenever she felt trapped, she thought of that horrible stretch of days. Eight months pregnant, buried under a massive pile of concrete, no fresh air or sunlight. She'd never take freedom for granted again.

"Almost done," the makeup artist said, aware that Penny was growing restless. "Purse your lips."

Penny made a dutiful moue, hoping the color wouldn't draw more attention to her mouth. She already had full lips and a wide smile. When she wore bright lipstick, it was like a neon sign on her face.

The chaos in the makeup room, along with her inability to move, increased her anxiety. Her mother was getting her hair styled in a chair nearby. Her sister, Raven, had shown up late. She was standing by the door, text-messaging her boyfriend on her iPhone. She seemed annoyed that she had to wait until Penny was finished.

Her youngest sister, Leslie, was trying to distract Cruz with a book. He didn't want to sit still in this cramped environment any more than Penny did. She hoped he wouldn't cause a scene during one of the speeches. In less than an hour, she'd introduce her mother in front of a huge audience at the San Diego Convention Center.

Millions would be watching from home.

"Done. You look beautiful."

"Thanks," she said, barely glancing at her reflection. She got up from the chair just as Cruz wiggled free from Leslie's embrace and grabbed a mascara wand. "Not so fast," she said, prying it from his little fingers.

"Mommy! I want to paint."

"Let's go for a walk," she said, putting the contraband out of reach. She shrugged out of the styling cape and grasped Cruz's hand. As she led him toward the exit, she smoothed the front of her jungle-print dress. It was green-swirled chiffon with a gathered waist and a halter top. The daring style wasn't typical for political conventions, but that was kind of the point. She'd been recruited to entice a younger, less rigid crop of voters.

Owen Jackson was standing by the door. He'd been a member of her father's security team for about six months. Now that Jorge Sandoval had Secret Service protection, Owen had been relegated to guarding Penny and her five-year-old son, Cruz.

Owen skimmed her body with the barest hint of interest before he moved on to Cruz. "What's up, little man?"

"It's boring here."

Owen's brows rose. "This place? It's a circus."

Cruz studied a trio of men in suits passing by, as if

searching for elephants. The convention center's main floor had an arched canvas ceiling that resembled a dozen circus tents, or maybe the sails of a thousand ships. It was full of interesting architectural shapes and bustling with people. Penny might have given him a tour if she wasn't worried about being recognized and accosted by reporters.

"Is there any space he can play?" she asked.

"Right this way," Owen said, leading them down the hall. He touched the communication device at his collar, relaying the details of their location change.

Tonight her father would be awarded the official nomination at the Republican National Convention. No Hispanic-American had ever won this honor. It was the most important evening of his life. His performance would have a direct effect on the outcome of the November election. The entire nation was watching.

Penny felt like throwing up.

She'd promised to attend for her father's sake, but she didn't care for the public scrutiny. Her status as an unwed mother hadn't gone unnoticed by her father's conservative base. He was known for "family values." Over the past few weeks, speculation about Cruz's parentage had run rampant. Religious groups had criticized her for having loose morals. Pro-life activists claimed her son was the product of rape.

Troubled by the rumors, Penny had agreed to a single on-air interview. She hadn't named and shamed Tyler, her son's father, but she'd been candid in her other responses. She'd even confessed that her parents had ordered her to leave their home when she was pregnant. Then she'd told the extraordinary story of Cruz's birth—days after the San Diego earthquake.

The public reaction to the interview had been overwhelmingly positive. Young people found her relatable. Everyone loved survivor stories. When her father had stood by her, expressing regret over his actions during her pregnancy, his approval ratings with women had soared.

It was just the boost he needed.

Although Penny hadn't wanted to get involved in the campaign, she felt obligated to make one last appearance on his behalf. It was the least she could do after he'd given her his unconditional support.

She followed Owen to a small outdoor terrace that offered a spectacular view of the San Diego Bay. It was closed in, with walls on both sides and a Plexiglas barrier in lieu of a guardrail. At sunset, the surface of the ocean rippled with golden highlights. Cruz's eyes lit up when he saw the fountain in the middle of the terrace. Water bubbled from the top of a stone pillar, cascading down its smooth facade.

"Let me take off your jacket," she said.

He endured the three-second delay with impatience, his little body leaning toward the fountain. As soon as he broke loose, he raced to the fountain's edge. She watched him play for a moment, her arms crossed over her chest. He gathered leaves from a nearby plant to make an armada of floating ships, sinking them with pebble bombs.

Focusing on Cruz helped her regain a sense of calm. He meant everything to her. Strangers said they looked alike, but his tawny-brown hair came straight from Tyler. It was thick and tended to curl at the ends, brushing the collar of his shirt. Sometimes, when his hair was freshly washed, she hugged him close and buried her face in it. Her love for him was boundless, almost frightening in its intensity.

She'd die without him.

Taking a deep breath, she moved her gaze to Owen. He was a tall, unobtrusive statue beside her. Away from the crowds, he didn't need to be on high alert. His manner wasn't exactly relaxed, but he seemed... present. As if he wouldn't choose to be anywhere else.

His appearance never varied: smooth-shaven jaw, close-cropped blond hair, inexpensive black suit. She knew from experience that there were hidden depths to his pale blue eyes, dark secrets lurking beneath his ill-fitted jacket and white button-down shirt. The faint scars on his neck and hand, remnants from laser-removed tattoos, told a very different tale than his clean-cut image implied.

Cruz thought Owen was some kind of secret superhero. She'd told him that Owen had rescued them during the earthquake, and helped track down criminals in Sierra National Park. Her son had started making up elaborate stories of Owen's other assorted feats.

She wondered if Owen was aware of the latest

rumors. A tabloid reporter had linked them romantically, suggesting he was Cruz's father. Which was impossible, because he'd been incarcerated at the time of Cruz's conception.

"My sister wants to pitch a family reality show to the cable networks," she said. "*Keeping up with the Kardashians* meets *The West Wing*."

He arched a brow. "Sounds like your dad's worst nightmare."

"Mine, too."

"The White House would never allow that kind of filming."

"Do you think he'll win?"

"Yes," he said after a pause.

The polls were even, but her father was gaining ground. He had momentum. If he continued to perform well, he could be the nation's first Hispanic president. The thought made her heart swell with pride.

"Would you move to Washington, D.C.?" he asked.

"No. Cruz is starting kindergarten next week, and I don't want to leave Palos Verdes."

Owen nodded, scanning the space between Cruz and the door again. Owen was often too engaged in his duties to carry on a real conversation. At this secure location, she didn't think that was a problem. Since accepting the role of bodyguard, he'd put up a wall between them. He was polite and distant, as if they had no personal history. As if he'd never kissed her, or assisted her in childbirth, or been her unlikely confidant.

Their interactions had become stilted.

Maybe he wasn't interested in furthering their relationship. If he was, he wouldn't have been so eager to work for her father. He had a college degree and firefighter training. Instead of applying to the LAFD, as planned, he'd settled for this.

She'd settled, too. Over the past five years, she'd been a dutiful daughter, grateful to her parents for welcoming her and Cruz back home. They'd taken care of her financial needs and spoiled Cruz rotten. Between getting her degree and being a single mother, she'd been too busy to disappoint them.

They'd never approve of her dating someone like Owen.

She fell into a contemplative silence as the sun set over the bay. It felt odd to be back in San Diego with Owen again. Before the earthquake, Penny had lived here for several months with her aunt, who had died in the freeway collapse. The convention center was less than five miles from the interchange, which marked the epicenter. Most of the damage had been repaired years ago. The city showed no signs of its former devastation.

Owen fashioned a paper plane out of a discarded advertisement for the convention and handed it to Cruz. Instead of launching it off the balcony, Cruz ran around in circles, lifting the jet high overhead.

"The clinic offered me a part-time position," she

said. "I'm going to be their new community health educator."

He looked impressed. "Congratulations."

She thanked him with a nod. Although she'd done a lot of volunteer work during her final semester of college, this would be her first paid job. She was freshly graduated, ready to make a difference.

"They're asking for you backstage," he said, touching the microphone at his ear.

Her stomach exploded with butterflies. She had the terrifying premonition that she'd trip over her dress, hyperventilate at the podium, or faint from an attack of nerves. "I can't do this," she said in a rush.

"You'll be great."

"Do I look like a clown?"

He examined her face, smiling. "No."

"You look good, Mama," Cruz said, gazing up at her. "As pretty as the ladies on Telemundo."

Owen laughed at this compliment. Perhaps he was familiar with the scantily clad female performers on the popular Spanish-language channel. When he saw her worried expression, he sobered, letting security know they were on the way.

An event organizer escorted the three of them through a maze of passageways until they reached the backstage area. Penny found her mark and stood there, taking deep breaths. She would enter on one side while her mother waited on the other. She didn't dare peek around the curtain to gaze at the crowd.

Cruz was supposed to sit with Leslie and Raven

in the family balcony. When her grandmother came to retrieve him, he hid behind Penny's skirt and refused to let go.

"You can't walk out on stage with me," she told Cruz.

"I'll stay behind the curtain with *Abuelita*."

Penny's grandmother agreed to this suggestion; she rarely said no to Cruz. He stomped toward her, purposefully noisy in his shiny new shoes. She held his hand and let him wander around backstage.

Penny was too nervous to argue. She hoped he wouldn't cause a scene during the introduction. Cruz didn't throw temper tantrums as often as he used to, but he had a lot of energy and got into his share of mischief.

"He'll be fine," Owen said.

She practiced her lines, heart racing.

"Can I get you anything?"

For some reason, his polite offer bothered her. She didn't want a bodyguard or a servant. She wanted a friend. A man. "Do I really look okay?"

"You've never looked better."

"The dress isn't…too much?"

His eyes traveled down the bodice and back up. "Not quite enough, I'd say."

The words held no judgment, only mild admiration. He was making a joke to put her at ease, not giving her his sincere opinion.

"I feel like a fraud," she whispered. "Or a whore."

This sparked an honest reaction in him: anger. "Why?"

"They're using me for sex appeal. Selling my image, my...tasteful cleavage."

He said nothing, unable to deny the truth.

"Do you think it works?"

"Yes."

"Are votes so cheaply had?"

"Some are."

"What about yours?"

His lips quirked into a smile. "I'd vote for you, if you were running."

She assumed he supported the opposition, but she didn't ask. He respected her father too much to admit it. Which was kind of ironic, considering the circumstances. It was no coincidence that her father had offered Owen a job as soon as he'd come to L.A. Jorge Sandoval expected his daughters to marry wealthy Latinos. He'd hired Owen to keep him under his thumb—and off-limits to Penny.

She was annoyed with her father for manipulating Owen, and with Owen for letting him. Most of all, she was frustrated with herself. She'd always felt stifled by her family's strict religious beliefs. If not for Cruz, she'd have left home long ago. She'd traded stability for independence, suppressing her own desires.

"People say I don't know who Cruz's father is."

"Fuck them," he said succinctly.

Her worst critics were members of the Freedom Party, an ultra-conservative group her father had courted and abandoned after winning the primaries. Now that he needed to focus on gaining ground with undecided voters, he could no longer afford to be affiliated with extremists. In recent weeks, his social media accounts had been inundated with suggestive comments about Penny, ethnic slurs and anonymous threats.

Maybe she'd spoken her mind during the interview in an attempt to break free from her family chains. But the move had backfired. Here she was, at another campaign event against her will. She didn't want to be put on display, or to help her father win. What she longed for was right in front of her. She wished she had the nerve to tell Owen how she felt. To shed her inhibitions and offer herself to him.

"What if they boo me?" she asked.

"They won't."

Penny pressed a palm to her stomach. If she choked, the media would have a field day. If she tripped and fell, the video clip would go viral.

"Try to picture the audience naked," he said. "I've heard it helps."

She started with him, her eyes trailing down his body. Years ago, she'd seen him bare-chested. He was lean and strong, built more like a runner than a weight lifter. She knew he'd had some of his tattoos removed. She remembered one on his shoulder, a three-leaf clover. It wasn't quite as offensive as the rest.

"Kiss me," she said, meeting his gaze. "For luck."

He stared at her in disbelief. She crossed her fingers and waited, pulse racing. When he realized she was serious, he glanced around to see who was watching. Her grandmother and Cruz were nearby, their backs turned. Her mother studied her cue cards on the other end of the stage, more than a hundred feet away.

She didn't know if he did it because she asked, or because he wanted to. But he stepped forward and lifted his hand to her face, indulging her request. His fingertips skimmed the side of her neck as he leaned in. She held her breath, longing for a tongue-tangling kiss. At the last second, he moved to the left, brushing his lips over her cheek.

Chaste. Respectful. Distant.

But when he retreated, she saw the heat in his eyes. The want.

After they broke apart, her grandmother approached with Cruz. "Leslie can't find Raven. I have to go look for her."

"Cruz can hang out with me," Owen said.

Penny didn't challenge the arrangement. Babysitting wasn't part of Owen's job, but neither was kissing, and she'd only be onstage for thirty seconds. While her grandmother went to search for Raven, Owen chatted with Cruz, avoiding Penny's gaze. His expression showed no indication that they'd just shared an intimate moment.

Penny focused on the heavy curtains, her anxiety spiking. An innocent peck on the cheek was the most action she'd had in the past five years. She could still feel his mouth on her skin, his thumb against her throat.

When the production assistant gave her the go signal, she glanced at Owen and Cruz. They both smiled at her encouragingly.

Taking the plunge, she walked out on stage. The crowd stretched into infinity, red signs waving, a blur of excited faces. She continued toward her mark, terrified. *Don't trip. Don't forget your lines. Smile.*

She reached the podium without incident. Gripping its comforting wood edges, she stared at the blinking red light on the center camera, aware that her image was being broadcast on a huge screen behind her.

Smile.

Her heart threatened to burst out of her chest. There were no boos or rude remarks. Someone in the far corner whistled, causing a ripple of laughter in the audience. Then her tension eased, and she stopped worrying about flubbing her lines.

She didn't value the opinion of the bigots in the Freedom Party, a vocal right-wing minority. Let them criticize her wardrobe, her figure or her conduct. The only thing that mattered was getting through the introduction and moving on with her life.

Channeling confidence, she leaned forward to start her introduction. Before she'd uttered a single word, an alarm sounded, splitting the air with high-pitched wails. She stepped away from the microphone, flinching at the loud noise.

The stadium erupted into chaos.

CHAPTER TWO

OWEN HAD NEVER WANTED to be Penny's bodyguard.

It wasn't that he didn't care about her. He'd give his life for her or Cruz in a heartbeat. He had self-defense training, rescue experience and an EMT certificate. After three years in prison, he'd learned how to read tensions in a crowd and anticipate violence. Even his entry-level position at Sierra National Park had been more dangerous than he'd anticipated.

But private security wasn't his field of interest, and he was a poor candidate for Penny, in particular. He'd had a crush on her for years. It was extremely difficult for him to focus on the surroundings instead of her. He found himself following her every move, studying her body language and facial expressions... imagining them together.

In protective services, getting emotionally involved with a client was a bad idea. Engaging in sexual fantasies about her was downright stupid.

She often tried to draw him into conversations with her, which didn't help. He was already distracted by her beauty. He liked her voice, her animated gestures, her smile. Her personality was irresistible.

And that *kiss*. Jesus.

He could get fired for touching her. There were cameras all over the place. If Sandoval heard Owen was sniffing around his daughter, he'd cut him loose without the recommendation Owen desperately needed.

Owen had developed a few coping strategies for keeping his cool around Penny. He avoided eye contact. He memorized her clothing details at a glance. When he had to look at her, he concentrated on her attire, not the body underneath. He treated her like an assignment, blanking his mind of their previous interactions.

It didn't always work, obviously. He was slipping.

After Penny walked across the stage, Cruz tugged at Owen's hand, pointing to a dark corner he wanted to explore. Owen might be biased, because he'd helped bring Cruz into this world, but the kid struck him as ridiculously cute. He had Penny's honey-colored complexion and big brown eyes.

Owen pressed a finger to his lips and shook his head. He couldn't let the boy wander off. There was a fleet of security personnel at this event, so he didn't have to monitor the audience, but he had to stay alert.

A second later, an alarm sounded, indicating an emergency that required immediate evacuation.

Penny.

He tightened his grip on Cruz's hand and strode toward the podium to retrieve her. She was already on her way backstage. As soon as she saw Cruz, she bent down and picked him up, her face tense.

The voice in Owen's ear told him what to do: find the closest exit. He was familiar with the layout of the building. A production assistant waved a group of people forward. Owen placed his hand on Penny's shoulder as they skirted around stage and lighting equipment. He looked for Penny's mother but didn't see her.

The alarm continued to go off in loud, intermittent blares. He couldn't hear any more instructions from his boss. Pressing the button on the microphone at his collar, he checked in. "Moving toward the exit," he said, reciting their code names and basic location.

They spilled out the door into a pavilion on the side of the main building. Audience members were emerging from multiple exits. Most of them headed west, to the area behind the convention center. It offered access to the harbor, parking lot and adjoining hotels. The production assistant went the same direction with the rest of the employees.

Owen didn't follow. Penny would get recognized in the crowd, and his team was prepared for this kind of situation. They had a driver waiting in the loading area in front of the building, ready to whisk them to safety.

"To your left," he said, squeezing her upper arm. It was early evening, just before dark, with good visibility. There were some random people milling around, along with a couple of photographers in casual clothes.

Owen hated the paparazzi even more than he hated

those Freedom Party rejects who criticized Penny for having a baby out of wedlock. At the last political event she'd attended, some jerk had thrown a water balloon at her, soaking her blouse to near transparency. Of course the cameras had flashed before Owen could remove his jacket to cover her. The photos had been posted everywhere online.

He'd heard that one of the sleazy gossip magazines had offered to pay top dollar for a "crotch shot."

Over his dead body.

Owen understood the public fascination with Penny. Her father was running for president. She'd grown up in the lap of luxury, made relatable mistakes and survived one of the worst natural disasters in U.S. history. She expressed herself sincerely. It didn't hurt that she had a movie-star face and a figure like a Victoria's Secret model. With her long legs, dark hair and radiant smile, she was stunning. The media loved her.

He spoke into his microphone once again to communicate their whereabouts, directing Penny toward the Cadillac at the curb. Secret Service had their own vehicles, so this one was used exclusively by Penny and her sisters. As they approached the car, Owen sensed a presence closing in on them. It was probably one of the photographers, hoping to get an angle up Penny's skirt as she climbed into the backseat. He opened the back door, urging Penny and Cruz inside. Their driver, Keshawn Jones, was at the wheel.

Before Owen could glance over his shoulder to assess the threat, he noticed a rush of movement by the driver's side. A masked man jabbed his fist through the open window, striking Jones in the neck.

The next few seconds passed in a blur. Owen reached for his mic just as he was tackled from behind. His fingers never found the talk button. A sharp pain hit his midsection, radiating through his torso like a bolt of lightning. Not a gunshot wound or a knife laceration. Electroshock. He was incapacitated before he even collapsed.

The man with the taser shoved him into the vehicle and climbed inside. Owen quaked like an epileptic. He couldn't fight back or even resist. His body shook uncontrollably, and his thoughts scattered.

He was vaguely aware of Cruz's muffled screams as Penny tried to quiet him. Everything else was pain. Pain in his torso, where the device had struck him. Pain in his muscles, which had seized up. His face contorted into a grimace, and his chest tightened. The pain went on and on, never ending.

Darkness edged in. Soon he'd be unconscious. Dead.

Owen didn't realize the man with the weapon was still stunning him until he stopped, taking the device away from his side. The door slammed shut, and the vehicle accelerated. Owen slumped over, his cheek mashed against the leather seats. The worst of the pain receded, but the twitching continued.

"You didn't have to tase him that long," someone said from the front seat. "You almost killed him."

Even in his fractured state, Owen recognized the voice.

It was Shane. His older brother, who'd just been released from prison. Shane must have pushed the driver aside and taken over.

"He's still alive," his attacker said. Then kicked Owen in the ribs for good measure.

Owen hardly felt the added insult, though he struggled to fill his lungs with oxygen. Cruz wailed in dismay, asking about Owen and sobbing his name repeatedly.

"Mommy, Mommy, what's wrong with Owen?"

"Shut that kid up."

Owen lifted his head to speak to Penny. His vision was blurry, his mouth slack. When he tried to speak, a string of saliva dribbled from his lips. "M'okay," he mumbled, forming the words for Cruz's sake. "I'm okay."

Penny looked horrified. Maybe he should have saved his breath.

The man put away the taser and cuffed Owen's hands behind his back. He couldn't move, couldn't think. His muscles felt like jelly. He wiped his chin against the fabric of his jacket. Lethargy drowned out most of his embarrassment.

"He's okay," Penny murmured to Cruz, rocking him in her lap. "He's hurt, but he's going to be okay."

"Where are we going?"

"To the hospital," she said immediately. "Owen needs a doctor."

She knew what was happening. Of course she knew. She wasn't dumb. Even he knew, and his brain was fried.

"What happened to him?" Cruz asked.

"He had a seizure."

"A seizer?"

"Seizure," she corrected. "Shaking you can't control. This man is helping Owen so he doesn't hurt himself again. Isn't that right, Mr....?"

"Dirk."

"Mr. Dirk."

It was a bullshit name, but it was a bullshit story. Owen should have been more careful approaching the vehicle. In his haste to get Penny and Cruz away from the paparazzi, he'd delivered them directly to...

The kidnappers.

He couldn't believe Shane was involved in this. He couldn't believe Shane was *here*. His brother had been living at a halfway house in Northern California. It went without saying that this violated the terms of his parole.

"The kid wasn't supposed to be with her," Shane said.

"What do you want to do with him?"

Penny tightened her arms around Cruz protectively.

"I can't drop him off on the street corner," Shane replied.

"Maybe he'll double our take," Dirk said.

Owen rested his forehead on the edge of the seat

and tried to recover his wits. His stomach churned with nausea as he sorted through the fuzzy details. Penny was the target of this crime, not Cruz. The disappearance of two Sandoval family members would be noticed and investigated at once.

Despite the mix-up with Cruz, this kidnapping appeared to be an organized effort. The fire alarm must have been rigged. They'd known Penny had been about to take the stage. They'd known she had a single bodyguard—him—and not an entourage. They'd been following her. Waiting for an opportunity to strike.

The ease with which they'd executed the plan appalled him. With lucidity came regret. He'd failed to protect Penny and Cruz. Failed on every level. He'd been tricked, overpowered and stunned into submission.

Cruz had a booster seat, but Penny didn't put him in it. Her arms were wrapped tight around him, her jaw clenched with determination. If anyone tried to take him from her, she'd claw their eyes out.

As the car went around a sharp corner, Owen slid towards Dirk. He wasn't trying to challenge him in any way, but he couldn't prevent his body from listing that direction. He had no control, no anchor.

Dirk gripped the back of Owen's shirt and slammed him facedown on the seat. Straddling his thighs, he ripped off Owen's communication device, which was hanging from his collar, and tossed it out the window. Then he checked him for weapons.

Owen gritted his teeth against the feel of another man's hands on him, diving into his pockets and thrusting between his legs. He didn't like incidental contact. Getting groped while he was restrained and vulnerable sent him over the edge.

He'd been held down before. Cheek smashed against the cold tile, wrists trapped in a cruel grip. He didn't want to travel to that dark place again. It was locked inside his memory, never to be revisited.

Dirk dispensed with Owen's jacket and relieved him of his cell phone, pepper spray and tactical baton. He also found Owen's money clip and confiscated it. "This rent-a-cop doesn't even have a gun."

"I told you he wouldn't," Shane said.

"What kind of bodyguard doesn't pack heat?"

Plenty of them. Some security experts used weapons, others didn't. Owen was trained in self-defense and close combat. His top priority was escorting members of the Sandoval family to safety, not getting into shoot-outs with assailants. He was also a convicted felon, so he couldn't own a gun. Being armed wouldn't have made a difference in this situation, anyway. He'd been incapacitated before he'd had a chance to react.

With a derisive grunt, Dirk continued the search, running his hands along Owen's thighs and circling his calves. He finished the pat-down, but the violation wasn't over. Dirk pinned Owen to the seat with his body weight, taking an aggressive rear-mount position. He slanted his forearm across the back of

Owen's neck, putting his mouth close to his ear. "I heard you were a little bitch in prison."

Owen clenched his jaw, not responding to the dig. It was a common insult for ex-cons; Dirk had no idea what he'd done inside. He was just trying to make Owen mad. Owen refused to give him the satisfaction. Dirk's opinion meant nothing to him.

Penny was another story. Owen didn't want her to see him like this. When he glanced at her, she was watching them. She'd cradled Cruz's head to her chest to prevent him from witnessing the disturbing scene. Her eyes glittered with unshed tears.

He closed his, feeling like a loser.

Fifteen minutes ago, she'd begged him to kiss her. For luck, she'd said, gazing up at him. He'd been floored by the request, but he'd also understood what prompted it. She'd needed an escape, a brief distraction. He'd fantasized about kissing her—*really* kissing her—a thousand times. The temptation to plunder her mouth was hard to resist. But he'd acted the gentleman, not mussing her pretty, painted lips.

In that fleeting moment, he'd fooled himself into believing he was good enough for her. In this one, he felt absolutely worthless.

"Quit fucking around," Shane said to Dirk. "I don't want to get pulled over."

Dirk climbed off Owen and returned to his seat, adjusting a black handkerchief around his neck to cover his face. His baseball cap and casual clothes made him resemble a member of the paparazzi, but his powerful build suggested otherwise. Owen pegged him as a recent parolee.

When Owen was capable of moving, he dragged himself upright and settled into the space beside Penny and Cruz. He couldn't help them escape, but he could put his body between them and danger.

They were on the freeway. Shane sat behind the wheel, wearing a motorcycle face mask. Keshawn Jones was handcuffed in the passenger seat. He appeared to be suffering from the effects of electro-shock, too.

Cruz twisted around in his mother's lap, studying him with solemn brown eyes. "Are you better now, Owen?"

"Much better."

"Why do you need those han'cuffs?"

"I don't have control of my arms yet. I might hit someone." He glanced at Dirk, his fists clenched behind his back.

"Can I hug you?"

Owen was touched by the request. "Sure," he said, clearing his throat.

Cruz let go of Penny and put his small arms around Owen's neck. He was a chatty kid, always full of questions and bouncing with energy. Penny encouraged him to be nice and mind his manners, but she also let him run wild when he needed to. She didn't try to smother his natural rambunctiousness or dole out harsh punishments. Owen respected Penny for raising Cruz with a gentle hand. It was clear the boy had never been mistreated in any way.

Cruz was so unlike how Owen had been at this age. Affectionate and expressive, quick to cry or laugh. Unselfconscious, unafraid. The way a child should be. Owen's gaze met Penny's over the top of the boy's head. He saw some of the same qualities in her.

The fact that Cruz cared so much about Owen, an employee, was deeply humbling. His little-boy empathy damn near broke Owen's heart. He'd be devastated if Cruz got hurt on his watch. And he wanted to tear Shane apart, limb by limb, for playing a role in this fiasco.

Owen couldn't go back in time to reverse the abuse he'd endured, or to erase the wrongs he'd done. He might not be able to heal his damaged soul or overcome his past. But if he could protect another child from harm, it would be a step toward salvation. If he could keep Penny safe, he could live with himself.

The alternative was impossible to fathom.

Cruz kissed his cheek before returning to Penny. The simple gesture caused pressure to build behind Owen's eyes. He took a deep breath, blinking the tears away. Shane noticed this exchange and issued a silent warning in the rearview mirror.

Owen understood the danger he was in. He had no value to the kidnappers. Sandoval wouldn't pay for his safe return. He was a liability. If he tried to defend Penny or Cruz, they'd probably kill him.

He wondered what Shane planned to do with him. They hadn't seen each other in eight years. Shane talked to their mother on a regular basis, and she sent him monthly care packages, but he hadn't stayed in communication with anyone else from the outside world. That included his own son, Jamie.

Owen studied the interior of the Cadillac, his heart pounding. It had master locks, so Penny couldn't open her door. The fire alarm had caused enough chaos to mask the kidnapping, but the security cameras in front of the convention center would show footage of the crime. There was a tracking device inside the car.

Shane pulled off the freeway, glancing in the rear-view mirror. He seemed confident that they weren't being followed. They continued to an industrial area, where he parked in a deserted lot next to a black SUV.

"Is this the hospital?" Cruz asked.

"No," Penny said.

"Where are we?"

"Shh."

Shane got out and opened her door. In addition to the half mask covering the lower part of his face, he wore a black handkerchief like a headband. His blond hair was shaggy. He was still lean, but he looked taller, and he'd put on weight. Those powerful shoulders were straight from the exercise yard.

He gestured toward the SUV, mock-chivalrous. "Your chariot awaits."

Penny turned to Owen for approval. He nodded for her to go ahead. She exited the car with Cruz and glanced around the empty parking lot. If they'd been followed, the police would have intervened already. But no shouts to halt rang out across the dark night. No officers swarmed the area, and no helicopter hovered overhead.

"Hurry up, princess," Shane said. "We don't have all night."

Penny couldn't run away in high heels with Cruz in tow; she got in the SUV. Dirk dragged Owen out of the Cadillac and shoved him into the backseat with her, climbing in after. She scooted over and put Cruz on her lap to make room. As discreetly as possible, she tried to lift the door handle on the opposite side of the vehicle.

It didn't budge.

Shane left Keshawn Jones handcuffed in the Cadillac and got behind the wheel of the SUV. Starting the engine, he drove out from the parking lot and headed east, away from downtown San Diego.

It was an uncomfortable ride. There wasn't enough room in the backseat. Owen was smashed against Penny's side. Cruz asked about the hospital again, but he sounded sleepy. She sang him Spanish lullabies in a soft voice, rocking him until he drifted off.

At some point, her son would wake up and realize they weren't going to the hospital. He'd wonder what was happening and get upset. Owen wasn't looking forward to the moment when reality struck.

He sat motionless and silent, his body thrumming with tension.

About twenty minutes later, Shane stopped by the side of the road. "Give me his phone," he said, reaching into the backseat.

Dirk located Owen's cell phone and passed it forward.

"Did you turn the tracking off?"

"Yes."

"You're going to talk to Sandoval," Shane said to Owen. "Tell him we want two million in a large duffel bag, unmarked. He has to bring it alone, no cops. We'll call back tomorrow with more instructions."

Owen couldn't refuse. He didn't have a choice.

Shane found Sandoval's number in Owen's list of contacts and pressed the button. Then he handed the phone back to Dirk, who held it close enough for Owen to speak into.

Jorge Sandoval answered with his own demand: "Where are you?"

Shane shook his head. *No details.*

"I'm with Penny and Cruz," Owen said.

"Put her on."

Shane nodded, allowing it. Dirk turned the phone toward Penny. "Daddy," she said in a tremulous voice. *"Estamos bien."*

It meant "we're okay," but Shane didn't know that. He made a sharp gesture across his throat. Dirk moved the phone back to Owen, who repeated their requests. Her father gave an immediate agreement, as calm and diplomatic as ever. Dirk ended the call.

Shane pointed a menacing finger at Penny. "You speak English or I'll cut your pretty little tongue out."

Owen's muscles went taut. He wanted to fly across the seat and attack his brother with his teeth, to smash his forehead against Shane's until they were both unconscious. But such an attempt would only result in him getting tased or beaten, and Penny would be no better off. So he curbed his fury and stayed still.

"Do you understand?"

"Yes," her mouth said. Her eyes said *fuck you*.

"What did she say?" Shane asked Owen.

"She said 'we're okay.'"

Shane turned around and started the engine again, muttering something about Mexicans. He continued to head east, toward the desert.

Owen noted the road signs and guessed their destination: The Badlands. It was a vast expanse of nothingness near Salton City, where they'd grown up. There were no witnesses and a thousand places to hide. Sandoval's security team would have a hard time finding them out here in the tumbleweeds. Cell phone service was spotty, rescue was unlikely, and an organized search effort would be difficult.

Owen's spirits sank lower with every mile. People who disappeared in the deep desert never came back. Shane had chosen this desolate place for a reason.

He hooked a right on the S-22, a winding highway between the Salton Sea and the U.S.–Mexico border. Dozens of sandy dirt roads led south, toward rocky hills, agave groves and mud caves. It wasn't the kind of terrain you wanted to get lost in. On an average August day, the heat was unbearable.

They traveled far from the main road, past the last vestiges of civilization, beyond the dirt roads. Few backcountry hikers would brave the late summer temperatures in the sun-ravaged badlands. Human traffickers and drug smugglers were active at night, but seldom seen. Even the border patrol didn't have the resources to cover this entire area. Its harsh conditions were deterrent enough for most criminals.

Owen couldn't count on Shane to spare him just because they were brothers. If he didn't create an opportunity to escape, he was going to end up in an unmarked grave out in the middle of nowhere.

CHAPTER THREE

PENNY HAD NEVER been more terrified.

Not even when she'd been under a freeway in the throes of labor without medical help. Her memories from the San Diego earthquake had faded with time, blending into a blur of unpleasant thoughts and images. She still smelled it, sometimes. The stench of gasoline and burning plastic, rainwater and decay.

A few years ago, her sister had broken her arm while Rollerblading. Penny had taken Leslie to the emergency room. Walking down the hallway, she'd detected the faint odor of singed flesh. Visions of her aunt's death had come flooding back to her, sucking the air from her lungs. She'd fled to the parking lot, sat behind the wheel of her car and sobbed.

Moments like that were few and far between, however. She enjoyed a life of luxury, if not excess. Cruz had everything he needed and then some. They were insulated from harm, isolated in a home so large it could have been called a compound. She did volunteer work, and interacted with people of various economic levels in her college classes. But, for the most part, she was surrounded by wealth and privilege.

She'd never even been camping.

The days after the freeway collapse had been excruciating. This situation was worse. Or maybe it was just *now*.

Five years of being an adult, not to mention a single mother, had given her some perspective. She worried more than she used to, about her place in the world and Cruz's future. She was no longer the center of her own tiny universe. What she remembered most about the disaster wasn't death or terror or hardship. It was the miracle of Cruz's birth. It didn't seem possible to love a child more each day, but she did. Maybe her fears had grown at the same proportion.

She'd do anything to keep her son safe. Anything.

Owen sat beside her, stiff as a board. He must have been suffering with his arms wrenched behind his back. Hers had grown numb from holding Cruz's sleeping weight. She had no idea where they were going or what they planned to do there. Would they kill her, torture her, hold her hostage? She took a deep breath, praying they wouldn't hurt Cruz. She couldn't bear it if they hurt Cruz.

She was afraid to examine either of the kidnappers. The driver had blue eyes, like Owen. They were about the same age and height. The thug sitting next to Owen was shorter, thick-necked and stocky with muscle.

She longed to rest her head on Owen's shoulder to comfort him, but she didn't want to draw attention. Her affection could put him in danger. The driver had already noticed Owen's sweet interaction with

Cruz, as well as his seething fury over the threats to Penny. The men had to know that Owen would fight for their lives, if he got the chance. She exchanged a glance with him, swallowing hard.

"I think these two are fucking," Dirk said.

Penny's stomach clenched with unease. She turned her head, staring out the window into the black night. Thank God Cruz was still asleep. He'd woken up early to watch cartoons and had spent the entire afternoon at the hotel pool.

The driver tugged down his mask and lit a cigarette. "Are you fucking your bodyguard, princess?"

"Leave her alone," Owen said.

"I didn't ask you, rent-a-cop. I asked her."

Penny said nothing.

The driver looked in his rearview mirror, as if searching for the answer on her face. "They're not fucking," he said, taking another drag. "He probably wants to fuck her, but she's too much of a daddy's girl to let him."

She tried not to flinch at the insult, which hit pretty close to home. The only men she'd gone out with since Tyler had been family-approved. Young Republicans from L.A.'s Hispanic Conservative Coalition didn't count as real dates, either. Penny and her sisters attended a lot of events on her father's behalf. She put on a pretty dress and smiled politely. None of her dance partners compared to Owen.

Even if Owen had been interested, her father wouldn't approve of her dating an ex-convict. Especially not during the campaign. The media already scrutinized her choices, which reflected poorly on her parents. She'd shamed them by getting pregnant at seventeen. She also felt somewhat responsible for her aunt's death. If she hadn't taken Penny in, she'd still be alive. They'd been on the way to a doctor's appointment when the earthquake struck.

Penny wasn't deeply religious, but she loved her family. Her parents had been wonderful with Cruz. In return, she'd given up some personal freedoms. She didn't have time for a serious relationship, anyway. Being single was part of her penance.

She snuck another peek at Owen, studying the pale tattoo scar on his neck. She'd often imagined putting her lips there and kissing away the hurt. Now the mark stood out in harsh relief against his flushed skin. Was he angry or embarrassed? If the driver's words rang true for him, she wouldn't have guessed it from his behavior. He never let his gaze linger on her body, never touched her for no reason.

Their trip through the desert ended at the mouth of a shallow, wind-carved canyon. The protected nook was surrounded by nondescript rock formations and covered with camouflaged netting. A trio of tents loomed in the shadows.

Penny counted three more men around a campfire. Most wore caps or beanies. Cowboy-style handkerchiefs shielded the lower halves of their faces.

The driver exited the vehicle, opening the door for Penny. It was difficult for her to maneuver with Cruz

in her arms, but she managed. Dirk dragged Owen
from the backseat and pushed him toward the campfire while the driver led Penny to one of the tents.
She carried Cruz inside and laid him down on a soft
blanket. As soon as he was settled, her captor gestured for her to come back out.

His crew gathered in a half circle around her. Although men had stared at her before, she'd never felt
this vulnerable, not even in a boisterous crowd. Public
reactions ranged from respectful comments to rude
catcalls and blatant groping attempts. Owen had a
hard elbow for the most aggressive types.

These men were more dangerous than a group of
rowdy extremists. And Owen couldn't help her if they
got aggressive.

"Search her," the driver said to one of the men.
"And take her shoes."

This order created a stir of excitement in the circle.
Owen strained against Dirk's hold, as if he wanted to
kick and head-butt and body-slam everyone around
him. His nostrils flared as a heavyset man in a fishing vest stepped forward.

Penny knew she couldn't struggle. Triggering
Owen's protective instincts might prove fatal for
him. If the kidnappers wanted to get paid, they had
plenty of incentive to keep her and Cruz alive. Owen
was dispensable.

She turned her head to the side, enduring the
stranger's touch. Her dress was thin and insub-
stantial, hiding nothing but expensive lingerie. He

skimmed his hands along her curves quickly. His friends seemed disappointed when he did a perfunctory job instead of sexually harassing her.

"What a waste," Dirk said.

"I don't think Gardener has a dick."

"Just a gunt," another man said, and they all laughed.

Penny could only guess what that word meant. She removed her strappy high heels and handed them over, her mouth thin. They were worth a small fortune, but useless here. She couldn't walk a quarter mile across the desert in those shoes. Barefoot, she'd encounter burrs and cactus needles in the first ten steps.

The leader gestured for her to go back in the tent, satisfied. "Make sure she stays there," he told Gardener, who sat down on a crate nearby. He zipped up the opening, blocking her view of the men outside.

She curled up next to Cruz and hugged her arms around her middle. The tent appeared large enough for three people, at most. There were two blankets inside. She started to tremble from stress, rather than cold. Now that the men couldn't see her, she had no reason to hold her emotions inside. Her face crumpled, and tears leaked from the corners of her eyes. She broke down in muffled sobs, her hand clapped over her mouth.

Someone switched on the radio in the SUV, settling for a Spanish-language station. She wiped her cheeks, listening. There might not be anything else available this close to the border, but she doubted these men enjoyed Norteño music.

They didn't want her to hear them.

She scrambled toward the front of the tent and lay flat on her belly. Unzipping a tiny opening at the corner, she peered through it. Owen was on the opposite side of the campfire. His wrists were still cuffed behind his back. The leader stood before him, smoking. His body language conveyed a challenge.

Owen shook his head, denying whatever he asked for.

The man flicked away his cigarette and stepped forward. Cuffing his hand around Owen's neck, he drew back his fist and punched him in the stomach. Owen doubled over, coughing.

Penny bit the edge of her fist to smother her scream.

PAIN SPREAD THROUGH Owen's midsection, settling like a ball of lead in his gut.

Although the blow wasn't unexpected, it hurt. It always hurt when his brother hit him. From a very young age, Shane had used brute force and intimidation to get what he wanted. He'd been violent and impulsive, quick to snap.

Owen had dismissed most of their childhood rumbles as sibling rivalry, fueled by testosterone and an extra dose of dysfunction. Boys were supposed to be physical. The toxic environment they'd been raised in had exacerbated the problem. Their father had instigated fights between them, encouraging Shane to attack weakness.

Back then, Owen hadn't stood up to either of them. He was younger than Shane, and nowhere near as aggressive. He'd never understood the appeal of hurting someone he loved. He preferred to run, hide and avoid conflict.

Now they were both adults and closer in size. He was handcuffed and at Shane's mercy, but he refused to cower. Owen might have a chance against Shane, one-on-one. He wasn't a scared, skinny kid anymore.

"Is that all you've got?" he wheezed.

Shane's eyes widened with disbelief. Instead of sucker punching him again, Shane squeezed the nape of his neck and let go, chuckling. "You've grown up, little brother."

He couldn't prevent the rush of warmth those words generated. Owen hadn't realized how much he'd missed Shane—or how much he'd craved human contact. His father's death had left a hole inside him. Shane's lengthy incarceration had made another, and his own stint in prison had gnawed him down to nothing.

Owen didn't trust Shane, but he would always love him.

Although they'd served time in different institutions, Shane and Owen had joined the same gang. The Aryan Brotherhood was the most popular white gang in the California penal system. Its members underwent a savage initiation process and swore allegiance for life. They were expected to continue to serve the AB on the outside.

After the San Diego earthquake, Owen had been transferred to a quiet, medium-security correctional facility. Penny's father had used his political connections to make the arrangements after Owen had helped rescue Penny. Owen would be forever in Sandoval's debt for the favor. At the smaller prison, he'd been able to distance himself from the AB. He'd taken advantage of college courses, therapy sessions and a work program. When he was released, he'd had a job waiting for him in a remote park where no one would find him.

Now, three years later, he was a security guard for a presidential candidate. He hadn't been worried about the gang coming after him. His mistake.

"You turned your back on the AB," Shane said.

Owen couldn't deny it.

"There's a punishment for deserters."

"What do you want from me?"

"Your compliance."

He wasn't sure how to respond. Did it even matter? These assholes would never believe he was on their side.

Owen had become a member the Aryan Brotherhood of his own free will. He'd engaged in gang fights and color wars. He'd used racial slurs without batting an eye and littered his body with offensive epithets. Although he regretted the necessity of these actions, he'd seen no other solution. He'd been eighteen when he'd gotten arrested. Male inmates preyed on young, attractive boys. Owen couldn't escape their attentions without help. And, unfortunately, only one group would accept him. There were no rainbow coalitions in prison. It was a segregated environment, and protection came at a price.

Owen wasn't a white supremacist, but ideological differences hadn't made it difficult for him to fit in with the gang. No, he'd adopted their ways easily. He'd been poor white trash his entire life. The men in the Brotherhood were just like him. They were the boys he'd played with after school, the desert rats with the faded clothes, the trailer park kids who came from nothing and ended up the same way.

Salton City was a backward place, full of poverty and prejudice. His father had been a racist fool, spewing ignorance on a regular basis. His mother didn't agree, but she'd known better than to contradict him.

Despite his upbringing, or perhaps because of it, Owen had rejected those views. He didn't want to take after his father. Long before he reached adulthood, he'd decided to be whatever Christian Jackson wasn't. Owen couldn't change the fact that he was white, male and heterosexual. In all other areas, he would diverge.

That was the plan, anyway. But he'd gotten caught up in his brother's world and drifted in the wrong direction. He'd started drinking heavily in high school, and he'd been a regular meth user by the time he was seventeen.

Since he'd left prison, however, he'd stayed on the straight and narrow. He had a stronger sense of who he was as a person. The idea of pretending to go along with Shane's scheme made him nauseous. Not only that, he doubted an agreement would give him any advantage. They wouldn't remove his handcuffs or let him go.

This was all just bullshit posturing. Shane had to prove his loyalty to the gang, and he had to do it with his fists. Dirk cracked his knuckles in a threatening manner. Owen knew what was coming: an epic beatdown. He studied each set of boots in his vicinity, expecting he'd be seeing them up close in the next few minutes.

"I told you he was fucking her," Dirk said.

"You might be right."

"Looks like he's had some tattoos removed."

"Strip him," Shane said.

Owen held still as one of the other men came forward, ripping his shirt down the front and letting it hang off his shoulders. The swastika on his hand and the script on his neck were gone. His other tattoos had been altered, rather than removed. He'd changed the Old English lettering that arced over his stomach to read Irish Pride, instead of White Pride. More telling, perhaps, was the cross on his chest. The flames were covered and the name Cruz was added underneath, transforming the hateful image into a tender tribute.

He still had a three-leaf clover on his shoulder, minus the AB initials. Green ink was hard to remove, and it was a symbol of his Scotch-Irish heritage, so he'd kept it. He was damned lucky to be alive after several close calls.

But maybe this was it. The last scrape.

Dirk pointed out the obvious. "This motherfucker isn't one of us."

"Are you with us?" Shane asked.

Owen didn't answer.

"Stand him up."

Two men dragged him to his feet. He looked Shane in the eye, his pulse racing. His brother hit him with an open hand across the face, knocking his head to one side. Pain exploded in his cheek and gums.

"Are you with us?" Shane repeated.

Owen spat a mouthful of blood on Dirk's shoes. "No."

"Son of a bitch!"

They took turns hitting him in the stomach and back, hammering his pride and bruising his luck. Shane didn't participate as much as the others, and his blows weren't quite as heavy. Owen wondered if he'd lost his appetite for violence. The malicious glint in his eyes had faded into resignation.

Whatever enthusiasm Shane lacked, his friends more than made up for. They held Owen upright and pummeled the hell out of him.

"Enough!" Shane roared.

They let him fall to the ground, writhing in pain.

"Leave us alone for a minute."

"Are you going to finish him?" Dirk asked.

"How about I finish you?"

Dirk walked away with the others, grumbling.

Shane crouched down next to Owen and lit a cigarette, one hand cupped around his jaw to block the wind. "I don't want to kill you."

Owen struggled for breath, rolling over on to his side in the dirt. The punches to his rib cage felt like fire. It was difficult to anticipate Shane's next move. He'd always been a loose cannon, acting in his own self-interests. But he'd defended Owen as often as he'd bullied him. He hadn't been as cruel as their father.

Shane changed the subject. "How's Mom?"

The question didn't soften Owen's sympathies any. Shane had a lot of fucking nerve, asking about their mother. "Better, now that Dad's gone," he said, spitting out another mouthful of blood. "I'll send her your regards."

He had the grace to look guilty. Their mom had a substance-abuse problem. Since their father died, she'd been clean, but Owen was worried she'd relapse. Difficult situations—like Shane busting parole—triggered her addiction. "Have you seen Jamie?"

"Yes. I visit him once a month."

"No shit?"

"No shit."

"Janelle won't even let me talk to him."

Owen didn't blame her. Jamie's mother didn't want her son to have anything to do with Shane, for good reason. He was a convicted killer. He'd only served eight of his ten-year sentence, which had been light to begin with. His brother had gotten off easy because the liquor store clerk had fired at him first—while he was running away with the contents of the cash register. The bullet intended for Shane had nearly hit Owen, who'd been sitting behind the wheel of the getaway car.

"Why are you doing this?" Owen asked, lowering his voice. "You'll spend the rest of your life in prison."

Shane took a drag of his cigarette, eyes narrow.

"Do you owe them money?"

Shane didn't answer. It was easy to get drugs in the pen if you had the right connections. Guards brought in the supplies while prisoners racked up debt. The AB was deeply involved in the underground narcotics trade.

"You could have gone to the police," Owen said.

Shane snorted at the suggestion. The Brotherhood might not track down and execute every ex-member, but they didn't mess around with snitches. If Shane gave incriminating information to the authorities, he'd have to enter a witness protection program.

"Fuck the police," Shane said. "I'll do the damned job and get it over with. Then I'll be free of them."

"Do you really believe that?"

"I don't have a choice, and neither do you. I told them you'd cooperate."

Owen refused to consider it. He had too much to lose. He wanted to make something of himself. Shane was asking him to throw his future away. "Not a chance. The last time we collaborated, I went away for three years."

Shane tossed his cigarette in the fire. The conversation hadn't gone the way he'd hoped, so he switched tactics. Shoving Owen facedown on the ground, Shane climbed on top of him. He hooked an arm around Owen's neck and applied a crushing pressure to his windpipe. Owen was trapped under his weight. He couldn't move. Couldn't breathe.

Shane continued to choke Owen until his vision went dark. "Tell Dad I said hi," he muttered, finishing him.

CHAPTER FOUR

PENNY EASED AWAY from Cruz and sat up, her ears straining for the slightest sound.

The men had finally quieted. She'd watched in horror as they'd beaten Owen to a pulp. When the leader had climbed on to his back and choked the life out of him, she hadn't screamed or broken down in hysterical tears. She hadn't unzipped the tent opening and rushed to his aid. She'd gone completely numb, her heart shrinking inside her chest.

She couldn't believe her eyes.

Someone dragged his body away from the fire, out of her line of sight. Then the men gathered in a circle and passed around a bottle. They didn't seem upset or anxious about the sequence of events. If anything, they were giddy. In the hours that followed, they'd celebrated their success, drinking beer and laughing like hyenas.

Now they were probably sleeping it off inside the other two tents. The guy who'd searched her was still awake, sitting outside. He'd been respectful, but she didn't fool herself into believing she was safe. Dirk had made several suggestive comments about Penny. What would stop him from trying to attack her?

These men were dangerous criminals.

She doubted her father would follow their instructions. There was no way he could keep this secret from the police. His profile was too high. He'd bring the money and *pretend* to cooperate. She swallowed hard, imagining a bloody shoot-out.

Even if everything went according to plan, which she doubted, the kidnappers might kill her before the money exchange was completed. They could take her father's money and kill him. They could kill Cruz.

Her thoughts raced with possible outcomes, none of which involved a happy ending. They'd *killed Owen*. Hadn't they?

Her head ached from tension. She refused to accept the fact that he might be dead. Maybe if she saw him up close and touched his cold skin, she could acknowledge it. Until then, she had to push the awful possibility from her mind.

She thought back to the dance she'd shared with Owen at his friend Sam's wedding. It was months before he became her bodyguard. Her sister Leslie had been helping Cruz eat a piece of cake at a nearby table. Penny and Owen had had a rare moment to themselves. But when the song was over, they'd broken apart.

Tears of regret spilled down her cheeks. If only she could go back in time and not let go. She should have hugged him closer, confessed that she wanted him. Instead, she'd withdrawn, waiting for him to make a move. He hadn't.

For too many years, she'd been passive and acquiescent, pleasing her parents. After surviving the earthquake and seeing so much devastation, she'd been overjoyed to be reunited with her family. She'd needed their love, comfort and security. Keeping Cruz safe was her main focus, and her father's house was very safe.

But her father wasn't going to rescue her tonight. Neither was Owen. She had to save herself—and her son. If she didn't try to escape, and they hurt Cruz, she'd never forgive herself. She had to act fast, while the leader and his cronies were inebriated.

Outside the tent, the guard made quiet crunching sounds. Slow, deliberate, infrequent. After a long pause, he started again.

Penny's stomach lurched. She'd been too nervous to eat before going on stage, and now she felt sick. She was also desperately thirsty, and her bladder was full. They hadn't been given any food or water, or allowed a bathroom break.

Cruz shifted beside her. "Mommy?"

"Be quiet."

"I have to potty."

Damn.

He sat up, rubbing his eyes. "Where are we?"

"We're camping."

Cruz had always wanted to go on a camping trip. Her father had taken them boating at Pyramid Lake once. Her son had been enthralled by the sight of tents and picnic tables on the lakeshore. This probably wasn't what he'd pictured, however. He had no pillow and only a blanket as a cushion. "I'm thirsty for water."

At least he wasn't hungry. Yet.

She unzipped the front of the tent and looked out at the guard. "Can we have a drink of water?"

He handed her a canteen, his eyes shifting in the dark.

A glance around as she accepted the offering revealed nothing but inanimate shapes in the moonlight. "Thank you," she said, helping Cruz get a drink. After she slaked her own thirst, her bladder screamed for relief. "We have to go to the bathroom."

"One at a time," the man said.

She urged Cruz outside, telling him to go right there, by the tent. He came back when he was done and curled up on the blanket, too drowsy to question the strangeness of this experience. "I'll be right back," she whispered, kissing his forehead. More tears sprang into her eyes, but she blinked them away, exhaling.

She could do this. She could think of a way to trick the guard. She could find a weapon. If she had to, she'd attack him with her bare hands. Owen had taught her some self-defense techniques.

Owen.

Heart clenching painfully, she stepped out of the tent. The sand was cool and gritty beneath her bare feet. She didn't want to push her luck by straying too far, but she wouldn't squat down in front of the guard.

He kept his eye on her as she balled the fabric of her skirt in her fist and crouched in the shadows by the canyon wall, next to a crumbling rock pile.

Rocks made good weapons.

It was difficult to pee and search for a blunt object at the same time. Her pulse raced with anxiety as her trembling fingertips touched a chunk of clay. It broke apart on contact. She tried again, reaching farther. The next rock she encountered was solid, about the size of a baseball. She held it in a tight grip as she rose, adjusting her clothing.

Now she needed a way to surprise him. If he saw her coming at him with a rock, he could shout out a warning or duck.

The rest of the men had to have been asleep in the tents, because she couldn't see them. As she walked forward, she pretended to step on a sharp object. Gasping in pain, she crumpled into a pathetic little heap on the ground.

"What is it?" the guard asked.

"I cut my foot."

He approached to take a look, kneeling beside her. Her skirt rode high on her thighs as she extended her foot, whimpering. When he bent his head to inspect the injury, she walloped him. Her first strike was weak, partly because she didn't really want to do it, but also because winding up would have caught his attention. The short swing and glancing blow failed to incapacitate him.

He touched his temple, dumbfounded.

Cringing, she hit him again. And again. The third one did the trick. He slumped forward on top of her, knocking the wind from her lungs.

Oh, God. Now she would die of suffocation underneath him. Saying a quick prayer, she asked for forgiveness. Then let go of the rock, which was wet with blood, and shoved him aside. He made an odd groaning noise that she hoped wasn't his last breath. Pulse pounding in her ears, she tugged off his boots and put them on her own feet. They were slip-on style, reaching just past her ankles, and only a size too large.

She hurried toward the tent, afraid he'd regain consciousness and start shouting. His canteen was sitting by the crate, along with the vest he'd been wearing earlier. Grabbing both, she stuck her head inside the flap. Cruz blinked at her in confusion. *"Silencio,"* she hissed. *"Vente, ya! Apúrate."*

He knew she meant business when she issued sharp orders in Spanish. Her family had a lot of Mexican pride, but Penny and her sisters were typical second-generation immigrants. They spoke English almost exclusively.

He scrambled out and grasped her hand, voicing no complaints as she yanked him along. She rushed past the SUV, searching for a set of ignition keys. She couldn't knock on the tent flaps, asking for him. She didn't see a cell phone lying around.

They had to leave on foot. Trying not to panic, she fled with Cruz, circling around the side of the canyon until they were out of sight. Faced with another immediate dilemma, she paused, taking a ragged breath. She didn't know which way to go. Following the tire tracks back to the road seemed like a reasonable option, but she doubted they would reach civilization before the kidnappers found them. The opposite direction was just as risky. Getting lost in the desert might be a fate worse than death.

Even so, she headed away from the tracks, dragging Cruz across the moonlit landscape. The terrain was difficult to navigate, full of loose pebbles and shifting sand. They ran until the camp was far behind them, and Cruz begged to stop.

"Where's Owen?" he asked, winded.

"I don't know."

"Are we lost?"

She couldn't lie again. "Those were bad men. They wanted to hurt us. We have to get far away and hide."

He started to cry, which wasn't unexpected. This situation didn't sit well with her, either. She hadn't wanted to leave Owen with those bastards, dead or alive. She was afraid to take her son into the deep desert. The ill-fitting boots were already bothering her.

"Drink," she said, passing him the canteen. "Don't let it spill."

While he sat down with the water, she rifled through the vest. She found a pocketknife, a pack of matches, ChapStick and a miniflashlight. All useful items. There was also a medium-sized bag of corn nuts.

She used the knife to cut strips from the bottom of her dress, making it shorter. The length inhibited her movements, and she needed the fabric. She wrapped up her feet and stuffed the excess into the toes of the boots. Much better.

That done, she put on the vest and canteen, adjusting the strap across her chest. Then she knelt, gesturing for Cruz to climb on her back. As soon as he was secure, she resumed jogging. It wasn't easy. He didn't weigh much, just forty pounds, and adrenaline fueled her every step, but she didn't have the strength to go all night like this. She wasn't a cross-country runner or an experienced hiker. Cruz tightened his arms around her neck, half choking her. She kept looking over her shoulder, expecting to see Mad Max.

After a few minutes, she realized that she was following a dry riverbed and leaving discernible footprints. Her trail would be easy to see. Switching directions, she traveled across a series of low hills, dodging the boulders and cactus plants that threatened to trip her up. She continued at a brisk pace, alternating between carrying Cruz and making him walk. They had to cover as much ground as possible before sunrise.

Hours later, the horizon turned pink with approaching dawn, and she slowed to a stop. Defeated, she let Cruz slide off her back. She had nothing left. Her arms felt like spaghetti; her thigh muscles were trembling and her feet were raw.

Cruz couldn't go another step, either.

She searched their surroundings for a place to rest. Like wounded animals, they needed to crawl into a hole and hide.

The hills in the distance looked promising. Tall mounds rose up toward the sky, their jagged surfaces resembling peaks of meringue. She'd been hoping to find a group of large boulders to duck behind, but perhaps these structures would suffice.

"This way," she said, grasping his hand. "Just a few more minutes, and we can sit."

He trudged along gamely, more cooperative than usual. Cruz had endless energy for fun activities, but no patience or endurance whatsoever on long, boring trips. He seemed to understand that this was neither.

Her spirits lifted as they got closer. There appeared to be a hole in the side of the hill, a tunnel of sorts, carved from wind or water erosion. She turned on the flashlight, inspecting the interior. What an amazing stroke of luck.

"It's a cave," Cruz said, excited.

"Let's explore."

They stepped through the opening, which widened out to a large area before narrowing again. The passage zigzagged along for several hundred feet. Penny had to turn sideways in some areas, and duck in others to avoid bumping her head. When they came to a fork in the path, she veered left, choosing the tighter squeeze. She dropped to her hands and knees, inching forward with the flashlight in her mouth. Cruz crawled behind her. They reached a section she could barely fit through. It opened up to a small room with a skylight.

She didn't think the men could reach them here. She couldn't get out, either, because the hole in the roof was tiny. But the little window comforted her, making the hiding place seem less tomblike and claustrophobic.

Penny hated enclosed spaces, for obvious reasons. "Here we are."

"We can stay?"

She nodded, resting her back against the wall. "We have to be very quiet."

"Will they come looking for us?"

"Maybe."

They shared the corn nuts, which weren't actually nuts, but roasted corn kernels, called *elotitos* in Mexico. She tried not to drink too much water, though she was thirsty. The canteen might have to last several days.

"Why do they want to hurt us?"

"They want money," she amended.

"For what?"

"I don't know."

"Do they touch kids?"

"I don't think so," she said, disturbed by the question. She'd told him about child molesters out of necessity. He had no fear of strangers, no shyness. One day he'd wandered off in the library when her back was turned. After a frantic search, she'd found him talking to a friendly older man. Later, at home, she'd explained the danger.

She doubted any of the kidnappers were pedophiles, but the threat of rape had felt very real to her. A woman of color surrounded by racist gang members was at high risk. She thought about the way Dirk had manhandled Owen, with threatening postures and suggestive insults. These men weren't above using sexual violence as intimidation.

She felt another pang of guilt for leaving him. This was all her fault. He wouldn't have taken this job under normal circumstances. Her father had probably appealed to his sense of chivalry, claiming she required special protection.

If she hadn't been such a coward and a pushover, none of this would have happened. She should have moved away from home three months ago, when she graduated. Or sooner, before her father announced his candidacy. She hadn't because her father claimed it wasn't *safe*. He'd insisted on enrolling Cruz in a private Catholic preschool for the same reason. After he offered to pay full tuition, how could she refuse?

Her father doted on Cruz, spoiling him with expensive gifts. He was like the son Jorge had always wanted. And Cruz needed a man in his life, so she didn't complain. If her father had his way, Penny would marry a young conservative—Cuban, perhaps, because there were so few Mexican-American Republicans—and move in next door.

She should have stood firm and been more independent. She should have told her father flat out that she had feelings for Owen.

Now it was too late.

She couldn't stand the thought of never seeing him again, never asking for another kiss. With a strangled sob, she touched her trembling lips, trying to recapture that tender moment. Her fingertips tasted like salt and something else, a dark tang. With horror, she realized that she had dried blood on her hands.

"I'm scared," Cruz said.

"So am I," she replied, hugging him close.

CHAPTER FIVE

"GET UP."

Shane woke Owen by kicking the bottom of his foot. He wrenched his eyes open, studying the tan nylon tent fabric inches from his nose. Dirk had dragged him inside last night, where he'd drifted in and out of consciousness. His mouth was dry and his throat ached. His midsection, which had taken the brunt of the blows, felt like raw hamburger. When he tried to raise a hand to his face, he encountered resistance.

Handcuffs. Now they were in the front.

Shane was standing outside the tent, smoking a cigarette. His motorcycle mask was pulled down to his neck. He had a 9 mm tucked into his waistband.

Owen's stomach roiled at the smell of tobacco. He groaned, trying to piece together the events from the night before. His brother had attempted to kill him, or maybe just scare him into believing his life was in danger. It had worked; he was scared. He'd only been knocked out once before, after the earthquake. Waking up under a collapsed freeway with a band of escaped convicts, himself included, had been pretty fucking horrible. Getting strangled by his own brother, even more so.

"Your bitch ran off with her kid," Shane said.

Owen blinked a few times, processing the information. He was glad Penny had escaped, but the badlands was a treacherous place for a woman and child with no shelter or supplies.

"Don't call her that," he said, rolling over and crawling out of the tent.

"A bitch or yours?"

He winced at the early-morning light. "How did she get away?"

Shane took another drag. "Went to pee, grabbed a rock and bashed Gardener over the head with it."

Owen spotted Gardener on the other side of camp. He had a purple goose egg on the left side of his forehead, and he looked nauseated. Owen had to give Penny credit for a simple, effective attack.

While the crew got ready to search for Penny and Cruz, Owen studied each member, memorizing as many details as possible. Most of them were wearing hats and sunglasses, with handkerchiefs over their faces. Next to Shane, Dirk was the strongest, medium height and loaded with muscle. Sometimes that kind of bulk could slow a man down, but Dirk's movements weren't clumsy. He was armed with a handgun, like Shane.

Gardener was the weak link, even before his injury. He had hound-dog eyes, a receding hairline and a rounded gut.

The other two men, Brett and Roach, were in between. Brett was small and wiry, tough like a bullfighter, with dusty-blond hair. Roach had longish dark hair. He was taller than Dirk, almost as tall as Shane. His pale skin and slouching physique gave Owen the impression that he played a lot of video games.

Owen rated them by threat level. Shane was a five, despite their family connection. Dirk, four; Brett and Roach, three; Gardener, one.

No one tried to guard Owen as he found a rock to urinate behind. He couldn't get far in handcuffs and wasn't going anywhere, anyway. Not without Penny and Cruz. He helped himself to a jug of water, rinsing the old blood from his mouth before taking a drink. Then he eased his shirt back on to his shoulders and fastened the single remaining button. Bruises were already beginning to form on his battered torso.

A few minutes later, they loaded into the SUV and followed Penny's tracks. She'd stolen Gardener's boots—clever.

They lost her trail quickly. She'd left the softer terrain of the wash and traveled across the hard-packed hills. Shane parked the SUV and got out, muttering under his breath. Going after her on foot would be a hassle. Penny couldn't outdistance them with a child in tow, but if she found a good place to hide, she had a chance of evading them.

She could also die from heat and dehydration. Fear stabbed Owen's chest. He didn't know whether to root for her or not. She might be safer with them.

Shane searched for a sign of her while the rest of them waited in the SUV. He cursed and kicked a cactus, annoyed with it for getting in his path. Then he looked south, his eyes narrow. "Let's check out the mud caves."

Owen wasn't familiar with every inch of terrain between here and the border, but he knew the mud caves. Situated a few miles away, the domelike structures offered a network of tunnels and caverns, formed out of dried clay. Beyond the caves lay a five-palm oasis with ample shade and a seasonal pool of water. From there it was a half-day's hike to the old railroad, which led back to civilization. If Owen got the opportunity to break free, he could orient himself and survive out here. He could guide Penny and Cruz to safety.

Shane drove south and parked as close to the mud caves as possible, walking the final mile. The early-morning sun was already blasting heat. Living near the coast for so long had thinned Owen's blood. Eighty degrees felt like a hundred. They were all sweating as they approached the cave's entrance.

One by one, they stepped out of the harsh sun and into the cave's cool, dark recesses. It was almost like entering an air-conditioned room. Owen squinted into the cave, letting his vision adjust to the lack of light.

Dirk bent to pick up a scrap of fabric on the dirt floor. He brought it to his face and inhaled, as if sniffing panties. "This is hers."

Shane inspected the blue-green material and turned to Owen. "Call out to her."

Although his body still ached from last night, he hesitated. He'd take another beating before he betrayed Penny.

His brother drew the 9 mm from his waistband and pressed it to Owen's cheek. This wasn't up for discussion. "Do it."

"Penny," he shouted, his voice hoarse with anger. Most of it was directed at Shane but some bled inward. He'd been warring with these feelings his entire life. This sick, dysfunctional mixture of love and hate. As much as Owen loathed his father, he'd also sought his approval in many ways. He'd learned welding, his father's trade, to earn a rare pat on the back. He hadn't wanted to be like his father, but he'd wanted be *liked* by him.

That desire had never quite faded.

He was furious with Shane for picking up where their dad had left off, and with himself for being unable to break this vicious cycle.

Penny didn't answer his call. She might not be able to hear him. She might not even be inside the cave anymore. Some tunnels went on for miles and offered multiple escape routes. Others were dead ends.

Shane returned his gun to his waistband, his eyes moving from Dirk to Brett. They were brothers, too, Owen realized. The younger, smaller Brett was a criminal-in-training.

"Give Brett your piece," Shane said to Dirk.

"What for?"

"I'm sending him in. They might be hiding in a narrow space. He'll fit through the tight spots easier than you."

Dirk handed his weapon to Brett, seeming to be disappointed. He wanted to hunt down Penny and terrorize her himself. "How will he get her out?"

Shane sucked on his lip, thinking. "Owen, you go first. Make her come to you."

"And if she won't?" Brett asked.

"Tell her you're going to shoot Owen in the head."

Brett's mouth went slack. He wasn't as hardened as Dirk, or as macho. "O-okay."

"If she still doesn't come out, shoot him in the foot," Shane conceded. The guy who'd pulled his punches last night was gone, replaced by the cold-eyed sociopath who'd choked Owen into submission. His brother was good at intimidating people, staying in control. He could flip the switch between charming and cruel in an instant. Penny's actions had challenged his authority—and this was payback.

Dirk smiled at Owen, enjoying the tension.

"You two, walk around the perimeter," Shane said to Roach and Dirk. "If you find another entrance, guard it. I'll stay here."

They followed his instructions, leaving the mouth of the cave. Brett trained the gun on Owen while Shane removed his cuffs. Owen needed free hands to navigate in the dark. Between the twisted tunnels, armed escort and men blocking the exits, he'd be a fool to try running away. Or so they thought.

Owen rubbed his chafed wrists, his blood pumping with adrenaline. He wasn't going to let an amateur like Brett shoot him in the foot. He'd take advantage of any opportunity to escape. He'd create an opening if he had to.

Shane had brought supplies from the SUV's glove compartment. They had walkie-talkies and flashlights. Brett clipped the walkie-talkie to his waist and held a mini-flashlight in his teeth, gesturing for Owen to precede him. The setup wasn't ideal. Owen's shoulders kept blocking the beam of light. Brett wasn't stupid enough to let him hold the flashlight, so Owen crouched as low as possible, picking his way forward.

He was comfortable in this kind of setting. Dark, confined spaces didn't bother him, even after his experience in the earthquake. Neither did heat, usually. During his firefighter training, he'd endured both better than most students. He'd grown up near the badlands, in Salton City. High temperatures and harsh conditions just reminded him of home.

They came to a fork in the tunnel. Owen stopped and listened, detecting the faintest hint of wind. He couldn't wait any longer. If they reached the end of the cave before he had a chance to strike, all would be lost.

"Bats," he shouted at the top of his lungs, flapping his arms around.

Brett looked up at the ceiling of the tunnel, where

there *were* bats. Sleeping bats, tucked up and motionless.

Owen seized the moment of distraction. He grabbed Brett's right wrist and slammed it against the cave wall, knocking the gun loose from his grip. It clattered to the floor, along with the flashlight from Brett's surprised mouth. Owen couldn't see his face, but he didn't need to. He drew back his arm and punched Brett in the stomach with full force. The air rushed out of him in an audible whoosh.

Brett doubled over, as men who'd been gut-checked often did. Owen grabbed Brett's head and brought it down on his raised knee, crushing the small bones and cartilage in his nose. The blow was delivered with enough force to knock him out, apparently. He slumped to the ground, unconscious.

Owen scrambled for the gun and flashlight. He also took Brett's walkie-talkie. Then he crept forward, his heart hammering against his chest. "Penny?" he called out, unsure which direction to take.

He had no idea how they would get out of this. His actions might have saved them or sealed their doom.

PENNY JOLTED AWAKE with a start.

She'd had a dream about Owen. He'd been calling out to her in the dark, crawling through the earthquake wreckage, searching vehicles full of dead bodies. She was pregnant again, sitting in the passenger seat of her aunt's car. Not trapped under the freeway, as she had been, but among the victims in the massive pileup outside. Owen had found her and reached inside. His grasping hand was blue-tinged, his forearm ropey with black veins.

Shivering, she cleared her mind of the disturbing image.

Cruz was about ten feet away from her, carving designs on the wall with a sharp stick. It was hard-packed clay, not crumbly, but it had a fine, siltlike surface. The powdery substance clung to her dress and skin. Cruz looked like he'd taken a bath in it. He was singing songs under his breath, not being quiet at all.

"Shh," she told him, straightening. "Did you hear anything?"

"No."

"Come here."

He dropped the stick with reluctance and returned to her side. The light coming from the hole in the ceiling seemed a little brighter. She took a sip of water, doubting she'd slept more than an hour. "How long was I asleep?"

"I don't know." He had no sense of time. Five minutes was an eternity to him.

She put her arm around him and listened, her pulse still pounding from the nightmare. Although she was exhausted, she couldn't believe she'd drifted off. She'd been quaking with tension and sorrow, tortured by the thought of Owen dying.

Catastrophic events made some people stronger. Owen had been a hero during the earthquake. He'd emerged from prison a reformed man. At his national park job, he'd proven himself again by rushing to help a female ranger in trouble. These experiences had inspired him to pursue a career in rescue work. He was naturally courageous.

Penny wasn't.

She'd had the opposite reaction to trauma, retreating from any hint of danger. Playing it safe was more her style. She didn't know how she'd drummed up the nerve to hit a man over the head with a rock. If not for the blood under her fingernails, she'd have suspected the episode was just another bad dream.

"I'm hungry," Cruz whispered.

Penny gave him a drink of water. It was the only thing she had.

"When can we leave?"

"Soon."

"What happened to Owen?"

She swallowed hard, unable to answer without breaking down. Although she had mixed feelings about prayer, she said a silent plea in her desperation, begging God to spare them.

"I'm bored," Cruz said.

"You don't like this cave?"

"I want to see the rest of it."

"I bet there are bats."

His brown eyes lit up with curiosity. He had clay dust in his hair and on his lashes, giving him an angelic look. "Where?"

Penny was about to answer when she heard a man

calling her name. He sounded frantic. He sounded like…Owen.

Cruz tried to respond, but she clapped her palm over his mouth. This might be a trick to draw them out. She also didn't trust her ears. She'd seen Owen's lifeless body. Heart racing, she stared at the narrow entrance, half expecting a zombie hand to reach through.

"Penny," he shouted, closer now. "Cruz?"

She released her grip on Cruz, trembling with emotion. "Owen?"

"Where are you?"

"Over here!" She scrambled toward the opening and stuck her arm out, waving to get his attention.

Then he was right there with her. The hand that clasped hers wasn't ghostly pale or black-veined. It was dirty and strong and vibrant. His skin was lightly tanned, not quite as dark as hers or Cruz's. She wept at the sight and feel of him.

He was alive! She didn't care how. He was alive.

Owen couldn't fit through the narrow space, so she climbed out to greet him. With a strangled sob, she threw her arms around his neck. His stiff shoulders betrayed his discomfort; he'd always reacted strangely to touch.

Penny had been friends with Owen since he'd gotten out of prison. She'd stayed in contact with all of the earthquake survivors. They exchanged emails and shared Facebook photos. She'd taken Cruz to visit Owen a few times in Sierra National Park. The three of them had a special connection. He seemed to enjoy their company as much as they enjoyed his. Penny cherished every moment with him.

Over the years, Owen had gained confidence. He no longer flinched at a simple handshake, but he still avoided overt displays of affection. She didn't think he was repulsed by the feel of her body against his. There was something else going on.

His behavior reminded her of an incident from her childhood. Their dog, Blanca, had run away on a rainy day, only to be captured and returned by a neighbor. Her mother had tried to thank the man with a hug, but he'd been wet and dirty, too polite to soil her clothes.

That was Owen, to a T.

She knew he'd had a dysfunctional home life. She knew he'd done things he regretted, in and out of prison. Maybe her father had told him, in no uncertain terms, that he wasn't good enough for her.

"I thought you were dead," she said, for his ears only.

"Shh," he said, patting her hair. "It's okay. I've got you."

When Cruz joined them, she released Owen, wiping the tears from her cheeks. He hugged her son with ease, proving his self-consciousness was reserved for grown-ups. Perhaps her, in particular.

A groan emitted from the shadows behind Owen. She froze, peering into the dark. He turned and directed his flashlight toward the sound. She could only guess that he'd harmed someone in order to break free.

"We have to go now," Owen said.

She gathered her vest and water, following as he led them back to the main tunnel. Owen took Cruz by the hand and skirted him around a prone figure on the ground. It was a semiconscious man, his face splattered with blood.

"Who's that?" Cruz asked.

"A bad guy," Owen replied.

"Did you hit him?"

"Yes."

"You must hit hard."

Penny hurried past him, cringing. They headed into the deep recesses of the cave, traveling a serpentine path.

"Is there another way out?" Owen asked.

She thought *he* knew where he was going. "I didn't check."

He stopped, considering. "They're going to come looking for that guy. If we don't find an exit soon, we'll return to your safe spot."

"You can't fit there."

"That's okay," he said, showing her the gun he had tucked into his waistband.

Penny stared at the weapon in dismay. She felt faint, as if she might forget to breathe and pass out from fear. Five minutes ago, she'd thought Owen was gone for good. Now they were together, but they weren't safe. The idea of him getting into a shoot-out and dying for them made her chest ache.

"Don't risk your life again," she whispered. "If it comes to that, surrender."

He nodded his agreement. Then he continued forward, into the dark.

AROUND THE NEXT CORNER, natural light beckoned.

The tunnel emptied into a large room with an opening at one end. It was exactly what Owen had been hoping for. Scrambling toward the narrow passageway, he got down on his hands and knees, ducking his head out. The area was deserted. They were on the opposite side of the mud cave, nowhere near the other entrance. A steep slope downhill could pose a challenge for Penny and Cruz, but it wasn't impossible. He'd sooner navigate rocky, crumbling terrain than tangle with members of Shane's crew.

"How does it look?" Penny asked.

"Like freedom," he said, straightening.

He was embarrassed by his reaction to Penny's earlier embrace, and by the tears that clogged his throat now. It had always been this way with her. Even casual hugs from friends made him uneasy, but he could handle it. He couldn't handle his feelings for her. They were too intense, too threatening to his self-control. Whenever she got close to him, he felt as if he was on the edge of something, ready to fall over. Her touch affected him on a deeper level, reaching the places he was afraid to access.

Instead of urging Penny and Cruz through the opening, he hesitated. They might be spotted as they fled the area. He needed to buy them a little more time. "I have to create a diversion so we can get away without being followed."

Penny gave him a curious look. Her eye makeup from last night was smudged, her pretty face streaked with dirt. "How?"

He had an idea, but he couldn't explain it with Cruz listening. So he gave her a watered-down version. "I'll shoot a hole in the tunnel. While the guys come in to see what happened, we'll climb out."

"Okay," she said.

"Stay here. I'll be right back."

She nodded, her mouth trembling. He didn't think she suspected what he really planned to do, but he avoided her gaze as he left the cavern. Heart racing, he returned to the place Brett had fallen. He was conscious now, sitting up with his back to the wall. Owen couldn't decide if that made his task easier or harder. He'd already broken the guy's nose. Now he was *really* going to jack him up.

He took the weapon from his waistband. It was loaded and ready; he'd checked. Raising the gun, he assumed a ready stance. The flashlight in his left hand supported his right.

Brett cowered against the cave wall, trying to scoot backward. "No," he cried, his voice muffled by the hand cupped over his face. "Don't, please!"

Owen took aim and pulled the trigger, shooting him in the foot. If he'd waited another second, he might have lost his nerve. It was probably the most difficult, most horrific thing he'd ever done—and he'd done a lot of shitty things.

Brett screamed at the top of his lungs, moving his hands from his broken nose to his ruined foot.

Owen was tempted to apologize, but he didn't. He just walked away. Brett didn't give a fuck how sorry he was. He'd spend the next few hours, if not days, in excruciating pain. He might be crippled for life. The fact that Brett was a kidnapper who'd agreed to do the same to Owen didn't ease his guilt any.

Shane shouted into the radio, demanding answers.

Owen engaged the safety and tucked the gun into his waistband. It sizzled against the small of his back. The burn wasn't worth wincing at, under the circumstances. His stomach lurched suddenly. He stopped in the middle of the tunnel and retched, emptying its meager contents. After his nausea abated, he wiped his mouth with the back of his hand and continued down the corridor on wobbly legs. This wasn't the first time he'd shot a man. It was the first time he'd shot a *defenseless* man, and the difference wrecked him.

"We haven't found another way in," Dirk said to Shane on the radio. "Do you want us to come back to where you are?"

"Yes," Shane growled. "Fuck!"

Owen turned down the volume on the radio. His risk had paid off, but he felt no triumph. When he re-entered the cavern, Penny flinched. Her arms were wrapped around Cruz, her hands covering his ears.

She seemed reluctant to let go, which was understandable. Brett's hoarse cries faded into the background as Owen came forward.

He wondered how he looked to her. Like a monster, not a hero.

Owen felt disconnected from reality, as if studying the scene from above. He didn't want to be the kind of person who shot a man as a strategy, instead of in self-defense, but here he was. He just wished Penny and Cruz didn't have to witness it.

"You climb out first," he said to Penny. "Cruz can go next."

She edged closer to the opening, kissing Cruz on the top of the head.

"Wait for us right outside," Owen said.

"Be careful, Mommy."

She had to get down on her hands and knees to pass through the narrow space. Her skirt impeded her progress, so she hiked it up to her waist. He watched her crawl forward, his pulse jackknifing. It was an incredibly inappropriate moment to ogle her. They were still in danger. He'd shot an unarmed man two minutes ago. Even so, his mind wasn't so detached from his body that he failed to admire her perfect backside, framed by lacy black panties. His libido was like the heat of the muzzle—irrelevant, but undeniable. Seeing her in this position appealed to the animal in him. He couldn't have averted his gaze if he'd tried.

When she reached daylight, she sat up and glanced around carefully before signaling for them to join her. Cruz climbed out next, followed by Owen. The path along the side of the hill looked much steeper from here.

"Don't stand up," he said to Penny. "Crouch down and slide on your butt if you have to. I'll take Cruz."

She did what he said, her movements clumsy. He winced as she half slid, half scrambled down the slope, probably scraping her hands and bruising her bottom in the process. But she reached the ground safely.

"Ready?" he asked Cruz.

The boy looked up at him with huge brown eyes. "I'm scared."

"I won't let you fall."

Cruz clung to his neck, trembling with fear. He made short work of the climb. Penny watched them descend, her face tense. She took Cruz away from Owen at the first opportunity. Making a strangled sound, she cradled her son to her chest.

He studied the hole they'd climbed out of, raking a hand through his dusty hair. Although he didn't want to push Penny too hard, they couldn't afford to delay. Brett's injury would create problems for Shane and his ragtag crew, but that didn't mean their ordeal was over. Someone would come after them.

"Let's go," he said to Penny as gently as possible.

She set Cruz on his feet and trudged forward, her shoulders trembling. She knew what he'd done to Brett. He'd exposed her to his true nature. She'd seen the ugliness inside him, the savagery he'd always tried to hide. He'd been raised this way. Infected with dysfunction, hardened by circumstances. He couldn't shed his criminal past. He was the kind of person who got off on the sight of a crawling woman. He'd just committed a stunning act of violence. There was no going back now.

He wasn't one of the kidnappers, but he wasn't one of the good guys, either.

CHAPTER SIX

"WHAT THE FUCK is going on in there?"

Shane released the talk button, listening for a response from Brett. Still nothing. Jesus. When he'd told Brett to shoot Owen in the foot, he'd been bluffing! He never thought Brett would actually do it. He'd just wanted to ensure Owen's cooperation. Maybe Brett had gotten trigger-happy. He was young and green and eager.

Shane didn't want to wait for Dirk and Roach to return to the entrance. "I'm heading inside," he said to Dirk on the radio. He turned on his flashlight and made his way through the narrow passageway, taking care not to bump his head or scrape his elbows. He could barely fit through the tight squeezes.

He should have taken Owen through the tunnel instead of Brett. Shane didn't trust Dirk—he was an arrogant bastard. Shane didn't trust himself, either. He couldn't shoot a family member. Owen clearly had feelings for this girl and her kid, which complicated the situation. Putting a gun to his brother's head had made Shane's flesh crawl as if a thousand centipedes had walked over his skin.

He hoped Owen wasn't dead. Their mother would

be devastated. She already thought Shane was responsible for ruining her life and for messing up Owen's. She'd been a shell of a person since they'd both gone to prison.

Fuck.

He couldn't get Brett to answer on the walkie-talkie, so he gave up and used a loud voice, calling out his name every few minutes. When Shane reached a fork in the path, he paused, pointing the beam of his flashlight in both directions. There was a dark, wet trail on the right, along with the telltale drag marks of a person with an injured limb.

Heart racing, Shane drew his gun from the back of his pants. "Owen!"

"Over here," Brett shouted.

Shane stepped around the soaked dirt and continued through the tunnel. Brett was around the corner, sitting with his back to the wall. His face was smeared with blood and dust. He'd removed his white T-shirt and tied it around his boot. The effect was cartoonish, like a giant bandaged foot.

"Where are they?" Shane asked.

Brett pointed into the dark. "I think they went that way."

"How far?"

"I don't know."

Shane stared down the twisted passage in disbelief. "I told you to shoot *him* in the foot," he said, even though he hadn't meant it. "Not yourself!"

"He shot me," Brett mumbled.

"What?"

"He took the gun and knocked me out. Then he came back and shot me."

No wonder Brett's face was mangled. On second glance, his nose appeared to be broken.

The radio at his belt sounded. "We're at the front of the cave," Dirk said. "Do you want us to come in?"

Shane didn't answer right away. He squinted at Brett, weighing his options. The shirt wrapped around his boot was soaked with blood. Shane didn't think he'd die in the next few hours, but he needed immediate medical treatment, and they were out in the middle of nowhere. Driving him to the emergency room would take all day. More importantly, hospitals reported gunshot wounds. His contact, Ace, would probably tell him to eliminate this problem right here, rather than risking capture.

Brett wasn't so naive that he couldn't see the wheels turning in Shane's mind. Perhaps getting shot had introduced him to cold, hard reality. He looked terrified and trapped, writhing in agony. But he didn't cry or beg. He would go out like a man.

After a moment of indecision, Shane let him live. Not because he'd shown a hint of courage, but because Brett reminded him of Owen. The kid had tagged along with his good-for-nothing brother and ended up in a world of hurt.

Explaining the second shot to Dirk would have been tricky, also.

"Yeah, come in," Shane said into the radio. "We're on the right side."

Brett slumped against the dirt wall, relieved.

"How did he take your gun?"

"I don't know. He just…attacked me."

"Did you try to shoot him?"

"I didn't get the chance."

"You had the flashlight," Shane explained. "He was in *front* of you."

"He said something about bats," Brett said, panting. His forehead was dotted with sweat. "I looked up for a second."

Shane stared at his misshapen nose, wanting to break it again. Every minute that ticked by gave Owen and that Spanish cunt a greater opportunity to escape. He wondered if his brother had lied to him about their relationship. They acted like a couple, and he had her son's name tattooed on his chest. What kind of sucker did that for a girl he wasn't even dating? Why get a tribute for a kid who wasn't his?

By the time Dirk and Roach reached them, Shane was seething. He'd been pissed at Gardener for dropping the ball, but confident that a woman with a child wouldn't get far. Now they had Owen's help. The three of them might leave this cave and walk all the way back to civilization.

Shane felt the situation slipping from his hands. These idiots were going to ruin everything, and the stakes were too high for him to back out. He owed the Aryan Brotherhood more money than he could ever pay. If he skipped town, they might threaten his family. It was a matter of honor, if nothing else.

Dirk went nuts when he saw Brett. He paced back and forth, plotting revenge on Owen. "I'll kill him," he repeated, baring his teeth. "When I find him, I'll cut off his head and piss on his neck."

"Shut up," Shane said wearily.

"I'll do his bitch, too. I'll do her right in front of him."

Shane fisted his hand in Dirk's shirt. "You won't do a goddamned thing unless I say so. Got that?"

Dirk didn't agree, but he didn't argue, either.

Shane let him go. "Stay here while Roach and I check the rest of the cave."

He sat down beside Brett, his nostrils flaring. Shane crept down the passageway with his gun drawn. They came to a large room with an opening to the outside. Cursing, he bent down and looked through the hole.

There was no sign of them.

As Shane straightened, the implications of Owen's actions began to sink in. His little brother had a gun. He knew the badlands as well as Shane did, if not better. Owen could survive out here. He could hide.

That wasn't Shane's only challenge. He'd planned to recapture this bitch and her brat before checking in with Ace. Now Shane had to deliver the bad news. He'd lost his quarry, *and* he had an injured man to deal with.

He turned to Roach, his eyes narrow. "Find their

trail and follow it. We can't afford to let them get away."

"What do I do if I see them?"

"Keep your distance. Watch them until we come back."

"Where are you going?"

"I don't know yet."

Roach left the cavern, armed with a jug of water and a walkie-talkie. Shane went back down the tunnel to rejoin Dirk and Brett. "They're gone," he said, clenching his hand into a fist. "Let's get him out of here."

Dirk helped Brett stand up and supported him on one side as they limped away. The return trip to the SUV took forever. Brett might have been prepared to face death like a man, but he handled a gunshot wound like a total pussy. He moaned every time his boot dragged along the ground. Dirk had to lift him up and carry him the last half mile.

Shane didn't slow down or offer to help. When they reached the SUV, Dirk loaded him into the backseat, elevating the injured foot. It was still bleeding.

"Should I take off his boot?" Dirk asked.

"Hell if I know."

"Don't touch it," Brett wailed.

Dirk removed the soaked T-shirt, to Brett's dismay. He had a small hole in the top of his boot and a slightly larger one in the sole.

"It went in and out," Shane said.

Brett grimaced. "Is that good?"

"It's better than ricocheting around in there, shattering bones."

Dirk wrapped another shirt around Brett's boot and gave him a bottle of whiskey, which he sucked on like a tit. "He needs to go to the hospital."

"Let's go," Shane said, annoyed.

He got behind the wheel of the SUV while Dirk climbed into the back with his brother. Brett made a sound of agony every time Shane went over a bump. He turned the radio up to drown out his whimpers.

Back at camp, he slowed down to talk to Gardener, another useless wretch. He was sitting in the shade, smoking a joint.

"Get in," Shane said.

Gardener blinked at him stupidly. "I just started this."

"Bring it."

As soon as he got in the passenger seat, Shane took the joint away, bringing it to his lips and inhaling deeply. He was going to smoke the rest without sharing, but then the mellow mood hit him and he handed it back.

"What happened?" Gardener asked.

"Brett got shot."

"Really?"

"Yeah."

They followed the road to the highway. It was a long drive, so long that they were sober again by the time they arrived. Brett hadn't lost consciousness, and his color looked better. Shane was glad; he didn't want to go to all this trouble for a goner.

While he drove, he tried to plan what he would say to the boss. Ace was really just a middleman, a connection between Shane and his unknown clients. Shane knew they were affiliated with the AB, but he'd never met any of them. He didn't want to meet them. He just wanted to do the job and get the hell out of Dodge.

Before he bit the bullet and called Ace, he took Owen's phone from his pocket, scrolling through his list of contacts.

Janelle was there. Owen had her home number *and* her cell phone number, unlike Shane. She refused any communication from him, even letters. She told him that he had to apply for visitation rights if he wanted to see Jamie.

Shane knew Janelle was friendly with Owen, but he'd never envied their relationship. Probably because he'd held an outdated view of his little brother, like an old picture he hadn't bothered to replace. Owen was a man now. The better man, according to Janelle. The man who was allowed to visit Jamie.

Shane dialed her number on his throwaway cell. She picked up right away, her voice raspy from sleep. The sound hit him like a main-line rush. She wouldn't have answered if she'd known it was him. They hadn't shared an uncontentious conversation in years. Shane wished he could ask to speak to his son.

Instead, he shoved the phone at Gardener. "Tell

her to take Jamie and go to her mother's house. Stay there for a few days."

Gardener repeated this message.

Shane listened as Janelle's tone turned shrill. She demanded answers and issued threats. This was the woman he knew, sharp and combative. But even her foulmouthed tirade elicited a pleasurable response in him, oddly enough. He remembered the good times, the passionate arguments and wild nights.

Clearing his throat, he ended the call. Then he dialed Ace's number. "We have a problem."

"I don't like problems."

Shane broke the news about Brett's accident and claimed he had the situation under control. No need to worry Ace with too many details. Shane was optimistic his brother wouldn't be on the loose for long. Owen had limited resources. The girl and her kid would drag him down. In this heat, they couldn't outrun Shane on foot.

"Let me talk to Roach," Ace said.

"He's back at camp. Keeping an eye on things."

"Just handle it," he said, and hung up.

Shane said he would. If he didn't, he'd be a dead man.

He had a third call to make, to Jorge Sandoval. It couldn't be traced, but it could be triangulated. The government might scrutinize all communication signals from the same basic area, and there was nobody else out here. He drove twenty more miles to the town of El Centro, pulling over at a dusty truck stop.

Shane got out and glanced around to make sure the coast was clear before dialing. Dirk waited in the backseat, an impatient look on his face.

"This is Jorge Sandoval."

Shane had planned for Owen to make this call. It was the only reason Shane had brought him along. He didn't trust Gardener to do it right, so now his only option was disguising his voice. "Do you have the money?"

Jesus. He sounded like Cookie Monster.

"I want to speak to my daughter," Sandoval demanded coolly.

His attitude pissed Shane off. "You think you're in charge?"

"You've made it abundantly clear who's in charge."

The way he said it suggested the opposite was true. Sandoval was a Mexican puppet, as far as Shane was concerned, but the man enjoyed a position of wealth and power. All men wanted those things.

"I have the money," Sandoval said. "Please, put Penny on the phone."

"We need a goodwill gesture first," Shane growled. "Drop out of the race. Make a formal announcement. When we hear the news, we'll get back to you."

He hung up before Sandoval could reply. The men Shane worked for had financial and political motivations. They'd take Sandoval's money, but they also wanted a different puppet in the White House. It didn't matter to Shane. He couldn't care less about politics. He'd been chosen for this job because of his connection to Owen.

Climbing behind the wheel, he continued a few more miles to a parking garage. He had a getaway vehicle stashed here. He'd kept it secret from the other guys. It was always good to have a solo escape plan. Although he'd recruited everyone on the crew except Roach, that didn't mean he wouldn't double-cross them.

Shane cleaned his prints off the cell phone and gave it to Gardener. "Take Brett to a hospital in Mexico. Before you cross the border, make a phone call. Dial a number from a billboard, any random number. Hang up when they answer. Then wipe the phone and ditch it in a trash can."

Gardener stared at him in disbelief. There were three glossy, purplish knobs on his forehead. He reminded Shane of the dead fish on Salton Sea Beach. They washed up in stinking piles, their eyes foggy and jaws gaping open.

"You got that?"

Gardener nodded, accepting the phone. Shane made him repeat the instructions twice. "How long should we stay in Mexico?"

"Until you get word to come back."

Dirk shook his head in protest. "Brett can't get operated on by a border doctor, man. They'll cut off his foot with a rusty knife."

Shane doubted it, but he didn't really care.

"We can find a hospital in Arizona and say he shot himself."

Even in Arizona, people asked questions. Who were you with, what were you doing. All it took was one slip, and Brett wasn't a practiced liar. Unlike him. "They're going to Mexico. Boss's orders."

"How the hell are we getting back to camp?"

"I have a backup vehicle parked here."

Dirk swore under his breath. He said a tearful goodbye to Brett while Shane gathered his belongings and got out. They stood and watched the SUV drive south, toward the border crossing in Calexico.

"This is fucked up," Dirk said.

"Yes."

"You should have sent me into the cave instead of him."

That might have ended more violently. Dirk had no finesse with guns or women. "It was a simple task."

"Yeah? You didn't tell anyone your brother was a psycho."

Shane had to admit he'd underestimated Owen. He'd always seen his little brother as skinny and weak. Gentle but ineffectual, like their mother. As a child, Owen had felt sorry for the dying fish on the shore, throwing them back in to the toxic sea. Once he'd tried to save an egret that got stuck in the mud.

He was…sensitive.

Shane had assumed that Owen landed the cushy security job because of his connection to the candidate's daughter, not because he was a qualified badass.

"My mistake," he said with a hint of admiration. "It never occurred to me that he'd fight back in these circumstances."

"Why not?"

"I didn't think he had the balls."

CHAPTER SEVEN

PENNY KNEW WHAT Owen had done.

She'd held her hands over Cruz's ears in anticipation of the gunshot blast, and had kept them there to muffle the screams.

She understood why he'd done it, too. A medical emergency was a serious diversion, affording them better opportunity to escape. These men would exact a bloody revenge on Owen if they got the chance, but she didn't blame him for taking the risk. She knew he'd do anything to protect her and Cruz.

Owen seemed troubled by his actions, his brow furrowed and his mouth drawn. She longed to put her arms around him, but she doubted he'd take comfort in her embrace. He would hold himself at a distance, as always.

They fled the scene in a rush, traveling on a footpath that zigzagged across the mountain of dried mud. Owen kept his shoulders low, seeming to expect gunfire to erupt at any moment. The sun bore down on them like an oppressive force. It burned the top of her scalp and sucked the moisture from her lips. She could feel the heat of the earth through the soles of her stolen boots. The dry air singed her lungs, and it was only midmorning. She was walking in an oven. Cruz couldn't keep up.

Owen carried him for about a mile. When they reached a shady spot in an adjacent canyon, he stopped, looking back the way they'd come.

"Do you think they're following us?" Penny asked.

"I don't see anyone."

She sat down on a rock next to Cruz, offering him water. His cheeks were flushed, his eyes half-lidded. He gulped the drink, but his normal excitability was gone. As soon as his thirst was slaked, he slumped against her, drowsy. His forehead felt cool against her palm, which was a good sign. Cruz wasn't used to this much strenuous activity, and he'd only slept six or seven hours the night before. He needed a nap.

"What now?" she said, passing the canteen to Owen.

He took a judicious sip. "We have to keep moving. There's a spring near here. It might be a puddle this time of year, but I think it's our best bet."

"Why? The water won't be safe to drink."

"We can use it to cool down, though. Higher ground is easier to defend, and I can see someone coming from far away. The palm trees also give off plenty of shade. It's a good place to rest until the sun sets."

"Then what?"

"There's an old railroad a few miles south. It leads to the 8 Freeway."

"The 8 Freeway," she repeated, cracking a smile.

He had a history with the 8. After escaping the earth-quake rubble, he'd ridden a BMX along that route until he'd found some National Guardsmen.

He didn't smile back at her. "If we walk all night, we might get there. If not, we'll rest during the day and try again."

"We'll run out of water today," she said, lifting the half-empty canteen.

"Maybe not. There are water stations every ten miles or so."

"Water stations?"

"This is a popular border crossing area."

She'd heard of people traveling from Mexico through the desert on foot. Now she could better imagine the difficulty. Before setting out again, they made some gear adjustments. She took off her boots to rewrap her feet. The scraps of fabric kept getting bunched up, and several blisters were starting to form. When she winced at the tender spots on her heels, Owen removed his socks and gave them to her.

"Won't your feet hurt?"

"Not as much as yours."

His basic black oxfords looked well-worn and com-fortable, so she accepted his socks. The combina-tion of soft cotton and stuffed toes felt much better. She applied ChapStick to her lips and face, doing the same for Cruz.

"Want some?" she asked Owen. "It has SPF 15."

He put it on like war paint, two slashes across his cheeks and one on his nose.

They needed more protection from the sun, so she examined the fishing vest, deciding it could be made into hats. At her request, Owen cut the sturdy, sand-colored fabric into two sections. Penny put one of the squares on Cruz's head and secured it with a strip from her skirt. Then she gave the other section to Owen.

"What about you?"

"I've got something else."

Taking the knife from him, she cut away another layer of her skirt, making a veil that covered her head and bare shoulders. Owen used his belt as a hatband. Soon they were all outfitted desert-sheikh style.

"You look like a shepherd," Cruz said to Owen.

Owen smiled, picking up a long stick to use as a staff. "So do you. Let's herd your mother up this hill."

Cruz grabbed his own stick, enjoying the game. She allowed herself to be "herded" for a few minutes before letting Owen take the lead. The hike was strenuous, and the temperature seemed to climb with the altitude. Cruz soldiered on. He walked behind Owen, mimicking his gait and matching his stride.

About an hour later, his strength was sapped. So was hers. They'd eaten nothing today, after a grueling trek last night. It was blazing hot, well over one hundred degrees, and dry as a bone. When Cruz dropped his stick out of fatigue, she lifted him into her arms. Black spots danced behind her eyes, and the world tilted.

She set him down quickly, fearing a fall.

Owen turned to study her with concern. His gaze traveled across the landscape before returning to her. "Okay now?"

Her vision cleared, but she didn't know how long it would last. "Yes."

"You want a horsey ride, Cruz?"

He nodded, climbing on Owen's back. Penny took the lead again, after drinking a few more sips of water. She trudged forward, putting one foot in front of the other. Owen encouraged her to move at her own pace. He kept saying they were almost there.

Almost there.

Almost there.

And then they were. She saw the circle of palm trees in the distance, the fresh green fronds and shady allure. It smelled like wet leaves and mud. If she wasn't so dehydrated, she might have wept at the sight.

The "oasis" was no fantasy paradise. It was a shallow, rocky pool about six feet wide, surrounded by towering palms. Palm fans littered the ground, their stems arched and spiky, like dinosaur backbones.

Owen let Cruz down, groaning as if his muscles ached. He took the fabric off his head and raked a hand through his short hair. Cruz did the same.

She approached the edge of the pool with Cruz. "You can't drink it."

"Why not?"

"It might have bugs."

He flopped down on his belly and stuck his arms

in the water, which was murky and moss-green. Making a frog noise, he hopped his hand along the surface, retreating into the safety of his imagination. He needed both rest and playtime, like all children.

Penny sat down next to him, her muscles aching. She removed her scarf and swished it around in the pool. When the cloth was soaked, she wrapped it around her head. Cool water streamed down her face and neck.

Heaven.

Owen investigated a wooden barrel that was stuck between two tree trunks. "Sometimes people put extra supplies here." As he opened the cask, his eyes widened with delight. He took out a sack containing three small water bottles, a can of apple juice, three boxes of raisins, and six dried sausage sticks. "Thank you, Boy Scouts of America."

"How do you know it was them?"

"They signed the notebook."

Penny accepted the goodies, her stomach growling. She tore open the sausage packet for Cruz and handed it to him. Then she bit into hers. "Oh, my God," she said, chewing rapturously. "This is so good."

Owen grinned, watching her eat with pleasure. The three of them wolfed down the sausage sticks and moved on to the raisins.

"Mmm," she said, gobbling them up. "I don't even like raisins."

"I don't, either."

They laughed as if raisins were hilarious as well

as delicious. Even Cruz ate a handful. Penny let him drink all of the juice, figuring that he could use the electrolytes. She wasn't full afterward, but she felt better.

Cruz took off his shoes and waded into the water. Penny followed suit, removing her boots and socks with a wince. She sank her aching feet into the sandy mud at the bottom, wiggling her toes. "You might have to carry me tonight."

"Whatever it takes," Owen said. Instead of joining them, he went to the edge of the trees to keep watch.

Cruz splashed around until his clothes were soaked. The pool wasn't deep enough to submerge fully, so he stretched out on his back and tried to float. Penny dipped her scarf into the water and used it like a washcloth, sponging her arms. The air was so hot and dry, even in the shade. The cool trickle was a revelation against her dusty skin. She didn't protest when Cruz used a palm stem to ladle water over her head.

Owen made a bed of loose palm fronds, snapping off the sharp stems and tossing them aside. Refreshed, Cruz started helping him. He dragged a half-dozen more fronds over to Owen. Soon they'd built a soft place to rest.

"Try it out, Mommy."

She stood, wringing the excess water from her hair. When Owen averted his gaze from her body, she looked down. Her dress was almost indecent. The wet fabric clung to her like tissue paper, revealing everything. But it wasn't as if she was naked underneath. Her bra and panties covered as much as a bikini.

Crawling on to the pile of leaves, she declared it comfortable. "We should take a nap."

Cruz settled in next to Penny and closed his eyes. Too warm to snuggle, she simply stroked his damp hair, smoothing it away from his forehead until he drifted off. He was a quick, deep sleeper. She waited beside him for a few minutes to make sure he stayed down. While they rested, Owen kicked off his shoes and climbed into the pool. She watched with interest as he knelt in the water and removed his shirt, keeping his back to her. He still had the clover tattoo, among others. His shoulders looked wider, his muscles harder. His ink-sleeved arms flexed as he dunked the shirt in the pool, soaking the fabric.

To her disappointment, he didn't linger. He put his shirt back on and stood, dripping. Rolling his pant legs up to his knees, he returned to his guard post.

Penny looked up at the swaying trees, filled with a mixture of peace and dread. They were alive. For now, they were safe. But they had a long way to go before this was over. She didn't know if they'd make it.

She reminded herself that she'd survived a worse situation during the San Diego earthquake. But what were the odds that she'd get lucky again? How many chances did people have in life? How many hours before time ran out?

Inching away from Cruz, she sat up and studied his precious face. It satisfied her soul to see him sleeping comfortably, lost in dreamland. Maybe because she'd spent so many nights rocking him as an infant, taking care of his illnesses, singing him lullabies. Heart aching, she leaned in to kiss his cheek. It was still baby-soft.

She rose and tiptoed away to find Owen. He was nearby, sitting under a tree with his back to a flat rock. He had a pair of binoculars.

"Where'd you get those?"

"In the barrel. A bird-watcher probably lost them."

She examined the trail they'd ascended. It had taken them all morning to hike up here, and she could see far into the distance, even without binoculars.

"You should lie down," he said, not looking at her.

"So should you."

"I can't."

She sank down beside him and turned her face to the breeze. Although warm, it felt pleasant now that she was wet. "Where did you shoot him?"

"In the foot."

"Will he die?"

"Not from the wound."

She wasn't sure she wanted him to elaborate. "What about the man I hit over the head?"

"What about him?"

"Is he okay?"

His blue eyes slid to hers. "Did he touch you?"

"No."

He let the binoculars drop, resting his arm on a bent knee. "He's fine."

There was a faint reddish band around his neck—strangulation marks, in addition to the old tattoo scar. She thought back to the disturbing scene by the campfire. The leader seemed familiar in a way she couldn't put her finger on. It occurred to her that he looked like Owen. "Who are they?"

He didn't answer.

"You know them, don't you?"

"I only know one."

"Which one?"

"My brother. Shane."

"He's the man who choked you?"

He inclined his head.

Penny recoiled in shock. Owen hadn't told her much about his family. She was aware that he'd grown up near here. His brother was a convicted killer. Their sibling relationship added weight to all of the decisions he'd made so far. Owen had chosen Penny and Cruz over Shane. "When did he get out of jail?"

"Prison," he corrected. "Last month."

"Did you see him?"

"No." He kicked at the dirt, making a sound of frustration. "I never suspected he'd do anything like this."

"Why would you? It's not your fault."

"I'm supposed to protect you and Cruz."

"And you have."

His mouth twisted with self-derision, but he didn't argue.

"Does your brother know about this place?"

"Yes."

"Then he knows where the railroad is."

"Of course."

"Is it safe to rest?"

He shrugged. "We have to conserve our energy during the day. You don't want to get heat sickness out here."

"What if he catches up?"

"Just because he's familiar with the area doesn't mean he can guess my every move. He might assume we're hiding. It would be a smart strategy. If you weren't in such good shape, I'd suggest that."

"You think I'm in good shape?"

The question invited him to take a closer look, which he did. Her dress was still damp, her skirt hanging in tatters. Once long and layered, it was now short and thin, riding high on her thighs. He tore his gaze away without answering, but the attention went beyond casual regard. There was a different sort of tension between them, as if this experience had stripped away the first layer of his defenses.

She examined his profile, replaying their exchange from last night. He'd kissed her on the cheek less than twenty-four hours ago. Would he do it again, if she asked nicely?

This wasn't an appropriate time or place to tell him how she felt. The conversation was bound to make him uncomfortable. There was a reason he put distance between them, and she doubted he'd volunteer the information. Maybe he was aware of her father's machinations, and accepted them because it was easier than moving forward. He wanted to stay in this limbo.

Close to her, but not quite touching.

She didn't think she'd imagined his desire after the kiss. She wasn't imagining it now. His eyes were gleaming, his shoulders taut.

"Cruz asked me if you were his father," she said.

He turned to stare at her. "When?"

"A few weeks ago."

"What did you say?"

"I said no."

"You've talked to him about his real father before?"

"Yes."

"How did that go?"

Her chest tightened at the memory. "He asked... why Tyler didn't want him. I said it had nothing to do with him. Tyler just wasn't ready to be a dad."

"Did he understand?"

"I guess not," she said wryly. "Maybe he understands, but he doesn't want it to be true. He likes to play make-believe. And he adores you."

Owen fell silent, soaking this in.

"Cruz also knows you were there when he was born. I think he decided you might have been there for the conception, as well."

His lips quirked into a smile. "Have you told him how babies are made?"

"Just the basics," she said, smiling back at him.

He'd never looked better to her, despite a dark bruise on his cheekbone and a scrape along his jaw. His wet shirt was semitransparent, blurring the lines of his tattoos. He had a lean, well-muscled physique. Even his feet were handsome, his calves dusted with hair.

He'd been twenty-one when they'd first met, boyish and awkward. Now, at twenty-six, he was all man.

His easy affection for Cruz made him more attractive to her. Owen avoided physical contact with just about everyone except Cruz. She wanted Owen to make an exception for her, too. She wanted him to want her.

He seemed interested in her sexually, but he wasn't easy to read. They'd been friends for years, and he'd never tried anything. Their most romantic moment had been that slow dance at Sam's wedding. She remembered the feel of his hard body, his heart hammering against hers. She'd imagined he would kiss her, right there on the dance floor. Or even better, take her out to the garden and press her back against the stone wall.

But when the dance had ended, they'd drifted apart. She'd had no idea what he'd been thinking. Her father had offered him a job a few months later.

Maybe he'd experienced nothing more than a mild panic attack when they'd danced. Maybe he'd have the same reaction to any woman pressing herself against him, showing off her legs…begging for a kiss.

She flushed at the thought, unsure of herself.

"Tell me about Salton City," she said. "The truth, this time."

His brows rose at this request. "Some of what I told you before was true."

"Which part?"

"The sea is blue."

"Like the sky?"

"Darker."

"What else?"

"It's beautiful from a distance."

"Not up close?"

"No."

"Why not?"

"Some of the beaches are pristine-looking, with what appears to be fine white sand. When you get closer, you see what it really is."

"What?"

"Bones. Crushed bones. Thousands of fish die on the shore every summer."

"Why?" she asked, stricken.

"It's too hot. The oxygen levels drop, and they can't breathe."

She frowned, unable to fathom such a thing.

"One year there was a really bad heat wave," he said, glancing across the desolate landscape. "Shane and I rode our bikes down to the shore to check it out. There were piles of tilapia. Mountains of them. The sea was silver with floating bodies. They said eight million fish died that day."

"How could there even be that many fish to begin with?"

"It's a big sea."

"Did every single fish die?"

"I don't think so. The next year there were plenty."

"That's unnatural."

He laughed softly, not disagreeing.

"Why is it so toxic?"

"Lots of reasons. It's an ecological disaster."

"What do you mean?"

"About a hundred years ago, there was a flood. The Colorado River busted one of its canals and filled up the salt basin."

"What's a salt basin?"

"A place where they used to mine salt. By the time they rerouted the river, the Salton Sea was forty miles wide. Some real estate developers came in with dollar signs in their eyes. They figured a huge lake in the middle of the desert would be a perfect vacation destination. And it was, for a while. But the water salinity kept increasing, and something went wrong with the fish. Then the birds got sick. The stench and decay attracts flies, not tourists. When the resort area washed out, they never bothered to rebuild it."

"That's sad."

"Yes," he said. "Now you see why I lied."

"I can handle the truth."

He didn't respond. She'd been scared, eighteen, and in labor. He'd chosen to spin a tale of fiction rather than disturb her.

"What can be done to fix it?"

"I don't know. They can't control the heat. Decreasing the salt content would cost a lot of money. The sea level gets lower every year. If they let it dry up, the sediment will make huge dust clouds over L.A."

She wondered if her father knew about this. He probably did. "So Salton City is hot and dry and it smells bad. Why does anyone live here?"

"It's cheap," he said flatly. "And the weather's nice in the winter."

"How is your mother doing?"

"She's okay," he said, setting the binoculars aside.

His father had died last year. Owen had gone to take care of things and pay his respects. When Penny had offered to accompany him, he'd refused. "Does she miss your dad?"

"I don't know why she would."

"Do you?"

He picked up a pebble and rolled it between his fingertips, considering.

"You told me he worked on cars."

"He was a welder."

"You said he rebuilt a Chevy for you."

"That was a lie."

"You lie a lot," she said, smiling.

He tossed the pebble away, his jaw clenched. She hadn't really meant it, but she could follow his train of thought. He'd also said he'd joined the Aryan Brotherhood by choice, not for self-preservation. They both knew it wasn't true.

"I rebuilt the Chevy," he said, glancing at her. "I worked on it by myself for months."

"Why?"

"He brought it home for me. It was a rusted piece of shit, but it was the only thing I remember him giving me. He said we'd work on it together. Then he got arrested for stealing auto parts and went to jail."

"So you did all the work?"

"Yes. I liked it. He taught me everything he knew about mechanics and welding, which was quite a bit. He let me borrow tools. We didn't get along in the house very well, but he tolerated me in the garage."

"Did your brother help?"

"No. Shane didn't have the patience for fixing things. It was the one area where my dad and I saw eye to eye, instead of Shane and him."

"What happened to that car?"

"He sold it for drugs."

She bit her lip, hurting for the boy he'd been.

"At the time, I was crushed. I was seventeen and I'd just gotten my license. I hadn't even driven it yet."

"And now?"

"Now, what stands out to me is how impressed he was when he saw the work I'd done. He was proud of me."

Owen hadn't lied to her about everything. He'd been honest about his father's physical and verbal abuse without going into detail. The story about the car disturbed her, but she was glad he'd shared it. She didn't blame him for loving his father despite his flaws. It wasn't the kind of relationship a child could opt out of—even though so many fathers did.

Owen's ability to find a scrap of good in everyone was a reflection of his kind nature. The tears he blinked away were a testament to his strength, not a sign of weakness.

Instead of pretending not to see them, she lifted her hands to his face. The hours she'd thought he was dead had been excruciating. She wanted to be with him, and she didn't care what anyone else thought about it.

Turning his head toward her, she brushed her lips over his scraped cheek. Tasting salt, she kissed the corner of his tense mouth. Her fingertips trailed down the side of his neck, grazing his tattoo scar and the tender bruise. She longed to twine her arms around him and press her breasts against his chest.

Instead of giving in to her, he grasped her wrists and held them tight, as if her touch pained him. She met his gaze and saw the want. The *need*. It was in his taut muscles and ragged breaths. But his hands said *don't*.

She retreated a few inches, stricken. He released her wrists.

"I'm sorry," she said, her throat tight. "I thought..."

"You thought what?"

"I thought you wanted me."

His gaze moved from the trail to the place where

Cruz was taking a nap. Then he returned to her, considering. "I can't touch you, Penny."

"Why not?"

"My contract, for one. I'm not allowed to have a relationship with you outside of work."

"You're kidding."

"No."

"I doubt that stipulation is in anyone else's contract."

He didn't argue.

No wonder he'd been so reserved. Even casual friendship was off the table. "You should have told me."

He fell silent for a long moment, studying her. "Did you sleep last night?"

"Not much."

After a short silence, he put his arm around her shoulders. It was a conciliatory gesture, not the passionate embrace she'd hoped for. But she appreciated the attempt to step out of his comfort zone and console her.

The emotions she'd been holding back caught up with her. Now that Cruz was asleep, she didn't have to pretend she wasn't scared anymore. Leaning on Owen, she buried her face in his damp shirt and cried.

CHAPTER EIGHT

JANELLE STARED AT the unlisted number on her phone, wanting to scream.

She'd tried to call the stranger back, to no avail. His curt orders rang in her ears. *Take Jamie and go to your mother's.*

It was Shane. It had to be Shane. Every problem in her life could be traced back to Shane. The fact that he was also responsible for giving her Jamie, the best thing that had ever happened to her, didn't excuse the rest. Shane was a worthless excuse for a father and an all-around jerk. He didn't even have the decency to speak to her himself. She'd told him not to call, but she'd have made an exception in this case.

She should contact the police and report his sorry ass.

Her thumb traced the emergency numbers, not pressing them. What could she say, except that she suspected her recently paroled ex-boyfriend was up to no good? The cops wouldn't care about this "anonymous" message. Her car had been broken into a week ago, and they hadn't even bothered to make a report.

She rubbed her weary eyes, glancing at the clock. It was already ten, and she'd agreed to do a double shift. Her mother's house was an hour away, in the opposite direction of the club. If she was going to drop Jamie off before work, she'd have to leave now. "Shit," she groaned, reaching for the cigarette pack on her nightstand.

It was empty.

Tossing the trash on the floor, she rose from the bed and padded down the hall, barefoot. She could hear her son playing video games in the living room. The sound of rapid-fire assault weapons amplified her hangover.

She shouldn't have gone out for drinks with Tiffany after work last night. But she'd had a hard week, and making wise decisions had never been her strong suit. She was better than she used to be, miles away from perfect.

The video game paused like a record skipping. "Mom!"

She startled, almost slamming her hand in the kitchen drawer where she stashed her extra cigarettes. "What?"

Jamie and his friend, Pablo, were sitting on the couch. Pablo's eyes widened at the sight of her bare legs. She was wearing her typical pajamas, a T-shirt and panties. Her son looked mortified.

How was she supposed to know he had company?

"Get ready to go to your grandma's," she said, grabbing a soda from the fridge. "We're leaving in ten minutes."

"I don't want to."

"Too bad."

"I have soccer practice!"

Damn. She juggled the soda and cigarettes, nearly dropping both. Jamie had begged to join a competitive soccer team all summer. Eventually she'd conceded. He was a good boy, smart and athletic, with that elusive responsibility gene she lacked. She didn't like him staying by himself when she was at work, but so far he'd been fine. He rode his bike to soccer practice with Pablo, their neighbor. The games didn't start until fall.

"You can miss one practice," she said.

He jumped up off the couch, incensed. "This is the most important practice. The first game is next weekend."

Already? Jesus, time flew.

"You said I didn't have to go to Grandma's anymore."

"I changed my mind."

"I can stay with Pablo."

She glanced at Jamie's friend, who didn't protest this suggestion even though it wasn't very reasonable. His family lived next door in a trailer smaller than hers. Jamie was always welcome there, which was nice, but Pablo had more brothers and sisters than she could count. There was no room for Pablo, let alone Jamie. If she said yes, Pablo and Jamie would just hang out here, like they always did.

"No," she said.

"This sucks," he yelled. "What about the game next week?"

"If you don't watch your mouth, you'll miss that, too."

Scowling, he threw down the video-game controller. It bounced off the coffee table and knocked over a bag of chips. Nuclear-orange particles spilled across the carpet. Pablo tried to pick them up. He was a sweet kid. He probably never talked back to his mother. The behavior was unusual for Jamie, too.

Janelle didn't want to argue in her underwear, so she walked away, aware that her T-shirt didn't quite cover her butt. At least she wasn't wearing a thong. Inside her room, she cracked open the soda and took a fortifying sip.

What if her son turned out like Shane?

Maybe Jamie's outburst was a harbinger of things to come. Once he hit puberty, his hormones could take over. He'd change from a sweet kid into a surly teenager. He'd have poor impulse control and violent episodes.

"No," she said, denying the possibility. "No, no, no."

After a quick shower, she got dressed in a pair of shorts and a tank top. Lighting a cigarette, finally, she shoved her feet into cowboy boots and grabbed her bag. She looked awful, but it didn't matter. She did her hair and makeup at work, piling on the products like a sexy mask. By the time she was ready to go on stage, she almost couldn't recognize herself. And that was exactly the way she wanted it.

She fished around for her big sunglasses and put them on, along with her straw hat. "Ready?" she asked from the hallway, hoping Jamie had calmed down.

He came out of his room with his backpack. It was stuffed with superhero comics and video games, maybe a real book or two. By some miracle, he liked to read and write. She wished she could say the same. Every page of her college course work had been a struggle for her. It had taken her four years to earn an AA degree.

They completed the drive to Niland in silence.

"I won't do it again," he muttered.

"Damn right," she said, glancing at his sullen face. He had Shane's blue eyes, paired with her freckled nose and brown hair. He was growing like a weed, taking after his father. In a year he'd be taller than her. "Do what?"

"We only looked at it once."

She gave him a blank stare.

"The magazine."

After a long pause, her sluggish brain supplied the answer. She'd found a *Playboy* stashed in the recycling bin the other day. She'd thrown it away without much thought. A short chain-link fence separated their tiny front yard from the sidewalk. Anyone could have tossed the magazine into their bin.

Apparently it was Jamie's. He took care of the trash

and the recycling. If she hadn't been digging around in the bin, searching for an empty water bottle to wash and refill, she wouldn't have seen it.

She studied her son with a mixture of chagrin and concern. He was only eleven. She'd had boobs when she was eleven, but he was a boy. They matured at a slower rate. He wasn't ready for this. *She* wasn't ready for this.

Oh, God. Jamie and Pablo had been ogling pictures of naked women. This morning's underwear accident seemed so much more inappropriate now. Her cheeks heated with shame. She hadn't even known they were curious about sex. They didn't talk about girls. They played sports, geeked out on comics and ate junk food.

Janelle suppressed the urge to crack the window and light up another cigarette. She tried not to smoke in the car with Jamie. It was a million degrees out, anyway, and her air conditioner couldn't keep up. Her side window was still broken. She'd covered it with clear plastic and duct tape, praying the highway patrol wouldn't pull her over for the violation.

A ticket was all she needed.

"I don't care about the magazine," she said, glancing in her rearview mirror. "I wouldn't punish you for that."

"Then what did I do?"

"Nothing, baby. I just didn't feel like leaving you alone." When she reached across the cab to ruffle his hair, he shied away from her. Sighing, she returned her attention to the road. Although she didn't want him to think he'd done something wrong, she couldn't tell him about the scary phone call. He had no idea his father was out of prison. Shane wasn't supposed to be paroled for another year.

At first she'd felt a twinge of guilt for refusing Shane's requests to visit. Now she knew her instincts had been spot-on. He was already in trouble again. And she would never let him bring that trouble to her son.

Never.

"You weren't worried last night," he said.

That wasn't true. She'd checked on him before sneaking out with Tiffany. Maybe she shouldn't have gone at all, but she had so many responsibilities, and so few opportunities to cut loose.

"I'm always worried. My car got broken into at work, and I heard there was a home invasion on the other side of town."

"Who would rob us? We don't have anything."

"You have an Xbox."

His eyes narrowed. "We should buy a gun."

She laughed, even though she felt like crying. "Maybe I can work something out with Pablo's mother." The only other option she could think of was Shane's mother. Sally Jackson lived in Salton City. They'd never had much of a relationship, maybe because Janelle hadn't felt comfortable around Shane's father. That wasn't an issue anymore. According to Owen, Sally worked long hours as a nurse's aide. She also had a drug problem. She wasn't an ideal babysitter, but Jamie didn't need close supervision.

They arrived at her mother's house a few minutes later. Renata Parker had rheumatoid arthritis, which limited her mobility. Her second husband had left five years ago, after the diagnosis. She lived on disability checks.

Renata wasn't affectionate or attentive, but she was steady. With Janelle's father and stepfather out of the picture, her mother's home was safe. Janelle appreciated that. It was what she'd longed for most at Jamie's age.

She stared at the pristine white gravel in the front yard, remembering.

"I'm already bored," Jamie said.

"There are worse things in life than being bored."

He glanced at her, contemplative. "Take me to work with you."

"Absolutely not."

"I can scrub floors or do dishes for money."

"You're underage."

"I'll hide in the back."

He thought she was a waitress in a sports bar. She wondered what he'd say if he ever found out the truth. Imagining that moment made her die inside, just a little bit. "Is there another reason you don't want to stay here?"

"Like what?"

"Someone hurting you?"

"Grandma, you mean? She can't hurt a fly."

"You could tell me if she did."

He gave her a puzzled look. She was glad he didn't know what she was talking about. Glad he didn't have to go through what she had.

"You can talk to me about anything," she said, feeling awkward. "Is there a question you want to ask me...about girls?"

Now he understood where this was going. He flushed red, shaking his head.

Janelle's face got warm, too. Despite her lack of modesty and her sleazy job, she wasn't comfortable with this topic. It was a conversation a boy should have with his father. Shane had let them both down in so many ways.

"What about your uncle Owen?" she asked, struck by inspiration. "Would you talk to him?"

"Oh my God, Mom," he said, getting out of the car. "Just stop."

"Should I call him?"

"No!"

"Okay," she said quickly. "I love you."

He mumbled the words back to her and slammed the door, hitching his backpack on one shoulder. She watched him walk to the front door, his unruly cowlick sticking up. He needed a haircut and new clothes, badly. His backpack was worn and frayed. Her mother answered, waving at her before they went inside.

It took Janelle several moments to pull herself together. When she felt as though she was in con-

trol again, not spiraling toward an emotional break-
down, she placed her hands on the steering wheel
and drove to the club.

CHAPTER NINE

OWEN ENDURED THE TORTURE for as long as he could.

After Penny had cried on his shoulder, she'd surrendered to exhaustion and drifted off to sleep. His arm ached from holding her, and his right hand had gone numb. Still, he didn't move, merely flexing his fingers until they tingled.

It wasn't that he didn't enjoy the feel of her body against his. He did. But his sexual frustration was at an all-time high.

His contract wasn't the only reason he kept his distance. Their connection was unlike anything he'd ever known. Her gaze seemed to cut right through him, delving into places he kept hidden. Her touch went deeper. As much as he ached to be with her, he feared the experience would break him. He imagined falling on her like a ravaging beast, unable to control the flood of pent-up desire. Every dirty thought and horrible memory would converge. The emotions he held inside would come pouring out, drowning them both.

Maybe that was a little overdramatic. The bottom line was he'd rather die than hurt her. He couldn't have casual sex with her; they were too close. His response to her was too intense. And her father would disown her. Owen refused to be responsible for a rift between them. They were a nice family. She was a nice girl.

He was supposed to be *protecting* her.

Sex shouldn't have been an issue with Penny. She was his client. Even if he'd been capable of a healthy relationship, she was off-limits. He hadn't considered asking her out before he'd taken the job with her father, either. Their mutual friends had teased him about her, saying she was interested, but he hadn't believed them.

Why would drop-dead gorgeous Penny Sandoval be infatuated with *him?*

He'd realized that she liked him as a person. They'd bonded during the earthquake. She was still close with Cadence and the others. A special friendship, even one between members of the opposite sex, didn't have to develop into something else. He'd always assumed that his lust wasn't reciprocated.

Her behavior just now suggested otherwise. Owen was no Lothario, but her signals seemed clear. When a woman put her arms around his neck and pressed kisses on his face, she was looking for more than a platonic hug.

He replayed her actions, searching for an alternate explanation. She'd turned his head toward hers, kissing the tender spots on his cheek and jaw. Then she'd inched closer to his lips, as if begging him to kiss her back.

Last night, before going on stage, she'd asked him

to kiss her, point-blank. Her mouth had been as red and ripe as a cherry. He imagined that mouth all over his body, leaving marks on his skin. He couldn't decide which was sexier, bare lips or painted. Bare, probably. Bare and natural and sweet-tasting.

He studied their surroundings for a moment before turning his gaze on her. Now that she was asleep, he felt safe ogling her. When she was awake, he tried to keep his eyes averted. He was usually more successful. The stress of the past twenty-four hours had taken its toll, weakening his resolve.

The dress she was wearing had been provocative in its original state. Not too provocative, but revealing enough to make a man look twice. "Tasteful cleavage," she'd called it. The enticing hint of fullness invited a closer inspection. Although he couldn't see much more from the waist up, he had an extensive mental catalog to refer to. His go-to favorite was of Penny's soaked blouse after the water-balloon incident. The wet fabric had clung to her breasts and exposed the dark circles of her nipples. His erection grew impossibly stiff against his damp pants as he continued his perusal.

From the waist down…he smothered a groan. Her panties were visible beneath a thin, ragged layer of fabric, which only covered her to midthigh. Her legs were long and luscious, honey-smooth. He'd love to feel them wrapped around his hips as he slid into her. Pulse throbbing, he glanced away.

It seemed as if he'd wanted her forever. The idea

that she might want him, in return, was almost beyond his comprehension. He'd learned at a young age not to get his hopes up. Her desire was too good to be true—and too hot to handle.

Maybe it didn't mean anything. She was scared and vulnerable. She'd needed comfort, and he was available.

Wincing, he moved his arm out from under her and scooted away. She murmured a protest and curled up on her side, facing the other direction. Unfortunately, the position offered another visual feast. Against his better judgment, he engaged in a more thorough inspection of her legs. Her tattered skirt and lacy panties didn't do a very good job of covering her pretty ass. She had pebbles and leaves embedded in her flesh.

His fingertips itched to remove them.

Instead of reaching out to her, he ground the heel of his palm against his hard-on. It didn't help, of course.

He stood and focused on surveillance for a few minutes. He was trained to study an area section by section in regular intervals. By the time he'd done two complete sweeps, the blood had cooled.

Penny slept for about an hour. He thought of several other reasons why he should stay away from her. The situation was inappropriate. He should be concentrating on survival. He didn't want her to see his tattoos. They weren't as offensive as before, but the reminder of his checkered past was disturbing.

He felt ugly, inside and out. Tainted. She was beautiful and innocent and pure. His touch would defile her. A hand that had once been marred with a swastika didn't deserve to caress her honeyed skin.

He was like the Salton Sea. Better at a distance. Filled with old skeletons, toxic to the depths.

Penny woke with a start, sitting up and searching for Cruz.

"He's still asleep," Owen said.

She went to check on him anyway, brushing off her bottom as she rose. He clenched his hands into fists, envying the dirt that fell from her skin. Her eyes were puffy and her hair was tangled. She looked a little wild and unkempt. He was fascinated by the sight, perhaps because she was usually so put-together.

What would it be like to see her every morning before she showered or brushed her teeth? To sleep beside her every night, to know her as no one else did?

He accepted the fact that he couldn't have her. He'd never touch her or give her pleasure or make her his. But as long as they all got through this alive, he'd be okay. Keeping her and Cruz safe was enough.

He lifted the binoculars to do another sweep. A flash of movement caught his attention. Pulse racing, he searched the same section again.

There.

A man ducked into the dwindling midday shadows near the canyon wall. Owen couldn't see his face, but he recognized the orange trucker cap. Roach sat down and stretched out his legs, as if planning a short rest.

Owen had considered best-case scenarios as well as worst-case. The worst was that Shane would deal with Brett by killing him. With Brett out of the picture, Shane and the others could catch up quickly. The fact that the group of men hadn't already arrived suggested that the worst-case scenario hadn't occurred.

Neither had the best-case.

Owen was hoping Shane would take Brett to the hospital and abandon the kidnapping plan altogether. Roach's skulking presence indicated that Shane hadn't quit. His brother tended to be tenacious, stubborn and greedy.

Owen lowered the binoculars, noting that Roach was difficult to spot without them. Owen doubted Roach could see him standing in the shade of the palms. Roach probably suspected they were hiding out here because it was a convenient stopover. He'd followed their tracks or caught a glimpse of them hiking.

Maybe Shane had taken Brett back to camp, where he was suffering in slow agony. Maybe they were waiting for nightfall to attack. Maybe they'd attack within the hour. Time was of the essence in a ransom situation. If the exchange didn't happen the first day or two, complications ensued.

Owen weighed their options, feeling grim. They could leave now and try to lose the tail. Or he could be more proactive and make certain they weren't followed. Ambushing Roach carried a greater risk, but it was always more advantageous to pick off opponents one by one, rather than taking them on as a group. He didn't think Roach was armed. Shane wouldn't have given him his weapon.

It wasn't an easy decision to make. Owen didn't enjoy hurting people. But Penny and Cruz's lives were at stake. Owen's life was at stake. Shane's investment in this plot didn't leave any room for brotherly love.

Penny returned to his side. "What is it?"

"We have company."

"Where?"

He handed her the binoculars, describing the general area.

"I see him," she said. "I'll wake up Cruz."

"Don't."

"Shouldn't we leave?"

"Not yet. I'm going to circle around the canyon and…surprise him."

She flinched, giving back the binoculars. "By shooting him in the foot?"

"No. Sound carries, so firing at him would be my last resort. I'll try to knock him out and tie him up."

"I don't like it."

"Do you have another idea?"

"Let's keep moving."

"He'll follow us."

Her mouth tightened with displeasure. "Maybe we should give up."

Owen had entertained the same thought, but he suspected the situation was even more precarious than she realized. First of all, Shane was no criminal mastermind. If he pulled off the job, he would probably be eliminated as soon as he delivered the goods.

Owen didn't want to care about Shane's welfare, but he did. Thwarting this plan might save his brother from death or prison. More importantly, it could save others. Innocent victims like Penny, Cruz…and her father.

"I've heard that the Aryan Brotherhood has connections to the Freedom Party," he said, his stomach churning.

"From who?"

"My security team."

"They know you were a member?"

"Yes."

"Are you implying that the Freedom Party is behind this?"

He leveled with her. "Your father is rich, but he's not that rich. You've been targeted for political reasons. The endgame might be an assassination attempt."

She stared at him in horror.

"If money isn't the goal, we're all expendable. You and Cruz are just bait."

This news changed her outlook, as intended. It also appeared to scare the hell out of her. "Would your brother really be involved in a scheme like that?"

"He might not know."

She took a deep breath, staying calm. As always, he admired her fortitude. Even in desperate circumstances, she didn't fall apart.

He glanced through the lenses of the binoculars again, aware that he had only a short window of opportunity to strike. When the shade receded, Roach would move to a different location. He decided to leave the binoculars with Penny, along with the pocketknife. "If I'm not back by sunset, go on without me."

She took the items without responding.

"Promise me."

"No."

He knew she'd go on without him. She'd do it for Cruz's sake, no matter what she said. But her refusal to promise indicated that she cared about him. It meant she'd never forgive him if he didn't return.

His throat closed up at the sight of her defiant eyes, brimming with unshed tears. He cupped her chin and swept his thumb over her mouth, which trembled at his touch. He couldn't let himself fall in love with her. Not today, not ever. But he could give her a small indication of how he felt, just this once.

When he lowered his head, she inhaled a sharp breath. Both of her hands were occupied, and she seemed angry with him. That made it easier somehow. He was in control. There was no possibility of sex.

He brushed his lips against hers, almost groaning at the sensation. He'd kissed her mouth once before, a chaste peck that had featured in his fantasies for years. Her lips were even softer than he remembered, parted in sweet invitation. He wanted to sink inside, to urge her back against the tree and plunder her with his tongue.

But he didn't. He barely tasted her before pulling away.

She stared at him, moistening her lips. Her mouth drove him crazy. He pictured it trailing down his body, her tongue gliding over his taut skin.

"Promise me you'll come back," she said, turning the tables on him.

"I'll be fine."

Her eyes filled with tears once again.

He had to go before he broke down and cried with her. Or he broke down and tried to fuck her. Either way, he'd embarrass himself.

Tearing his gaze away, he put on his shoes and secured the gun in his waistband. The walkie-talkie he'd stolen could be used to call for help when they got closer to the road, but he didn't dare turn it on now. Some models had GPS, like cell phones. He left all of the water for Penny and Cruz.

To avoid being spotted, he jogged in a wide circle around the back side of the canyon before cutting across. The heat was like a dragon breathing down his neck. His damp pants dried quickly, the dark fabric soaking up sunlight. Last night's beating had weakened him. He was sore and stiff, his ribs aching. Several times, he had to slow down to breathe.

When he reached the outcropping Roach had been resting under, the shade was gone. And so was his target.

Cursing, Owen ducked behind a rock and searched his surroundings. Roach wasn't on the trail leading toward the summit. It was blazing hot, and he was lazy. He'd gone back downhill in search of shelter. Owen's expectations for success went with him. He thought he'd waltz up, wave the gun around, and take care of business. Now he was worried. If Owen went looking for Roach and ran into Shane and Dirk, he might not be able to keep his promise to Penny.

His gaze settled on a group of potato-shaped boulders in the distance. They were adjacent to the trail, and appeared to offer a tempting bit of shade. After studying a few less likely locations, he decided to approach the boulders. Again, he avoided the direct route, choosing a rocky scramble.

He crept across the jagged earth lightly, his shoulders hunched low. It was more difficult to maintain stealth than to run upright. His muscles burned with every step, his skin on fire. He paused at a short cliff above the boulders, his ears straining. He couldn't see into the shadows, and the wind was blowing the wrong direction. If anyone was crouched there, they could probably hear Owen. Every scrape of his shoe, every sliding pebble.

Fuck it.

There wasn't enough room for three men to hide, and he could handle one. He might have given himself away already. It was time to attack.

He jumped from the cliff to the top of the boulder, hoping to regain the element of surprise. It was about a six-foot drop to the ground below. Sure enough, Roach was sitting there. Owen drew his weapon before his eyes had a chance to adjust to the shade. "Don't move," he said, aiming in Roach's general direction.

Roach dove sideways, out of range.

Shit.

Owen leaped down to Roach's level, forced to pursue. The impact with the ground was more jarring than he'd expected. He lurched forward drunkenly and almost lost his balance. With a growing sense of panic, he realized that the odds were piling up in Roach's favor. The clumsy ambush had tipped off his opponent. The fact that Owen hadn't fired his weapon yet had also broadcast his intentions.

Roach was no dummy. He took advantage of these mistakes. Before Owen recovered from the near stumble, Roach went on the offensive.

Instead of running, he turned to fight.

Owen raised his gun a second too late. Several seconds too late; the safety was still on. When Roach grabbed Owen's wrist and slammed his hand against the boulder, the weapon didn't even discharge. It dropped from his slack grip and landed in the sandy dirt. Roach followed up with a hard right, connecting with the sore spot on Owen's jaw.

Pain rocketed through his cheek. Owen pushed off the side of the boulder and spun away, struggling to stay upright. He'd anticipated an easy target, like Brett. Maybe Roach had learned a few things from video games. His lack of muscle tone was deceiving. He had quick reflexes and good striking power.

Keeping his center of gravity low, Owen waited for Roach's next move. Roach glanced at the gun but didn't make a grab for it. He reached into his back pocket and drew out a wicked-looking knife.

Owen couldn't waste another second. He tackled Roach full force. They rolled like tumbleweeds down the side of the canyon, over sharp rocks and clusters of cactus. Dust filled Owen's nose and mouth, choking him. His knees and elbows banged against the hard ground. They slowed to a stop, each scrambling for the top position.

Roach won it. He straddled Owen's waist and lifted his arm high. Sunlight glinted off the blade, blinding Owen. He blocked the first stab, barely. The cutting edge glanced off his forearm, slicing through his shirt. His skin also, judging by the searing sensation and warm trickle. Owen's adrenaline was pumping so high he didn't feel the pain. Before Roach could slash him again, Owen landed a left hook across his chin.

Roach leaned to one side, dazed. Owen shoved him over and climbed on top. He gripped Roach's wrist, twisting it cruelly. Roach let go of the knife, but he didn't give up. He dislodged Owen with a bucking motion and took a wild swing. His fist glanced off Owen's ear.

Then the situation got ugly. Real ugly.

They fought over the knife, punching and clawing and crawling across the sandy ground. In the end,

Owen came up with it. He hadn't intended to use deadly force in this altercation. He'd planned to knock Roach out, tie him up and take his boots. A man with a concussion and no shoes couldn't follow them.

That wasn't what happened. Gripping the knife's handle, Owen flipped onto his back and pointed it skyward. Roach jumped on him, unaware of the danger. The blade's sharp tip penetrated his chest and sank to the hilt.

Roach let out a grunt of shock. He wore a startled expression, as if he knew this was it. Blood gushed over Owen's hands, soaking his clothes. Roach's gaze turned glassy. He slumped forward, his muscles slack.

As Roach lost his life, Owen flashed back to another time. Another limp body, another brutal violation.

When the memories faded, he returned to the present, which was no less horrific. He shoved the corpse aside, his heart hammering inside his chest. He didn't vomit, though the violence he'd just done sickened him. His thoughts scattered, and he shivered uncontrollably, letting out a strangled sob. The blood turned tacky on his fingertips as he studied the man he'd killed without comprehension.

Roach offered no answers, no forgiveness. His dead eyes stared up at the blazing sun, unblinking.

CHAPTER TEN

PENNY LOST SIGHT of Owen a few minutes after he walked away.

Pulse pounding with dread, she lifted the binoculars to watch the man in the shade. When the shadows receded, he left, probably in search of a better hideout. He traveled downhill and around the canyon, out of view.

Then there was nothing to look at. She studied the stark contrast of dirty beige hills against the vivid blue horizon. Flecks of yellow-green dotted the landscape. Some were barrel cactus, short and squat. Others looked like spiky teddy bears with rounded ears and bent arms. She wished for a view of the Salton Sea. It sounded unpleasant, but she wanted to see it for herself. Up close and personal, not just from a safe distance.

Dropping the binoculars, she glanced at Cruz. He was still asleep.

The heat had reached a plateau. Her dress fluttered in the wind, dry as a bone. Restless and worried, she thought of Owen's kiss. It had been too reserved, too chaste. As always, she ached for something more.

An hour passed with no sign of him. She finger-combed her damp hair and braided it, tying the end with a fabric scrap from her boot. Then she caught a glimpse of a figure on the trail. She peered through the binoculars, making a sound of distress. Owen's shirtfront was bright red with blood. He looked like he'd been shot.

She leaped to her feet, tugging on the boots she'd discarded. He continued uphill, moving at a brisk pace for a man with a bullet in his gut. She hadn't heard gunfire, come to think of it. When he got close to the summit, she ran out to meet him.

"What happened?"

He didn't answer, didn't even make eye contact. "Is Cruz awake?" he asked, glancing over her shoulder.

"No."

"Good. I don't want him to see this."

"Are you hurt?"

"I'm fine."

"You're covered in blood."

"It's not mine."

She studied the large red stain on his stomach. His shirtsleeves were drenched. If his pants weren't black, they'd have showed more carnage. She didn't think a person could survive after losing that amount of blood.

"He's dead," she said flatly.

There was no denying it. He walked past her, stripping off his ruined shirt. Wincing, he peeled the wet fabric away from a cut on his forearm. His tattooed torso was smeared red and marred by bruises.

She followed him to the pool, feeling a mixture of relief and unease. He'd killed a man, perhaps intentionally. She studied his guarded expression, remembering how he'd looked when they'd first met: tall, intimidating…scary. "You said you were going to knock him out."

He swished his shirt around in the murky water.

This morning, he'd told her he was going to shoot a hole in the wall. Maybe he'd lied again to protect her. "What happened?"

"He pulled a knife."

While she watched, he removed the knife from his back pocket and scrubbed the blade. Then he set the weapon aside, along with the gun. Jaw clenched, he splashed water onto his face and stomach. The Old English lettering that used to read White Pride now spelled out Irish Pride. Another big change caught her attention. The cross over his heart looked newly detailed, with a bold outline and a red banner that said CRUZ.

There were other, less conspicuous tattoos. Scrawls of black script on his biceps had been transformed into Celtic designs and tribal bands. The overall effect was edgy and eclectic, emphasizing an already eye-pleasing physique.

As he washed off, the wound on his arm welled with fresh beads.

"Let me," she said, kneeling beside him. She used her moistened scarf to sponge the blood from his skin. Red-tinged water streamed down his chest and into the waistband of his pants. When she touched the cloth to his abdomen, his muscles tensed. Although it seemed inappropriate to admire his blood-streaked body, she couldn't help herself. Maybe lust was a normal survival response.

She flushed, trying to ignore her primitive reaction to his warriorlike sex appeal. After cleaning the wound, she wrapped several dry strips around his forearm and tied them in knots. "You need stitches, but this is better than nothing."

He made a fist, rotating his wrist. "Thanks."

Her gaze moved from the bandage to the cross on his chest. She lifted her hand, tracing the red banner with her fingertip. His heart thumped hard underneath the ink, his flat male nipple just inches away. "When did you get this?"

"About a year ago."

"Why didn't you say anything?"

Shrugging, he glanced away. He seemed traumatized by the violence he'd done, his eyes haunted. She wished he'd let her in, rather than hiding his feelings from her. His contract with her father wasn't the only obstacle between them. He was keeping his distance, physically *and* emotionally.

He'd allowed her to care for his wound, though. That was progress.

She removed her hand from his chest, her pulse racing. If she had more nerve, she'd venture lower, splaying her fingers over the lettering that arched across his stomach. Not to tease him; they were in dire straits, and this was no time for games. But she wanted him to accept her comfort and acknowledge her desire.

"You don't have to protect me from everything," she said.

"Protecting you is my job."

"Is that the only reason you do it?"

"No," he admitted. But didn't elaborate.

"I told you I could handle the truth."

"I haven't lied to you in years."

She wasn't so sure. "You share very little of yourself. It makes me wonder if you think I have anything to offer you in return."

His brows rose with surprise. "I don't have anything to offer *you*."

"Because I have money, and you don't?"

"Penny—" He broke off, shaking his head.

"What?"

"I just want what's best for you."

She knew what that meant. Anyone but him. "You sound like my father."

When he flinched, she suspected that they'd discussed her. They'd made decisions without her input.

She fell silent, frustrated with the men in her life. And with herself for letting them set the tone in their relationships. Tyler had taken her virginity, gotten her pregnant and left without a backward glance. Her father loved her, but he'd tried to shape her into a mold that didn't fit. Her son, by no fault of his own, had become the center of her world.

She had no control over anything. Least of all Owen, who'd put her in the friend zone. He'd kissed her on his terms, not hers. Now he'd retreated again, protecting her from himself. She didn't appreciate the gesture.

"Just be honest with me," she said. "Keeping me in the dark is like telling me not to worry my pretty little head about it."

He stood abruptly, wringing out his wet shirt. "I lied about shooting a hole in the wall of the mud cave. But that was for Cruz's benefit, not yours. I didn't plan what happened with Roach. I messed up the ambush and dropped the gun. He came at me. If I could have escaped without killing him, I would have."

She crossed her arms over her chest, nodding. "I believe you."

"Good."

"It wasn't easy for me to watch you leave," she said, her voice hoarse with emotion. "I was a nervous wreck the whole time you were gone. When you came back, covered in blood…I assumed the worst."

His expression softened. "I'm sorry."

"I hope you don't blame yourself."

"Who should I blame?"

"Them."

He struggled into his wet shirt. The fabric was stained and torn, but no longer red. Most of the buttons were missing. "If I attack first, it's not self-defense."

"I attacked Gardener," she pointed out.

"Gardener is still alive."

"If he wasn't, would you blame me?"

"No. You did what you had to do."

"So did you."

The comparison gave him pause. He seemed to consider her actions fair, while his were reprehensible.

"Don't be so hard on yourself," she said softly, touching his arm. He frowned at the sight of her hand on his skin, but he didn't argue or pull away. She was glad they'd talked. It was a step in the right direction.

"We need to get going," he said. "I want to make it to the railroad by sundown."

"Won't they follow us?"

"They might, but we'll have a good head start, and there are lots of places to hide along the tracks."

"I'll wake up Cruz."

When she crouched down next to him, he rolled over on the rustling palm fronds. "Mommy?"

"Hey, sleepyhead," she said, smoothing his disheveled hair. "It's time to leave. We're going to see an old railroad."

Cruz loved trains, so this sounded like a grand adventure to him. While Penny helped him get ready, putting on his shoes and socks, he asked Owen a dozen questions. "Will there be a train to ride on?"

"Not an operating train," Owen said. "The tracks have been closed for years. But there are some abandoned railcars and rusted parts."

"Cool!"

She reapplied the ChapStick to Cruz's lips and face as well as her own. The dry wind sucked every ounce of moisture from their skin. Owen filled the canteen with water from the bottles. The sun was still brutal, burning hotter than ever. They put their headgear back on and set off into the distance like desert vagabonds.

SHANE RETRIEVED THE JEEP from the parking garage and grabbed some lunch with Dirk before heading back to camp.

He clenched his hands around the wheel as he navigated the bumpy dirt roads, his anxiety growing. This job had been a clusterfuck from the start. He hadn't wanted to take the kid, but they couldn't just leave him behind. He'd put Gardener in charge of the girl because he was a dickless chump. Shane hadn't trusted the other men with her.

His mistakes with Owen were even more pronounced. Shane hadn't felt like hitting his brother last night. He'd unlocked Owen's cuffs this morning, assuming an unarmed man wouldn't attack an armed one. Maybe he was getting soft.

Since when did he care about women, or kids or brothers? He'd spent most of the past ten years in prison. He was scrubbed clean of feelings, empty to the core. His sole concern, other than getting paid, was getting out of this godforsaken desert alive.

Fuck Salton. Fuck Owen. Fuck everything.

"What did Ace say?" Dirk asked.

"About what?"

"Isn't he mad?"

"I told him I had it under control."

Dirk wasn't stupid enough to dispute that, though he looked skeptical. Like Shane, he'd never even met Ace, but that didn't stop him from making presumptions. Shane was tired of Dirk questioning his decisions and mouthing off. Dirk never knew when to shut up. Shane didn't appreciate having his authority challenged.

Shane turned his focus back to the road, annoyed. If things continued to go south, he'd blame Dirk—aka Derek Peters—and his dumb-ass brother. Dirk had recommended Jerome Gardener. Both Gardener and Brett were inexperienced and incompetent. Roach was Ace's buddy, maybe his spy.

Shane assumed that Roach would give Ace all of the details eventually. If Shane executed the plan, it wouldn't matter. If he didn't, he'd be screwed anyway. He entertained a brief fantasy of ditching Dirk and crossing the border.

But, no. He couldn't run.

He could try to reel Sandoval in without the bait. That would be more difficult, because people liked to see what they were getting for their money. The main problem with failing to recapture the escapees was that they might not survive the desert. Owen was strong, much stronger than Shane had given him credit for, but a little kid and a spoiled rich girl didn't have a chance out here. Water was scarce, and there wasn't a damned thing to eat. Unable to provide sustenance, Owen would have to keep them moving. The heat was deadly, the sun brutal, and the terrain rugged.

They didn't call this the badlands for nothing.

If the boy or his mother didn't make it, Shane could be charged with murder. He refused to spend the rest of his life in prison, so surrendering wasn't an option. Neither was running; Ace would hunt him down and kill him. He might even go after Janelle and Jamie. Shane's choices were pretty much limited to death or success.

When they got closer to camp, Shane tried to call Roach on his walkie-talkie. There was no answer, and no GPS signal registered.

The lack of response didn't surprise him. Nothing worked in this Bermuda-Triangle shit hole. Cell phones were useless. Even high-end communication devices didn't function at full capacity in mountainous areas, and these walkie-talkies were middle grade.

He tried again near the mud caves, to no avail. The batteries might be low or the transmissions were jammed. He wasn't an expert in technology. Phones had changed so much in the past decade, he felt like an old man. The chick he'd visited last weekend had brought him up to speed in more ways than one. She wasn't as hot as the picture she'd sent him in prison, but he hadn't minded. She'd been energetic and eager to please. He'd worn her ass out.

He'd also grown bored with her quickly. Listening to Janelle's voice had reminded him that all women weren't interchangeable. It was a shame that the best ones always seemed to require more work, because he was an instant-gratification kind of guy.

"I'm still not getting a signal," he said, staring at the blank screen.

"That's not good."

Shane felt a prickle of unease. Owen had taken Brett's walkie-talkie and turned it off. Had Roach met a similar fate? The last thing Shane needed was another man with a gunshot wound to deal with. "I told him to follow at a distance," he said, shaking the device. "Doesn't anyone fucking listen?"

"You can track his movements," Dirk said, taking the walkie-talkie. He fidgeted with the buttons, bringing up a map and coordinates.

Shane was confused by the information. "That's where he is now?"

"That's where his last signal was transmitted from."

He couldn't get there by driving, so they exited the Jeep, bringing their hats and a jug of water. It was a bitch of a hike. The sun was relentless. Shane and Dirk had kept in shape by lifting weights in prison, but heavy muscles were more of a hindrance than an asset here. Dirk, with his gorilla-like frame, had even more trouble. The extra bulk slowed him down.

After what seemed like hours, Shane spotted a cluster of palm trees at the summit. He vaguely re-

membered visiting a pool of water here as a kid. There
were a handful of springs and mud caves in the area,
and many of the landmarks looked alike, so it was
hard to tell. Whether he'd been there or not, he felt
certain that they were on the right track. Owen would
seek a shady resting place during the hottest hours
of the day.

They reached the coordinates that the GPS indicated. It was a safe distance from the summit, well
out of range of a 9 mm handgun, but Roach wasn't
in the vicinity.

"Looks like a scuffle," Dirk said, pointing at the
ground.

Shane squinted at a few dark spots on the path. He
bent down, rubbing the grit between his fingertips.

"Blood?" Dirk guessed.

"I think so."

A crow swooped down the canyon, leading them
straight to the body. Roach was lying on a pile of
rocks about fifty feet down, already being picked at
by the black-feathered scavenger. His T-shirt was torn
and bloody, his eyes blank.

"Son of a bitch!" Dirk said. "Your brother killed
him."

Shane raked a hand through his hair, stunned. This
was so much worse than he'd expected. He was a dead
man, as dead as Roach.

"Ace is going to shit," Dirk said.

Shane grasped the front of Dirk's shirt. "We can't
tell him."

"What?"

He would draw his weapon if Dirk refused to play along. There was too much at stake. "He's already gone," Shane said, pointing at Roach. "As long as he doesn't get found, no one will ever know what happened to him."

Dirk stared at the corpse, his throat working in agitation. For all his bluster and bravado, he wasn't as cold-blooded as Shane.

"It's easy to get lost out here," Shane said.

"What will you say to Ace?"

"That he took off, and we never saw him again."

After a short pause, Dirk nodded. Shane released his grip on Dirk's shirt, watching the wrinkled cotton untwist. He didn't trust Dirk to keep this secret under duress, but he'd deal with that problem later. Right now, he needed Dirk's help. He was down three men. One more and he'd have to abandon the plan altogether.

"Your brother fucked up," Shane reminded him. "I did him a favor by sending him to Mexico."

"You said Ace ordered that."

"He didn't."

Dirk's mouth tightened at this news. Shane hadn't been concerned about Brett's welfare, but he could exploit this side benefit. More importantly, his words acted as a warning that Shane was still in charge. He wasn't afraid to lie to the boss, and Ace would believe Shane's version of events over Dirk's.

Shane considered Dirk a friend. They'd done time together and had each other's backs in prison. Even so, Shane would double-cross him in a heartbeat. He didn't have feelings for Dirk. He didn't have feelings, period.

"What about *your* brother?" Dirk asked.

"What about him?"

"You said he'd cooperate."

"I thought he would."

"You were wrong."

Shane had promised to take care of Owen if he caused trouble, but he'd never intended to follow through. He wasn't worried about his brother indentifying him to the police. Shane wouldn't stick around to get arrested.

"You know what needs to be done," Dirk said.

"And I'll do it," Shane replied, wishing he'd shot Brett in the head. "Let's bury this motherfucker."

They made their way into the canyon, with some difficulty. It was a steep slide down a cactus-riddled hill. When they reached the body, Shane crouched next to him, inspecting the wound in his chest.

"That's not a bullet hole," Dirk said. "He was stabbed."

Shane glanced up at the trail, trying to imagine what happened.

"Maybe your brother came to shoot him, but the gun jammed or something. Roach pulled a knife to defend himself."

Ace hadn't wanted the crew to be heavily armed.

He'd said that too many guns meant too many problems. Shane had allowed Dirk to bring one, but he'd
insisted that the other men leave theirs at home, along
with their cell phones. Roach had been carrying a
knife instead; it was his preferred weapon.

"They wrestled and rolled downhill," Dirk continued. "Roach bled out here."

"Why is there blood on the trail?"

Dirk considered the location of the drops. "I think
it's your brother's blood. He left it walking away."

Shane doubted Owen was seriously injured, judging by the small amount of blood. They wouldn't find
him holed up at the summit, nursing his wounds. He
was probably several miles down the trail by now.

They didn't even try to dig a hole. Under a thin
layer of pebble-strewn sand, there was hard-packed
desert clay, which presented too much of a challenge.
During a rainstorm, the stuff would suck the shoes
right off your feet, or give you a pair of concrete
boots. In dry conditions, it was as impermeable as
brick.

Shane dragged the body about a hundred yards,
where they wedged it into a crevice between boulders. Then they piled rocks and dirt into the narrow
space until no hint of skin or clothing was visible.

"You think that's good enough?" Dirk asked.

Shane nodded, dusting off his hands. It would have
to be. The only people who came out here were desert hipsters, driving their hybrid cars and searching

for inner peace. They liked the wildflowers in spring. By that time, Roach would be bones.

They hiked the remaining distance to the summit. He saw a pair of kid-sized footprints in the mud by the pool of water, along with a scrap of sheer green fabric. Dirk picked up the cloth and launched into a graphic description of sexual acts he wanted to force on the mother. Shane didn't really see the appeal of an unwilling woman. There were plenty of sluts to choose from. Whores, if you were desperate.

"You talk too much," he said, weary.

"Wouldn't you take a turn on her?"

"No."

"Why not?"

"It feels better when they want it."

"Shit," Dirk said, throwing the scrap down.

Shane decided he was full of it. Dirk didn't have a girlfriend, which was no surprise. Maybe he was intimidated by women or frustrated with his inability to score. He probably had a small dick. His big muscles and big mouth reeked of overcompensation. So did the fake name he'd chosen.

Shane walked to the highest point and looked down the opposite side of the mountain, figuring Owen had gone that direction. There was an old railroad to the south. Their dad had taken them to the tracks to search for salvage materials once or twice.

"When was Roach's last signal transmitted?"

"Noon," Dirk replied.

It was almost six now. Owen and his cozy little

family had a significant head start. Shane didn't know if he could find their tracks in the dark, let alone catch up with them. But he could cut them off at the other end.

CHAPTER ELEVEN

PENNY TOOK THE LEAD AGAIN, with Cruz in the middle and Owen bringing up the rear.

The downhill grade was much easier to traverse. After a few hours, the temperature finally began to drop, but Cruz lost momentum when the trail evened out. Owen carried him on his shoulders for the next several miles.

They stopped at dusk for dinner, sharing another sausage stick and the last box of raisins. The snack woke up her taste buds but failed to satisfy the gnawing ache in her stomach. They were all hungry. Cruz was cranky and lethargic. Penny didn't think she could go much longer, but she held her tongue. They weren't even to the railroad yet. The real hike would begin once they found the tracks.

She wanted to quit. To lie down and give up.

The feeling was a new one for her. She'd never pushed her physical limits this way, except maybe during childbirth. But labor was a faded memory with a happy ending. This was a grueling, torturous slog. Cruz had never gone without food before, either. Being unable to provide for him was heartrending.

As a mother, it was her job to keep her child healthy and safe. For the first time in her life, she was failing.

The obstacles seemed insurmountable, the trail endless.

In a small corner of her mind, she was aware of how lucky she'd been until now. She'd done hours of volunteer work and interned at a women's clinic, but she hadn't been familiar with suffering on a personal level.

Owen seemed to endure the hike with ease, despite carrying extra weight, which emphasized the differences between them. He accepted hardships as if they were his due. She stumbled along as if she were dying.

"This is what it must be like to cross the border illegally," she said.

"Same terrain," he replied. "We're only twenty miles from Mexico."

"How many miles from the main road?"

"I don't know. Ten."

"How many have we traveled so far?"

"Seven, maybe."

Penny's spirits plummeted. There was no way she could walk ten more miles.

Owen stopped and put Cruz down, studying her discouraged face. "Are you okay?"

When she tried to answer, the words stuck in her throat. She wanted to be stoic and calm. For her son.

"Can you carry my mommy?" Cruz asked Owen.

"No, he can't," Penny said. She was tall and slender, but not small. As fit as Owen was, he couldn't bear her weight for miles.

Cruz didn't believe it. "Can you?"

"I can carry her to the railroad," he said. "It's close."

"How close?"

"Less than a mile, I think. Traveling along the tracks will be easier because it's flat. We'll find a place to rest for the night."

She nearly swooned at the word *rest*. Maybe she could drag herself as far as the railroad before collapsing in a boneless heap on the tracks. Taking a deep breath, she said, "I'll try to make it."

"Are you sure?"

"Yes," she said, grasping Cruz's hand.

"I'll help you, Mommy."

"Thanks, *mijo*."

They started off again, her muscles weeping with every step. Owen told Cruz the entire history of the Carrizo Gorge Railway. Apparently the line had transported supplies between the U.S. to Mexico before it fell into disrepair. Penny listened with one ear, trudging forward to the sound of Owen's steady voice.

"Look," he said finally, perking up. "A loading dock."

She spotted a crumbling concrete ramp in the distance, next to a windblown shack. Rusted wheels and gears littered the area leading to the tracks. The sight of the railway didn't lift her morale. It appeared to go on forever, winding through a deep desert gorge. She inspected the shack, which had no roof.

They couldn't stay here.

When they reached the ramp, she sank down on the rubble, numb. She didn't even have the strength to cry.

Owen and Cruz, however, found the energy to explore the scattered wasteland. They came back with an old wheelbarrow. It had sturdy wooden handles and a modified metal wheel, flanged to ride along the track. "Hop in."

She sipped water from the canteen. "You can't be serious."

"I'm dead serious."

"You're going to wheelbarrow me down the track like a pile of rocks?"

"You and Cruz."

"I'm too heavy."

He studied her slender figure appreciatively. "You're not heavy at all, and pushing a wheelbarrow is a piece of cake. Easier than carrying you, or even carrying Cruz on my shoulders. I only have to balance the weight."

She squinted at him, evaluating his sincerity.

"Scout's honor," he said.

"You're not a Scout."

"Can I be a Scout?" Cruz asked.

"We'll see," Penny said, taking a seat in the bin. She gripped the edges, feeling silly. "Try it with just me first."

Owen guided her along the track without difficulty.

Cruz hopped in with her, sitting on her lap. They stayed in the middle so it wouldn't tip. "How's your arm?" she asked, glancing at the bandage.

"It's all right."

She held on for the ride, too exhausted to protest. His increased breathing pattern indicated that the task wasn't as undemanding as he'd claimed. He smelled like sweat and blood. As the sun dipped below the horizon, she grew drowsy.

At least it wasn't hot anymore. Over the space of an hour, the night air had become mild and pleasant. She sang songs to Cruz to stay awake. If she slumped over, she might fall over the side of the wheelbarrow and take a hard tumble into the gorge.

When they reached the first tunnel, Owen paused. It looked dark and spooky inside. Warning signs were posted at regular intervals along the tracks. This was an unmaintained railway. No safety inspector had declared the route passable, and no rescue crew would come to their aide if it collapsed.

Owen turned on the flashlight and handed it to Cruz. "Hold it steady, okay?"

"Okay."

They couldn't go around the tunnel, so this risk was unavoidable. Heart racing with anxiety, she hugged Cruz tighter as they entered the dark passage. It smelled of damp wood and rust and something unpleasant, like cobwebs or rat droppings. Her imagination conjured bats on the ceiling, and spiders the size of mice scuttling along the tracks. She couldn't see beyond the weak beam of light. Her feet dangled over the edge of the wheelbarrow. About halfway through, she felt a sharp pain in her calf, like a bite.

Gasping, she brought her leg up to inspect it. The discomfort increased as her muscle seized, hard as a rock.

"What's wrong?" Owen asked.

"Leg cramp," she said between clenched teeth.

He pushed them through the end of the tunnel quickly. Once they were out, he put down the handles and massaged her calf. She extended her leg, tears squeezing from the corners of her eyes. It hurt more than a regular cramp, and lasted longer. Cruz hugged her tight, worried. Finally the spasm eased.

"Drink some water," Owen said.

She lifted the canteen to her lips and drank, letting the cool water ease her parched throat. Fearing they'd run out, she'd been taking small sips all day. Saving water for Cruz. In retrospect, that hadn't been smart. Muscle cramps were a sign of heatstroke, along with light-headedness and nausea.

If she started vomiting, she'd only get more dehydrated.

Owen picked up the pace after that. He seemed to want to get as far down the tracks as possible before they stopped to rest. She didn't blame him for preferring to travel under a blanket of night. She wished she could contribute, but she couldn't even stay alert.

Her limbs were heavy like sand, her eyes grainy from lack of sleep.

The railway gorge was surreal in the moonlight. Although the tracks were smooth and flat, they crossed through tunnels and skirted steep cliffs. Falling off the edge would mean certain death. Between canyons, there were wooden bridgelike structures Owen called trestles. There were no safety rails, just a braided steel cord.

He paused when they came to a section of abandoned railcars. They loomed in the dark next to the tracks, too huge to be moved. Penny had seen rusted cars and junkyards before, but not on this scale. It was almost beyond comprehension, like the Salton Sea. This barren wasteland killed everything it touched. Even the most immense, powerful structures were useless here, reduced to nothing.

Owen pushed the wheelbarrow off the tracks and hid it behind the railcar before they ventured inside. He checked the interior for signs of life, directing the flashlight beneath the rows of seats. There was an open area in the back of the car, where someone had collected a pile of torn seat cushions.

Deeming it safe, Owen led Penny to the cushions. He gripped her elbow, as if afraid she'd pass out on the way there. She could barely walk. When he lowered her to the cushions, she moaned with relief.

"I'm sorry," she murmured.

"For what?"

She was too tired to answer.

"I'm going to check the other cars for supplies," he said.

"Can I come with you?" Cruz asked.

Owen looked to Penny for permission.

"Okay," she said, closing her eyes. She was overly protective of Cruz, rarely leaving him alone or letting him out of her sight. He didn't go anywhere without her, but she trusted Owen with their lives.

Before they'd left the car, she was asleep.

JANELLE PARKED NEAR the club's front entrance, hoping the manager wouldn't notice.

She wasn't supposed to take the best parking spots, but she preferred to stay close. She didn't like walking past drunken creeps in the wee hours of the night. Now she feared an intruder would climb through her broken window and wait for her.

She needed another job. Badly.

Before she'd transferred from Indio Community College to a "real" university in San Bernadino, she'd held down two jobs. She'd worked afternoons as a massage therapist—no happy endings—at a fancy resort. But the extra commute and more demanding classes had meant she had to quit the weekday gig. She couldn't do both, and she earned twice the money in half the time dancing.

The business wasn't as lucrative as it used to be, either. The best clubs in L.A. paid really well, but many of their girls were professional dancers or aspiring actresses, young and fresh and beautiful. In

Coachella, a sprawling industrial city near Palm
Springs, the women were like Janelle. Single moms
and washed-up tramps, making their way the only
way they knew how. Since the recession hit, she was
lucky to pocket a few hundred dollars a night. Less
on Sunday, but she was required to cover some slow
shifts.

Grabbing her bag, she locked up her car even
though the plastic-covered window wouldn't deter
theft. Her bag was heavy, full of makeup and outfits.
She hurried across the hot parking lot and into the
dark recesses of the club. Vixen was a tacky place
with flashing strobe lights and red neon, faux leather
and mirrored walls. The familiar stench of booze,
cigarettes and male sweat hit her nostrils even as a
blast of cool air ruffled her hair.

She nodded at the bartender and headed to the
back, where the girls got ready. They kept the side
entrance locked now. Last year, Tiffany's estranged
husband had walked in with a gun. He'd held her
hostage for several hours, claiming he was going to
kill himself if she didn't come back home. The police
had finally talked him down with a sandwich and a
six-pack. He'd had an axe, a shovel and a map of the
badlands in the back of his truck, belying his claim
that he meant to commit suicide. He'd be in prison
for a while.

Vixen wasn't an upscale establishment, but neither
was it a sleazy dive. They served alcohol, so the girls
went topless only. The customers couldn't touch, not

even in the VIP room. These rules were strictly enforced by the bouncer and owner, Chuck Finch. He was a Hells Angels type of guy with a gray ponytail and a thick mustache. He'd married one of his dancers twenty years ago, and he treated the others well.

His brother, Kevin, wasn't as nice. He managed the club and often took in girls who gave him sexual favors.

Janelle couldn't do anything about that, so she ignored it. She didn't have to suck Kevin's dick or anyone else's. They kept her on because she was a good performer and the customers liked her.

She'd agreed to cover two shifts today, early and late. On slow afternoons, she served more drinks than lap dances. The girls could either work as independent contractors or earn an hourly wage plus tips. Janelle had chosen the second, which meant she had to move her ass even when she wasn't on stage. During the hectic evening shifts, she didn't waitress because Kevin wanted her to be available for VIPs.

Tossing her bag down at an empty makeup station, she said hello to the other girls, Tiffany and Ginger.

"You look like I feel," Tiffany said.

Janelle grimaced at her own reflection. "You must feel like shit."

"I'll do your hair after I finish mine," she offered.

"Thanks. I'm running late."

Instead of rushing to get ready, she fidgeted with her cell phone, sending Owen a text message. Maybe he could call Shane and find out what was going on. She wanted to see if he'd talk to Jamie, too.

Owen had been the positive male role model in her son's life. Sometimes it broke her heart to see them together. He bore such a strong resemblance to Shane. They were nothing alike on the inside, praise Jesus. Owen might not be able to give Jamie any advice about sex. He was so shy and reserved, she'd wondered if he was a virgin.

Last summer, Tiffany had stopped by while Owen was throwing the football to Jamie. "Who is *that?*" she'd asked.

"Jamie's uncle."

"Hook me up with him."

Owen had seemed interested—all men liked Tiffany—so Janelle had made the arrangements. Tiffany had been through a lot, and she deserved a nice guy. Janelle hoped they'd hit it off, but they'd only gone on one date. When Janelle asked how it had gone, Tiffany had claimed she didn't kiss and tell, which was a lie. Tiffany usually dished all the details. For some reason, she stayed mum about Owen.

If he wasn't Jamie's uncle, Janelle might have tried to flirt with him herself. He was boy-next-door handsome, tall and lean and hard-muscled. She didn't care about hurting Shane, but Jamie loved Owen, and her son needed a decent man in his life. Janelle wouldn't do anything to jeopardize their relationship.

After she donned her waitress outfit, black satin shorts and a pink spandex top, she slathered on makeup. Tiffany teased her hair into a fluffy mane. For the next few hours, she alternated between serving drinks and dancing.

It was a busy night, so she left the floor early. During a solo number, she noticed a man sitting alone at a corner table. He wasn't in the mandatory tip area by the stage, where she normally focused her attention. She didn't cater to outliers, who wanted to look without tipping. Even her awareness of the front row was muted by the invisible wall she put up. They saw her as an object. She saw them the same way. Not as individuals with unique traits, but as wallet holders with bills of different denominations.

This man was watching her. His broad shoulders hunched forward as his eyes followed her across the stage. Something about him made her stomach coil with tension. He reminded her of Shane, in size and physical presence, if not looks.

She tried to pretend he wasn't there. Just another face in the crowd.

After her set was finished, she hurried backstage to cover up. "Table five wants a VIP," Kevin said, jerking his thumb at her.

For some reason, Janelle hesitated. She could refuse to perform this service, but she rarely exercised that right. Private dances were part of the job. The only time she ever said no was when the guy was sick or unwilling, being dragged to the VIP area by his buddies. The guy at table five had just arrived. He appeared stone-cold sober.

"He asked for you," Kevin said.

She nodded, letting out a slow breath. There was no point in getting fully dressed, but she put on a bra top and vinyl skirt over her sparkly G-string. The customers always wanted to see her take something off. Heart pounding with trepidation, she strode to table five. In the early days, she might have downed a shot of tequila first. Alcohol numbed her senses, but falling off stage was a real hazard in high heels, and no one tipped a sloppy dancer. As she'd gotten used to stripping for strangers, she'd learned to disassociate from her body.

The man at table five watched her approach, smiling a little. He had coal-black hair and cold blue eyes.

"Hey, there, big guy," she said, fluttering her lashes. It was her typical greeting, and fitting in his case. In addition to being large, he was attractive and well-built. His T-shirt stretched across a powerful chest. "You ready for a dance?"

"How much is it?"

"Twenty a song."

"I'll pay ten."

A haggler. This kind of behavior raised red flags. It indicated he wanted to test her limits, to get more bang for his buck. "Twenty's the bare minimum, sugar."

"Will you make it worth my while?"

"I'll give you a good dance."

"Nude?"

She shook her head, letting her earrings jangle.

Even topless dancing was prohibited in private rooms at clubs that served alcohol. That rule wasn't enforced, however, and all of the girls knew the customers tipped better if they saw the naughty bits.

He seemed disappointed that she had standards. Perhaps he preferred his women cheap and desperate.

"Should I come back later?" she asked.

"No," he said, rising. "I can't stay long."

She slipped her arm into his, noting his height and strength as she escorted him to the VIP room. He paid Chuck, who stood by the beaded entrance, and they slipped inside. "Have a seat anywhere you like."

He chose a black armchair in the back booth. They were all alone. The room had a security camera, and Chuck checked in routinely, but Janelle didn't feel safe here. She never would. Ten years in this business had taught her how fast a man could go from respectful to insulting, placid to angry, gentle to violent.

"Hands on the armrests," she said, noting that he had tattooed knuckles and a spider's web on his elbow.

He'd probably done time.

She wasn't surprised or put off by that. The strip club was a place for outcasts. Maybe she'd picked up on his prison vibes and overreacted because of Shane. She was still a little hungover, her nerves on edge.

Trying to relax, she waited for the next song to start. He looked at least thirty, with a coarse complexion and scarred motorcycle boots. Maybe he was a trucker, or an oil rig worker. His clothes were clean. He was intimidating but not repugnant.

When the music started she sort of…floated up, and away. It was almost as if she was watching the scene from a distance. She became someone else. Her dancer-persona shimmied between his splayed legs and turned, brushing her bottom over his lap. She bent over and wiggled suggestively, aware that her sparkly thong barely covered her sex. Then she straightened, facing him again. Lifting her high-heeled foot to the top of the chair, near his shoulder, she unzipped her micro-mini and let it fall away. She pushed her breasts together and gyrated slowly, moving her hips to the beat. The flare of interest in his eyes, along with the bulge in his pants, told her he liked what he saw.

Almost done.

During the last twenty seconds, she dropped to her knees and simulated oral sex. Sometimes the sight of male arousal excited her. Dancer-girl's cheeks flushed with heat. Her hair spread over his thighs, dragging across his fly. She pulled her bra down a little, revealing her breasts to the nipples. His hands clenched on the armrests.

Then the song was over.

Janelle rose, adjusting her top. She returned to her body in a flash, all business. After giving them both a moment to recover, she glanced at him. He seemed impressed and annoyed, as if he hadn't expected to enjoy her performance enough to get frustrated by it.

And there was the rub of a good lap dance, no pun intended.

"Care for another?" she asked.

"Only if you blow me for real."

She didn't bother to say no. He was already on his feet, wincing as he dug into his pocket for a tip. Instead of handing the bill to her, he held it up jauntily. She knew this trick. If she reached for it, he'd pull away.

"Will you be here tomorrow?"

"Yes."

He caressed her face with the edge of the bill, touching her the only way he could. When she closed her hand around the money, he let go. "Maybe I'll come back."

She watched him walk away, hoping he wouldn't return. If she wanted a scary, unsettling ex-con sniffing around her, she'd call Shane. The back of his shirt said Ace Demolition. As soon as he was gone, she glanced down at bill her in hand.

Five dollars.

Her pride came cheap these days.

CHAPTER TWELVE

OWEN DIDN'T FIND ANYTHING useful in the other rail-cars.

There were signs that other people had been inside. They'd left behind trash and graffiti, but no food or clothing. He headed back to the main car with Cruz, studying the deserted structures and silent tracks in the distance. Moonlight illuminated the area, pouring through the large windows of the train. It was a defendable space. He could guard the entrance while Penny and Cruz slept.

Owen decided to remove a few more cushions for them to rest on. He took out his knife and sliced one of the seat covers away, exposing the soft padding underneath.

"Can I help?" Cruz asked.

Owen had two knives now, Roach's combat weapon and the pocketknife Penny had stolen from camp. He gave Cruz the pocketknife, showing him its features. It had a dull blade and a couple of other tools.

Cruz held it in his little fist and made a stabbing motion, puncturing the seat.

"Not like that," Owen said, stilling his hand. "This

blade doesn't lock, so it can fold up and cut your fingers." He showed Cruz how to hold the knife safely and to cut away from his body. With Owen's guidance, Cruz separated a seat cover from the cushion, his brow furrowed in concentration. Then he did one on his own while Owen supervised.

Penny wouldn't have approved of this activity. Cruz seemed to know that and to revel in the illicit thrill.

When Cruz was finished, Owen held out his palm.

Cruz hesitated. "Can I keep it?"

"For what?"

"So I can protect my mommy."

Owen's throat tightened with emotion. "If someone attacks your mommy, you should run away and yell for help."

Cruz stared at the knife, conflicted.

"If someone attacks you, you can bite their hand or kick them in the nuts. You know what I mean?"

He nodded. "Mommy calls them *canicas.*"

Owen hid a smile. Marbles. Only a woman would call them that. "Let's practice. Pretend I'm going to attack you."

Cruz stood across from Owen in the aisle and fumbled with the knife. His little fingers couldn't get the blade out. He transferred it to his other hand and tried again, accidentally dropping the knife on the ground.

If he'd managed to get the blade ready, Owen would have shown him how easily he could be overpowered. But he didn't feel it was necessary now.

Cruz couldn't use the knife for any purpose. He didn't have the fine motor skills.

"See how hard it is? You could have just kicked me in the nuts and ran away."

Cruz picked up the knife and studied it in the dim light. Mouth pursed with concentration, he figured out how to extend the blade.

"Good," Owen said, surprised by his tenacity. "But you still can't hold it that way. Like I told you, the blade doesn't lock."

The boy moved his fingers out of the way. When he found the correct position, he frowned, seeming to realize that the knife wasn't made for stabbing.

"It's not a weapon," Owen said.

"What do you mean?"

"You can't use it to defend yourself. You can cut string with it or sharpen a stick, maybe. That blade is pretty dull."

He looked crestfallen.

"Look," Owen said, stepping forward. He molded Cruz's fist around the handle and let the blade stick up between his fingers. "This is the way to inflict damage. Punch someone in the eye like that and you'll stop them."

Cruz jabbed the seat cushion a few times to practice. He grinned, as if this was fun.

Owen took the knife back, aware that he'd made a mistake. Instructing a child to stab someone was too gruesome, too potentially traumatizing. He couldn't stop reliving the sensation of Roach's blood running over his hands. "It's not a toy."

"I know," Cruz said, stricken.

"You're better off using your body's natural weapons."

"How?"

Owen humored him with a quick demonstration on how to attack vulnerable spots with his fists, teeth, elbows and knees. Cruz listened carefully and mimicked his every move, relishing the lesson. Owen decided to let him keep the pocketknife, just for tonight. Cruz was scared for himself and for his mother. Owen could sympathize.

They collected a pile of cushions and seat covers, carrying them back to Penny. She shifted in her sleep but didn't wake. Owen suspected she had a touch of heat exhaustion. He hoped it wouldn't turn into full-on heatstroke.

"I'm hungry," Cruz whispered.

"We'll eat tomorrow. Lie down and get some rest."

He stared up at Owen with big brown eyes. Just like Penny's. "What are you going to do?"

"I'm going to guard the front of the car."

"I want to come with you."

Owen shrugged, leading Cruz down the aisle. They sat side by side, with Cruz by the window. They couldn't see much outside, other than moon-washed hills. So they just rested there, sharing the quiet.

"Is this train from the olden days?" Cruz asked.

"No, it's fairly new. The railway reopened about

ten years ago. Then it went bankrupt and closed again."

"Why did it go to bankrup'?"

"The owners ran out of money," he said, balancing his elbow on the back of the seat. The wound on his forearm throbbed like a son of a bitch.

"Have you been here before?"

"Not in this car. But along the tracks, yeah. When I was about sixteen, my dad brought me out here looking for scrap metal."

"What's that?"

"Machine parts that can be melted down and reused."

"Did you find some?"

"Yes," Owen said, shuddering at the memory. His dad had made him carry twenty pounds of rusted iron for ten miles. He'd ended up sunburned and sick, vomiting his guts out, so he knew how dangerous it was to get heatstroke.

"Is your dad old, like my grandpa?"

"Older. He was fifty when he died."

"He died?"

"Last year."

Cruz didn't know what to say about that. "Was he nice?"

"No."

"Why not?"

Owen tried to think of an appropriate answer for a little boy. "He yelled at me and called me names."

"Like what?"

Sissy. Faggot. Weakling. Cocksucker. "Words you shouldn't hear."

"He lived with your mommy?"

"Off and on," he said. Christian Jackson had spent a lot of time in jail, mostly for domestic violence and drug charges.

"Did he leave…because of you?"

"No," Owen said, startled by the question. He remembered what Penny had said earlier about Cruz thinking his father didn't want him. "Some people just aren't cut out to be dads. It's never the kid's fault."

He squinted up at Owen. "Did he love you?"

"Yes," Owen said, after a pause. For all his faults, his father hadn't been a sociopath. He'd had anger issues, a drug problem and poor impulse control. He'd probably thought he was doing Owen a favor by toughening him up. And maybe he had. Without that harsh upbringing, Owen might not have survived in prison. "He was a mean son of a bitch, though."

Cruz mulled this over. "Is it better to have a mean dad or no dad?"

"I don't know. That's a good question." Owen could forgive his father for slapping him around, but he couldn't look past the abuse his mother had endured. Far too often, she'd been used as a punching bag. Owen knew this: a bad *husband* was worse than none. "You're lucky to have such a great mom."

Owen glanced toward the area where Penny was sleeping, contemplative. Cruz had no experience with cruelty or abuse. He'd never been neglected. His fa-

ther's absence was the only mistreatment he was familiar with. Because of this, he didn't see Penny as
anything special, but he would. Someday, he would.

"Mommy says you're not my dad," Cruz blurted
out.

Owen studied the boy's hopeful face, his heart
breaking. He still couldn't believe Cruz had ever cast
him in the role. A role he so desperately wanted. Pressure built behind Owen's eyes. "I'm not," he said,
clearing his throat. "I wish I was."

"You do?"

"Yeah."

"Do you like my mommy?"

"Yes. Very much."

"She likes you, too."

His pulse accelerated. "How do you know?"

"I heard my tía Raven talking to her about it."

Raven. Owen knew not to take her seriously.
"What did she say?" he asked anyway.

"She said she wanted to go riding with you."

"Go riding?"

"Uh-huh. Mommy got mad and told her to leave
you alone. Tía said Mommy just wanted you for herself."

"And what did your mother say?"

"She said that was true. Then Tía said okay, she
wouldn't take you for a ride as long as Mommy went
with you."

"Was this conversation in Spanish?"

"Yes."

"What word did they use for ride?"

"Montar."

He laughed, rubbing a hand down his face. It didn't surprise him that Raven would initiate a naughty discussion. Even religious, well-bred girls talked about sex. He doubted she was serious about wanting to "mount" him, however. More likely, she had just been teasing Penny. The fact that Penny cared enough to warn Raven away from him was flattering. Did she really want him that way?

"Are you going to leave us?" Cruz asked.

"I don't know," he said, sobering. If Penny was too weak to continue, he'd have to make the difficult journey on his own. It was what he'd done after the earthquake. "I might have to go get help. But I'll come back."

"Promise?"

"I promise."

Cruz accepted those words, seeming comforted. "Mommy didn't want to leave you, either. We looked for you by the tents before we ran away."

"It's okay. She made the right decision."

Cruz curled up against his side and fell asleep. Owen stared out the window, lost in thought. He wondered if Penny wanted a man for herself or a father for Cruz. Owen loved Cruz as if he was his own son, but he'd never imagined having children of his own. He wasn't even in the market for a girlfriend, so marriage and parenthood seemed beyond his scope. For the first time, he considered how his intimacy issues affected others. He hadn't realized Penny was interested in him.

He'd assumed that stress and fear had caused her to cling to him. Seeking physical comfort was a normal reaction. But, according to Cruz, Penny had discussed him with Raven. She'd wanted him *before* the kidnapping.

He thought back to their earlier conversation. What could he offer her, other than his complete devotion to her and Cruz? Owen didn't have much going for him. He had no savings and limited prospects.

She'd brought up a point he hadn't considered. What did he think she could offer him? The question made him uneasy. It wasn't that he thought he had to bring more to the table in a relationship because he was a man. It wasn't *just* that, anyway. They were from different backgrounds. She was gorgeous and graceful and classy. She could date a movie star or a billionaire if she chose to. He was a convicted felon, a trailer park reject from the tumbleweeds. Of course he didn't understand what a woman like her would see in him.

She deserved someone better, someone healthy and stable. He couldn't support her in the style she was used to. If he kept his distance, she'd find the right person. She'd meet a decent man from a nice, respectable family. They'd live happily ever after. And he'd die of longing, watching her slip from his grasp.

He picked up Cruz's sleeping form and carried

him to the back of the rail car, setting him down beside Penny.

About a year ago, Owen had done a background check on Tyler Forsythe, Cruz's father. He was a law student at Yale, handsome and athletic. Cruz looked like him. He had Tyler's golden-brown hair and thick, straight eyelashes. Cruz resembled Penny more, but his features were a blend of two beautiful people.

As far as Owen knew, Tyler had never contacted Penny, never inquired about his son. Maybe he didn't care.

Tyler was the kind of person Penny's father approved of her dating, with the exception of his non-Latino heritage. It occurred to Owen, somewhat belatedly, that Tyler wasn't his equal. Owen would treat Penny ten times better than a spoiled, unfeeling bastard.

After staring at the sleeping pair for several moments, Owen returned to the front of the car, his chest aching. He wanted them so bad he was choking on it. Tyler had thrown them both away and never looked back.

CHAPTER THIRTEEN

Penny dreamed of trains.

She was running along the tracks with Cruz, trying to escape the oncoming train. She pushed him to safety, but her foot got caught between the railroad ties. Stumbling, she fell down. The whistling juggernaut struck her at full force, cutting off her legs.

She woke with a start, sitting up and gripping her calves. They were both cramped, the muscles rock-hard and quivering.

Owen loomed above her, his eyes silver in the dark. "Let me," he said, crouching down to massage her legs. She smothered a moan as he worked out the kinks in her muscles. Cruz was asleep beside her, tucked into a little ball. He had a blanket made of wool seat covers wrapped around his body. It was cold.

When her cramps eased, Owen straightened. He watched her for a moment, as if expecting her to go back to sleep.

"What time is it?" she whispered.

"Near dawn, I think."

Careful not to wake Cruz, she crawled away from him, keeping one of the seat covers as a shawl. Owen helped her up. Her knees threatened to give out. She clung to his arm, swaying on her feet. Her soles felt bruised and tender, as if she'd been walking barefoot on sharp rocks. Her belly ached from emptiness.

"Okay?" he asked.

She nodded, letting him lead her to the front of the railcar. Once there, she sat again, clutching the fabric over her chest. Her hair had come loose from the braid.

"Are you cold?"

"Yes."

There was just enough moonlight to see the concern in his expression. He put his arm around her, offering her a drink from the canteen. "The temperature is comfortable. Warm, by L.A. standards."

She took a thirsty gulp of water, aware that she was showing signs of dehydration. Her stomach jerked in protest, screaming for something more substantial. Then the quivering settled, and the fluids stayed down.

"How do you feel?"

"Like I got run over by a train."

"Sore?"

"My whole body is," she said, resting her head on his shoulder.

"That might get better as your muscles loosen up. You slept for several hours."

"I had a bad dream."

"You were whimpering."

"It was scary." She told him about running down the tracks and pushing Cruz to safety.

Owen smelled of sweat and dust and rusted metal. Old blood, perhaps. They were quite a pair. With her own soiled clothes and tangled hair, she felt about as fresh as an old rag. She inched away from him, self-conscious.

"Do I stink?" he asked.

"No."

"Right," he scoffed.

She squirmed in discomfort. "I just have to pee."

"I'll help you."

Her cheeks burned at the thought, but she didn't think she could manage on her own. So she let him guide her down the steps, into the cool predawn air. Squatting was beyond her current capabilities. He seemed to know this.

"There's a cinderblock," he said, pointing. "You can sit on it."

With his assistance, she hobbled to the concrete form. "Check for spiders."

He kicked it over and stuck his arm through the hole to show her it was clear. Then he set it upright and brushed off the top. She wiggled her panties down to her knees. Keeping his gaze averted, he lowered her to the impromptu toilet.

"Now go away," she said.

He turned and walked about ten feet.

She emptied her bladder quickly, embarrassed.

When she was finished, he glanced over his shoulder. "Done?"

"Yes."

He came back to lift her up.

"Thanks," she said, her voice wavering.

"What's wrong?"

She pulled her panties into place, blinking the tears from her eyes.

"Did it hurt?"

"No."

He put his arm around her and guided her inside the railcar. She sat down and stared out the window, wallowing in self-pity. Although seduction was the last thing on her mind, she wanted him to see her as sexy and irresistible. Instead she felt like an invalid.

"I'm sorry," he said.

"For what?"

"Everything. This whole fucked-up situation."

"It's not your fault."

"You shouldn't be out here, hungry and weak and…peeing on concrete."

"I'm not too fancy to pee outdoors, Owen."

"You're upset."

"Because I feel dirty and…unattractive."

"Unattractive?"

She refused to elaborate.

"You could pee *on* me, and I wouldn't consider it unattractive."

"Really?"

"Maybe not on my face. That would be degrading."

Her mouth dropped open. "People do that?"

He smiled, shaking his head. "I don't care how dirty you are, and I'm not disgusted by anything you do. I saw a baby come out of you, remember?"

"I wish I could forget."

"If that didn't turn me off, nothing will."

She wasn't sure why she started laughing. Maybe it was the combination of shock, discomfort and stress. Maybe it was his strange, honest admission. Maybe it was just the bizarre complexity of human behavior.

He laughed along with her, so something must have been funny.

When she regained control of herself, wiping the tears from her cheeks, she remembered that she'd also seen him during some vulnerable moments. And she found him more appealing for it, not less.

"I don't care if you smell bad," she said.

"That makes one of us," he replied, smiling wryly.

"I'd kill for a shower."

"Me, too."

She'd also kill for a cheeseburger, but she didn't want to torture him by continuing a conversation about things they couldn't have.

His gaze caressed her face. "I was worried about you last night."

"Why?"

"I've had heatstroke before. I got really sick."

She was stiff and sore, not sick. "I'll be fine. I'm just not used to hiking all day, especially in this kind of weather."

"Should I go on without you? I could probably reach the highway in a few hours."

"How long will it take with us?"

"Six, maybe more."

She didn't want him to leave her. The idea of sitting here without him scared her. When the sun came up, the interior of the train would get hot. They had no food and only a little water. "What do you think?"

"I'd rather stay together."

"Even if you have to push me in a wheelbarrow?"

"Yes."

"Then I guess you're stuck with me," she said, squeezing his hand. He didn't pull away. His eyes met hers, and a familiar heaviness hung between them. The feeling had shifted from unrequited to unspoken, however.

Instead of *I wish,* her heart whispered, *soon.*

Although he hadn't admitted to anything, she'd seen the desire in his gaze. The kiss he'd given her yesterday afternoon had been smoldering with it. His reasons for holding back might be complicated, but she no longer thought he wasn't interested.

"Do you still want to be a firefighter?" she asked, tentative.

"Yes."

"Why did you take this job?"

He hesitated before answering. "Your father promised me a recommendation letter to the Los Angeles Fire Department. I don't have a chance of getting hired without it."

"Why not?"

"I'm a convicted felon, and it's a competitive market."

She'd wondered about that. Another friend of theirs from the earthquake, Sam Rutherford, had helped Owen get the job at Sierra National Park. Of course he needed a reference to gain entry to the LAFD.

"Your father also arranged for my transfer from Santee Lakes to Pleasant Valley. I owe him big for that."

It was the least her father could do, after Owen had risked his life for Penny and the others trapped under the collapsed freeway. She was sure her father would come through with the recommendation, as well. Assuming they survived this horrible experience. Owen had gone above and beyond in his bodyguard duties.

"Speaking of letters, you never responded to mine." She'd written him several times at Pleasant Valley State Prison. She'd asked him about it once, years ago. He'd merely said that he'd read them and changed the subject.

"I promised your father I wouldn't contact you."

She frowned at this unexpected news. "Why?"

"It was one of the terms of the transfer."

"And after you got out?"

"I was a free man," he said, shrugging. "As powerful as your father is, I doubted he'd get me thrown back in prison for being friends with you."

He said this jokingly, but her father's actions didn't sit well with Penny. It felt like a conspiracy, an attack on her autonomy. Had he suspected she had a crush on Owen, even then? Her cheeks burned with indignation. She couldn't believe Owen had gone along with all of this and never told her about it. She suspected that her father's sneaky machinations fed into Owen's lack of self-worth.

He thought he was doing the right thing by keeping his distance.

Instead of continuing the conversation, Owen got up and prepared to leave the train. She woke Cruz while he took some of the seat cushions to the wheelbarrow, making a comfortable padding. Penny climbed in with Cruz, who went back to sleep on her lap.

"How's your arm?" she asked Owen, glancing at the bandage.

"It's not bad."

She took that to mean it hurt. He needed first aid and antibiotics. The man he'd…killed…had probably bled all over his open wound. The risk of contracting a communicable disease that way was small, but not insignificant. It was more likely that he'd get parasites or a bacterial infection from the water he'd used to wash with.

The injury didn't seem to slow him down. He pushed hard as the sun blossomed over the horizon, shining warm rays across the barren landscape. Cruz woke up, hungry and irritable. He walked along the tracks until he got bored.

Penny's muscles started to feel better as the temperature rose. She traded places with Cruz, stretching her legs. It was difficult to keep pace with Owen. Her feet hurt and she was hungry. But sitting in the wheelbarrow gave her a claustrophobic vibe that reminded her of the San Diego earthquake. In this vast wasteland, escape seemed impossible. There was rubble everywhere, death around every corner. No end in sight.

A blue flag fluttered in the distance. "What's that?"

"Water station," Owen said, wiping the sweat from his brow.

When they reached it, he removed the lid from a blue plastic bin. There were rocks inside to weigh down the bin, along with a gallon jug of water. Owen unscrewed the top and took a long drink, his throat working. Then he handed it to Penny, who shared with Cruz. As he reached up to steady the jug, an object slipped from his grip.

She bent to retrieve the pocketknife. "Where did you get this?"

"I gave it to him," Owen said. "I forgot to ask for it back."

"He could have cut his fingers, or tripped and fallen on the blade."

Owen replaced the lid on the bin, appearing contrite.

"Can I keep it?" Cruz asked.

"No," she said, appalled. "Didn't you hear what I said? You could hurt yourself playing with knives."

His brown eyes filled with tears. "I wasn't playing with it."

"What were you doing with it?"

"Just holding it. In case I needed to protect you."

She looked at Owen, whose gaze reflected her heartache. *"Mijo,"* she said, curving her hand around her son's neck. "You can protect me when you're all grown up."

He jerked away from her, refusing to be consoled. "I want to protect you now. Owen showed me how."

"Great," she muttered.

"I won't get hurt."

"You can't have the knife, Cruz."

He stared at Owen, his mouth trembling. When Owen didn't offer any rebuke, he turned to Penny. "Owen said I could."

"He's not your mother," she said, touching the center of her chest. "I am."

"I wish you weren't!"

She'd heard this kind of outburst before. Cruz had temper tantrums when he was tired or overexcited. Once, at Disneyland, he'd kicked her shin because she'd refused to wait two hours in the line for the Dumbo ride. Although she knew that this behavior was normal for children, especially during stressful situations, it made her feel like a failure. Maybe she wasn't meeting his needs as a single parent.

Cruz stomped away from the tracks. He lay down on the ground and cried, his little body full of frustration.

She crossed her arms over her chest, sighing.

"He doesn't mean it," Owen said.

"I know."

He snapped the flagpole in half, struck by inspiration. "Can he play with this?"

She smiled weakly. "Yes."

They let Cruz blow off steam for a few minutes. When Owen approached him with the new toy, she tucked the pocketknife into her bra. Cruz wasn't as excited about the flag, but he accepted it. He sat in the wheelbarrow, waving it back and forth.

About a mile down the tracks, something far more magnificent caught his attention. A huge bridgelike structure stretched over a steep gorge. The flag and the knife were forgotten in an instant. Cruz scrambled out of the wheelbarrow to look.

"World's largest trestle," Owen said, staring across the expanse.

"What's it made out of?" Cruz asked.

"Redwood."

An intricate maze of rust-colored wooden beams supported the tracks. They were as thick as railroad ties, crisscrossed like lattice. It must have been two hundred feet high, and three or four times as long. Not only that, the structure curved to the right. The tracks disappeared into a dark tunnel on the opposite cliff.

"Whoa," Cruz said.

"Hold my hand," Penny ordered as they got closer.

Cruz didn't argue. It was an intimidating tangle of wood, sturdy-looking but old. The only thing separating them from the edge was a railing of thin metal cord.

"Is it safe?" she asked.

"Sure," Owen said. "It was made to bear a lot of weight."

"What if the wood is rotten?"

"It's not. They built it in the early 1900s, and there were trains running this track five years ago."

She hesitated to step forward, her pulse pounding.

"I'll push you across in the wheelbarrow," he offered.

"No."

"You think I'll dump you over the edge?"

She shook her head. "I just want to go at my own pace."

"This is the last tunnel," he said. "On the other side, we're home free."

"Close to the road, you mean?"

"Just a few miles."

"It's all right, Mommy," Cruz said. "I won't let you fall."

She kissed the top of his head, forgiving his earlier misbehavior. "In that case, I'm ready."

"I'll go first," Owen said.

He pushed the wheelbarrow while they walked on an aluminum grate next to the tracks. She couldn't look down. Every step felt risky. Her stomach clenched with anxiety, empty and shriveled from lack of sustenance.

This would be a very bad place to faint.

When they got to the other side, she almost wilted with relief. She stopped to look back at the deep gorge in amazement. Owen put his arm around her, and she held on to Cruz's small shoulders. They were like a family at the Grand Canyon.

After a quiet moment, they turned and headed toward the tunnel. Penny and Cruz followed Owen, who was pushing the empty wheelbarrow. She got the flashlight ready. Before they entered the dark recesses, a figure flew out and tackled Owen. They rolled across the tracks, perilously close to the cliff's edge.

Penny screamed and pulled Cruz closer to her body, protecting him on instinct. But there was more than one attacker. A second man grabbed her from behind. He clasped his palm over her mouth and barred her waist with his arm. She was wrenched away from Cruz, yanked into the shadows of the tunnel.

She sank her teeth into his rough, salty skin.

"Goddamn it!"

Tasting blood, she bit harder.

Releasing her mouth, with some difficulty, he employed a different tactic: pressing the barrel of a gun to her temple. "Be still."

She went still.

Cruz watched this, his eyes wide with terror. He couldn't run away even if he wanted to. Penny and her captor where blocking the tunnel. Owen and Dirk were wrestling on the dusty ground in front of the trestle. Cruz was trapped between two horrifying struggles.

"Let go of my mommy!" Cruz said.

"Shut him up," the man behind her said. Shane, she figured.

"I'm okay," she choked out. "Stay right there. Stay quiet."

He clenched his little hands into fists but obeyed. She shuddered to think of what he might have done with the pocketknife.

Shane probably meant to control Owen by threatening her, but Owen had his hands full with Dirk. He appeared to be fighting for his life, trading punches next to the overturned wheelbarrow.

When Owen drew the gun from his waistband, Shane inhaled a sharp breath. "I've got your woman, brother!"

Owen glanced at Penny. In that second of distraction, Dirk pounced. He straddled Owen and grabbed his wrist, slamming it against the ground. The weapon discharged with an earsplitting boom and tumbled over the edge of the cliff.

The battle would have been over at that point if Cruz hadn't interfered. To her absolute horror, her son ran toward the melee. He drew back his foot and kicked Dirk in the ribs, hard enough to make him grunt.

When Dirk raised a hand to retaliate, Penny's world came to a grinding halt. The next moment unfolded in slow motion. Dirk struck her son across the face and sent him flying. Cruz landed near the front of the tunnel, crumpled in a heap. His eyes were open but dazed. Penny screamed his name, reaching out to him.

Shane swore under his breath and tightened his grip.

Owen went nuts.

With a feral growl, he slammed his fist into Dirk's stomach and shoved him aside. Dirk scrambled to his feet, coughing. Owen jumped up and pulled a knife from his belt. He advanced, slashing it at the other man's midsection. His opponent leaped backward just in time. Dirk retreated toward the trestle, waggling his fingers at Owen in a clear invitation to bring it on. His nostrils were dripping blood, his eyes wild.

"Enough," Shane yelled, dragging Penny from the shadows. "I have a gun to her head, you dumb fuck!"

Penny wanted to tell him not to surrender, but the words died in her throat. Even if Owen defeated Dirk, Shane would decide how this ended. Maybe he'd have mercy on Owen. Maybe he wouldn't.

Owen looked over his shoulder at Cruz, wiping blood from his mouth. Her son was curled up in a little ball, crying. A muscle in Owen's jaw clenched at the sight. He tossed his knife in the dirt, defeated.

"Turn around and get on the ground," Dirk shouted. "Facedown."

Owen followed those instructions, his eyes dead.

Dirk picked up the knife and rushed forward, stepping on the back of Owen's neck. Owen bared his gritted teeth as Dirk applied more pressure, smashing his cheek against the ground. "You're not so tough now, are you, motherfucker? You're not so tough without a gun to shoot someone in the foot, or a knife to stab them with."

Penny hated to watch this. She hated for *Cruz* to watch this. Her son continued to weep quietly, tears leaving tracks in the dust on his face.

Dirk lifted his boot up and grabbed Owen by the collar, dragging him toward the edge of the cliff. Shoving Owen's head under the thin metal guardrail, Dirk crouched on top of him, pressing his knee between Owen's shoulder blades. He gripped Owen's short hair and touched the tip of the blade to his taut throat.

"No!" Penny wailed. She pummeled her fists against Shane's arm to get free, but he wouldn't budge.

"How tough will you feel, watching your blood spill out?"

"Not in front of Cruz," Owen rasped.

"What did you say?" Dirk asked.

"Not in front of the boy. Please."

Dirk deferred to Shane. "Do you want to finish this? If you're not going to take care of business, I will."

"Is that my brother's kid?" Shane asked Penny.

Penny wasn't sure how to respond. Anyone who could do basic math would know Cruz wasn't Owen's son. Shane must be an idiot.

He dug the barrel into her temple. "Is it?"

"Yes," she sobbed. "Yes!"

"Cover his eyes," Shane said, shoving her toward Cruz. She stumbled and fell down hard. Tears blurring her vision, she crawled to her son on her hands and knees. Her entire body quaked as she drew Cruz into her embrace. Turning him away from the carnage, she cradled his head to her chest and closed her hands over his ears.

The sound of a gunshot bounced off the walls of the gorge, making her jump. She felt it penetrate, straight through the heart.

CHAPTER FOURTEEN

OWEN STARED AT the bottom of the gorge, his bile rising.

He was determined not to glance at Cruz or Penny. He didn't want either of them to get hurt in a futile attempt to help him. Better to just take a deep breath, let his mind go blank and accept his fate. Hold steady. It would all be over soon.

Instead of cutting his throat, Dirk merely nicked him. Blood coursed over his Adam's apple in a thin trickle. A couple of drops splashed on the rocks below. Owen heard Penny's agonized sob as Shane shoved her aside.

His brother came forward. To kill him.

In his peripheral vision, he saw Penny crawling across the dirt, toward Cruz. She cowered at the mouth of the tunnel, protecting him with her body. Cruz was also crying. He didn't appear to be badly injured. If the boy had been knocked unconscious, Owen would have gutted Dirk like a fish.

He wasn't sure he'd made the right decision by dropping the knife. Sacrificing himself for Penny and Cruz was a no-brainer, but he didn't want his life to end like this. Not at his brother's hands. Not facedown and helpless, staring at his own blood.

Pebbles crunched under Shane's boots as he approached. Owen smelled rust and sweat and cigarette-stinking fingers. The unpleasant odor reminded him of his father. He squeezed his eyes shut, holding the tears at bay.

How fucking stupid, to care about looking like a wimp before he got his head blown off. What insidious, asinine macho bullshit. Even at the cusp of death, his father's words haunted him so much that he refused to beg and blubber.

Like it mattered. Would he rather be a corpse or a coward? If he had a choice, he'd take coward. It wasn't as if he'd always stayed strong or held his head high. Some of the things he'd done in prison—well, he'd proved the old man right.

Shane stepped up to finish him. His brother didn't mess around with big talk and intimidation, like Dirk. It was cold comfort, but Owen knew Shane wouldn't savor this. He'd carry the guilt with him to the grave.

Owen flinched as the gun went off. The sound ricocheted throughout the canyon, oddly flat and lacking impact.

He hadn't even felt the bullet.

Dirk let go of the knife and slumped forward, on top of him. Something warm and sloppy slid across the back of his neck, soaking the collar of his shirt. Owen opened his eyes, realizing he hadn't been shot. Dirk had.

The scene was like a Picasso, difficult to process. He blinked a few times until his brain solved the gruesome puzzle. What was left of Dirk's face rested right next to Owen's. The top of his head was gone, his scalp hanging loose.

Owen recoiled in shock.

Shane shoved the corpse aside with his foot. It toppled over the edge, glancing off rocks and turning cartwheels before hitting the bottom of the gorge with a sickening thud. Owen rolled away from the guardrail and retched. A small amount of water and stomach acid came up, burning his throat.

Shane wrenched Owen's arms behind his back and snapped cuffs on his wrists. Owen was too traumatized to struggle. He didn't even understand what his brother wanted to do to him. Maybe Shane had another bullet with his name on it.

Shane picked up Roach's knife and stuck the blade in his boot. Apparently his brother intended to go through with the money exchange and whatever else the plan called for. Shane might have chosen Owen's life over Dirk's, but he wasn't giving up. Once he committed to a crime, he didn't quit.

Owen dragged his gaze toward the entrance of the tunnel. His head throbbed from hanging off the edge, and his ears were ringing. The sun was too bright for his bleary eyes. Penny had her back to him. She appeared to be weeping.

"Get up," Shane said, yanking him to his feet. "Walk."

Owen stumbled toward Penny. Keeping Cruz's head cradled to her chest, she looked over her shoulder. When she saw him, her tears cut off like a switch. She stared at him for a long moment, her lips parted in wonder. Then her face crumpled, and she starting crying again. With relief, perhaps.

"Let's go, princess," Shane said.

Wiping her wet cheeks, she rose. Although she was clearly shaken and still weak from the day before, she lifted Cruz into her arms. Shane took out a flashlight, waving at her to precede them into the dark passageway. They walked down the tracks in silence. There was a light at the end of the tunnel, but it didn't lead anywhere peaceful.

A dun-colored Jeep was parked on the other side. Shane shoved Owen into the passenger seat and secured the safety belt, trapping him there. Then he opened the glove compartment and removed a roll of duct tape. He pointed at the space behind Owen. "Put your kid there."

Penny stood rooted to the spot, uncooperative.

"We can do this the hard way or the easy way," he said. "I won't hurt him, but I'll use the taser on you if I have to."

Mouth trembling, she carried Cruz forward and sat him down, latching his seat belt. Owen cranked his head around to study him. Other than a red mark on his cheek, the boy seemed unharmed. Owen didn't know what to say. Cruz might not be injured, but he wasn't okay. Nothing about this would ever be okay.

Penny allowed Shane to tape her hands behind her

back. He wrapped her crossed wrists several times and loaded her into the Jeep.

Owen stared at the dashboard, his mind numb. He hadn't figured on Shane coming from the south side of the tracks. It was the longer route and a gamble. There was no trail to follow. Owen might have gone the opposite direction. The more distance he'd put between them and the palm oasis, the more comfortable he'd felt. He'd grown complacent.

Shane started the engine and headed down a narrow wash. He looked tired and angry, as if shooting Dirk had ruined his whole day.

"Where's Brett?" Owen asked.

"Mexico."

Gardener must have driven him. There was no one else. Both Roach and Dirk were dead. It was just brother versus brother now. Owen didn't know if he had the heart to challenge Shane. He couldn't imagine killing him. In any fight, they'd both lose.

He was drained, physically and emotionally. The past three days had been worse than the San Diego earthquake. Back then he hadn't given a shit about anybody, least of all himself. Caring made everything harder.

Owen was exhausted. His clothes were filthy. He had blood and gore on his neck, some of which wasn't his own. The inside of his mouth ached from multiple blows, and hunger gnawed at the pit of his stomach. His palms were blistered from the wheelbarrow, his feet hurt and the cut on his forearm burned like fire.

Maybe *he* had heatstroke.

These minor discomforts were nothing compared to his inner turmoil. Seeing Dirk raise his hand to Cruz had affected Owen deeply. It had filled him with rage and impotence, for the boy Cruz was and the boy Owen had been. Neither deserved the abuse.

Owen couldn't change the past, but he wanted to control the future, and prevent *this* child from ever being struck again.

It wasn't Cruz's fault that Dirk hit him or Tyler didn't want him. It wasn't Jamie's fault that Shane was a reprobate. And it wasn't Owen's fault that his father had been abusive. None of their fathers' actions reflected on them.

He realized now that he'd never been a coward. His father had been the coward for choosing weaker targets. Whenever Owen had flinched or shied away from him, he'd been beaten for it. He'd been punished for being scared, which was a natural response to violence. Shane had been punished for fighting back. Their mother had been punished for doing nothing. No one had escaped unscathed.

But they could overcome. *He* could overcome.

Owen needed to stop listening to the voices inside his head, the ones that whispered the same things his father had. By letting his bad experiences dictate the rest of his life, he'd given them too much power. He had to rise above the trauma and move on.

"Wake up," Shane said, shoving his shoulder.

Owen straightened abruptly. He'd closed his eyes for a moment and drifted off, slouched in the passenger seat. They were already in Salton City, parked in front of his mother's modular home. Her car was gone, indicating that she was at work. His father's old fishing boat was sitting there, covered with a green tarp.

Owen glanced at Penny, who stared back at him with an inscrutable expression.

Shane got out of the Jeep, motioning for her to do the same. Then he went to open the passenger door. Owen stood up with a wince, his body stiff from sleep. Cruz unlatched his seat belt and followed them toward the house.

Shane let Penny in first, then Cruz and Owen. She walked a few tentative steps, stopping when she reached the kitchen. His stomach rumbled at the thought of food. He could smell bread and bananas and coffee grounds.

"I have to go to the bathroom," Cruz said.

Shane pointed at a nearby door. "In there."

Owen also wanted to relieve himself, but he could hold it, and he doubted Shane would unlock his cuffs. With Shane's help, he sat down at the kitchen table.

"Can I go, too?" Penny asked.

Shane seemed to consider her a minor threat, easy to overpower and control. She wouldn't run off without Cruz. He removed the knife from his boot and turned her around, preparing to cut through the duct tape. But perhaps he remembered that she'd walloped Gardener a good one, because he hesitated. "You carrying any weapons, wildcat?"

She shook her head, cheeks flushed.

He searched her anyway. He was thorough, and not particularly respectful. She winced as Shane cupped her breasts crudely.

Owen tried to remain calm, but his blood boiled with fury. He suspected Shane was doing this to taunt him. Owen wanted to leap to his feet and head-butt his brother for touching her. Shane dug into her bra, removing the pocketknife with dirty fingers.

"Look what we have here," he said, tossing it on the table. "Maybe I should do a full cavity search."

"Leave her alone," Owen said through clenched teeth.

The harassment was cut short by Cruz, not Owen. When the boy returned to the kitchen, Shane's manner changed from menacing to mild. He sliced through the tape at Penny's wrists and stepped back.

"I'm hungry," Cruz said.

"Make us some food," Shane told Penny.

She rubbed her wrists. "Can I use the bathroom first?"

"Sure," he said, winking at Owen. He pocketed the army knife and accompanied her, standing right outside the open door. Her mouth was thin with discomfort as she walked back into the kitchen and looked in the fridge.

"Mommy doesn't know how to cook," Cruz said.

"Oh, yeah?" Shane asked. "Why is that?"

"We have a chef."

"They have a chef," Shane said, arching a brow at Owen. "Of course. What does he make?"

"Tacos, pizza. Anything we want."

"How nice for you."

"There's lunch meat and cheese slices," Penny said. She rifled through the drawers. "Some fruit. That's about it."

"What to drink?"

"Milk."

"No beer?"

"I don't see any."

Shane shrugged. "Bring it all. I'm starving."

She brought everything she could find. Ham, processed cheese, apples, bananas, white bread and peanut butter. They were too hungry to wait for sandwiches. Cruz fed himself and Owen slices of ham and cheese. Penny slathered peanut butter on bread, and Shane quartered apples with his new pocketknife. It was a white-trash feast.

"That's mine," Cruz said.

"This?" Shane said, holding up the knife.

"Owen gave it to me."

"Is that right?" he mused.

Cruz nodded.

A smile played on his lips. "If I give it back to you, will you stab me with it?"

"Not unless you hurt my mommy."

Shane must have liked this answer, because he shoved the knife across the table. "Here. Keep it."

And with that single gesture, Shane won Cruz over. The boy tucked the knife into his pocket like a sacred object while Penny stood by, silent. Now Owen understood how she'd felt this morning. He was angry with Shane for presenting a weapon to Cruz—one that he'd yanked from her bra—as a gift.

"Can Cruz watch cartoons?" Penny asked.

Shane nodded his permission. She took him to the couch and turned on a kids' show. Owen wondered what she thought of his childhood home. It was as clean as always, but cheaply furnished and shabby. The carpet was threadbare, the linoleum outdated.

Shane lit up a cigarette and stood. He looked through all of the drawers and cabinets, slamming them in frustration.

"Try the boat," Owen said. "Dad kept a bottle under the tarp."

"You sure?"

"I took a swig of it myself after the funeral."

"Go get it," he told Penny.

She didn't like being bossed around any more than she liked being manhandled, but she acquiesced to his demands. When she returned with the bottle of whiskey, Shane gulped down a few swallows. Owen said nothing. Although his brother was a mean drunk, like their father, they'd have a chance to escape if Shane got wasted.

Drink up, brother. Drink up.

"What's your plan?" Owen asked.

"The exchange was supposed to happen today, but that went to shit."

"Why?"

"I don't have any help, thanks to you." He flicked his ashes into an empty cup. "I need at least one other guy to pull it off."

Owen didn't feel bad about throwing a wrench in the works. Nor did he consider it his fault that Dirk was dead. He'd defended himself during the first strike. Then he'd defended Cruz. His only regret was letting his brother cuff him so easily. But he'd been sick and stunned, overwhelmed by the bloody mayhem.

Shane lit another cigarette using the cherry of his previous one. "Dirk was my friend."

"I'm your brother."

"Right now, you're a fucking thorn in my side."

"Why did you get even involved in this?" Owen asked, frustrated. "Do you *want* to go back to prison?"

"I had no choice."

"You still have a choice. You can turn yourself in."

"No, I can't," Shane said. "They'll go after Jamie."

Owen studied Shane from across the table, his pulse pounding with animosity. Shane had gone forward with this plan, knowing it might endanger his son. His actions were unconscionable. Owen calculated the possibility of disarming him, but decided against it. In these close quarters, bullets might fly.

And…he was weary of violence. He didn't want to attack his brother in their childhood home.

"Who are they?" Owen asked.

"I don't know. They're affiliated with the Brotherhood. The guy I answer to is just a middleman."

"What's his name?"

Shane didn't answer.

"Do they want to assassinate Sandoval?"

"No," Shane said. He rose, grabbing a folded newspaper from the countertop. Reading the front page, he tossed it down. "They don't need to."

Owen glanced at the bold headline: Sandoval Drops Out. The accompanying article included a vaguely worded press release from his campaign, citing a family emergency. Speculation was rampant that his wife had a recently diagnosed terminal illness. Sandoval's top competitor, the runner-up for the GOP nomination, was slated to take his place. "You're responsible for this?"

"That was one of the conditions," Shane said. "It was supposed to be a simple exchange, no problems. Your girl and the kid would be home right now if you hadn't decided to play hero. We never meant to hurt them."

Owen stared at the newspaper, stunned.

Shane took another drag of his cigarette, glancing across the room. Penny was sitting on the couch with Cruz. "Is she your girlfriend?"

"No."

"Liar," Shane said.

"I care about her. You can't understand that because you're a heartless bastard."

"You have her son's name tattooed on your chest."

"So what?"

"She says he's yours."

"He might as well be."

Shane made a skeptical noise.

"I'll help you if you let him go," Owen said.

"What?"

"You said you didn't mean to take Cruz. So, give him back."

"How?"

"Mom can drive him. She'll be home from work soon."

"She can't deliver him to their front door," he said, shaking his head. "They'll arrest her on the spot."

"She can put him in a cab at LAX."

Penny was listening to their conversation. She turned her gaze to Shane, hopeful. Owen would have liked to bargain for them both to go home, but his brother would never agree to that. Shane needed someone to ransom.

"You know it's the right thing to do," Owen said.

"Since when have I ever done the right thing?"

"Do it, just this once. Think of Jamie."

Shane didn't like the idea, but his options were limited. If he wanted Owen's cooperation, this was the only way to get it. "Shit," he said in a defeated tone, swigging whiskey.

CHAPTER FIFTEEN

PENNY KISSED CRUZ on the head and rose, leaving him to watch cartoons.

The thought of leaving without him made her anxious, but not as anxious as him staying here with Owen's brother.

Shane was handsome, like Owen, but his shaggy blond hair and pumped-up muscles didn't appeal to her. Although they shared the same pale blue eyes, Shane's held no warmth or depth. A hint of sensitivity softened Owen's strong, angular features, while the lack of it lent Shane a cruel edge.

He stared at Penny, his expression flat. "Bring me the phone."

She went to get the cordless receiver from the console, passing it to Shane. She slid into the chair beside him.

"Call Janelle," Shane said to Owen. "I told her to take Jamie to her mother's, and I want to make sure she did it."

Owen dialed the number and listened. "No answer. She's probably working."

"Where at?"

He hesitated, seeming uneasy with this topic. "Club Vixen."

Shane's face went slack. "Since when?"

"Since you went away."

"Did Mom know?"

"Yes."

"Why didn't she tell me?"

"You'll have to ask her."

"She can't find a job that doesn't involve showing her tits?"

"Kids are expensive," he said. "You've never paid child support. She has to make ends meet somehow."

Shane stood, swearing under his breath. It was the first display of emotion she'd seen from him. He'd executed Dirk without batting an eye. He had no qualms about kidnapping and murder, but this bothered him? Penny couldn't tell if he didn't want his child's mother stripping for selfish reasons, or if he felt guilty about being a deadbeat dad.

A bit of both, perhaps.

Owen called Janelle's mother to confirm that Jamie was there. He asked to say hello to Jamie, at Shane's request. Shane took the phone and listened to his son's voice for a moment. Although his face didn't reveal it, Penny imagined that he felt something. She tore her gaze away before her sympathy reflex could get triggered.

Shane handed the phone back without speaking. Owen had a short conversation with Jamie about soccer and hung up.

"Does Dad's boat still run?" Shane asked, looking at Owen.

He shrugged. "It's been sitting idle for over a year."

"Can you get it started?"

"Probably."

"We have to go."

Before they left, Shane allowed Penny to grab a change of clothes and some first-aid supplies from their mother's bedroom. There were several metallic disks on top of her dresser, like award medals. One of them said Ninety Days.

Shane picked it up, turning to Owen. "When did Mom get back in the program?"

"About a year ago."

"What program?" Penny asked, curious.

"Twelve Steps," Shane replied. "It's like rehab, for poor people."

"I've heard of it," she said.

"She never mentioned it to me," Shane said.

"Maybe she wanted it to be a surprise."

Penny looked through the drawers, finding some old clothes for her and Owen. She put the items in a plastic bag, along with underwear and some bandages. Shane didn't protest when she added a few toiletries to the mix.

He removed Owen's handcuffs, letting him use the restroom and wash up. When Owen came out, bare-chested, he put on the clean shirt Penny offered. Shane watched him like a hawk, even though Owen had promised to cooperate. At least Shane cuffed his hands in front, which was more comfortable.

"Get some food from the pantry," he told Penny. "And a cup of ice."

While she followed those instructions, Shane sat down to write a note for his mother.

He slid the paper across the table to Owen. "I need the kid's info."

Penny didn't want to leave Cruz. She'd hoped Shane would have a change of heart and decide to let them both go. He was a father and a son, but he seemed barely human. Her throat tightened as Owen jotted down her full name, address and phone number.

"Can I say goodbye?" Penny asked, swallowing hard.

Shane nodded, so she walked into the living room, kneeling in front of the couch. "Owen's mother is going to take you to the airport."

Cruz's face lit up. "Will I fly in an airplane?"

"Not this time. You'll get in a taxi and ride home by yourself."

The novelty of a solo taxi ride didn't appeal to him as much as an airplane. "Where are you going?"

Her heart clenched inside her chest, like water being wrung from wet cloth. "I'm going with Owen."

His little mouth trembled. "I want to stay with you."

Now that she was well hydrated, the tears didn't build slowly. They gushed into her eyes and spilled over as she hugged him tight. "I know you do. But try to be a big boy, for Mommy. I'll be home soon." She choked out the last words. "I love you."

"I love you, too."

She didn't want to let him go, but she was afraid he'd pick up on her anxiety and make a scene if she held on too long. As soon as she released him, Cruz ran into the kitchen and flung his arms around Owen.

"I'll protect her," Owen said. "Don't worry."

"Do you promise?"

"Yes."

Penny bent down to kiss her son's cheek. "Go watch TV until Owen's mother gets here," she said, ruffling his hair.

Cruz obeyed with reluctance.

Shane poured coffee over ice and used the phone to call his mother. Apparently, she was already on her way home.

They went into the garage to examine the condition of an old fishing boat. Penny stood by the Jeep, sniffling, while the brothers discussed which set of tools to bring. Shane grabbed a large bucket and tossed a garden hose into it, among other things. Owen climbed into the backseat and Penny took the front. Shane hitched up the boat trailer. Then they were riding down a lonely road. She felt hollow to the core, having left her baby—her heart and soul, her reason for living—alone in a trailer in Salton City.

Owen held her hand, stroking her fingers to comfort her. Shane noticed this and grunted, lighting another cigarette. He was drinking iced coffee now instead of booze, but she didn't trust his driving.

"You think Mom will call the cops?" Shane asked.

"She might."

He drove for about an hour, brooding in silence. When Penny's tears dried up, she acknowledged that Cruz was in a much better situation. Her son would get home safe, whether Sally contacted the police or not. But Penny couldn't take a deep breath until she knew for sure. Concern for him weighed heavily on her chest.

Although they passed by the Salton Sea, she couldn't see it. The shore was on the driver's side and only visible at brief intervals. She didn't want to crane her neck toward Shane to catch a glimpse. She could smell it, however. The odor reminded her of the salted cod available in Mexican markets, mixed with the unpleasant stench of a Baja fish factory.

Soon they reached another small town. Shane pulled over at a deserted campground and parked in the day-use area. He turned off the engine, tossing Owen the handcuff keys. "Lock her to the wheel."

Owen removed the cuffs and attached one of her wrists to the wheel, giving her an apologetic look. Then he pocketed the keys and got out.

She understood Shane's strategy. It was the same one he'd used with her and Cruz. Owen wouldn't leave her, so Shane didn't have to worry about him running away. Owen might make a grab for the gun if he got the chance, so Shane wisely kept his distance. He wasn't as stupid as she'd figured.

Shane sat down on a picnic table under a shade structure while Owen got to work. He filled up a bucket with water from a spigot and stuck the propeller into it. After tinkering with the engine for a while, adding fuel and oil and spraying some gunk on the parts, he cranked the ignition cord. It turned over.

Shane grinned around the butt of his cigarette, pleased. "I knew you could do it."

Owen's expression was more difficult to read. Penny couldn't tell if he felt pride or shame or resignation. He seemed to bask in his brother's praise and resent it at the same time. "Now what?"

Shane checked the time on his phone. "It's almost four, too late to do the exchange. We'll hide the boat somewhere and find a motel in Bombay."

Owen dumped out the bucket and gathered their supplies, placing them in the backseat.

"Lock your wrist to hers," Shane ordered.

He used the keys to remove the cuff from the steering wheel and snapped it on his wrist, attaching his right hand to her left. It was an uncomfortable arrangement. He had to extend his arm from the backseat and she was forced to keep hers bent.

Shane hopped behind the wheel, his mood punchy. As they left the campground, he glanced at Penny. He'd seen her before, but he'd never really *looked* at her. "Why did you say your son was Owen's?"

"You had a gun to my head," she said stiffly.

"Are you sleeping with him?"

She flushed with anger, refusing to answer.

"Lay off," Owen said.

"Who's the real dad?" Shane persisted.

"Some jerk," she shot back.

"That kid likes you," Shane said to Owen. "What's the harm in telling him you're the father?"

"How would you feel if Janelle did that with Jamie?"

He mulled it over. "Maybe he'd be better off thinking I was someone else."

"Too late," Owen said.

Shane dropped the subject. He didn't seem upset, just contemplative, as if his feelings were buried so deep, he couldn't access them. After a few minutes, he reached into his pocket for a cell phone. "Tell your dad to bring the money to the Texaco gas station in Brawley at 10:00 a.m. He has to come alone, with his phone. Repeat that back to me."

Penny did.

He handed her his cell. "Remember to speak English. This is America, even if it looks like Mexico."

"Mexico is part of America."

"What?"

"Mexico is in North America, along with Canada and the United States."

"Just make the call, smart-ass."

She dialed the number, her heart pounding. About three hours had passed since she'd left Cruz in Salton City. He probably hadn't arrived in L.A. yet.

"This is Jorge Sandoval."

"Daddy," she choked, instantly emotional.

"Gracias a Dios," he said. "Where are you?"

She gave him the instructions, word for word.

"I'll be there," he promised. "A cabdriver just called me from the airport. Cruz is coming home."

Shane grabbed the phone and hung up before she could respond, but it didn't matter. She let out a strangled sob. Her baby was safe.

"He said he'd heard from a cabdriver," she told Owen. "Cruz is on the way."

Owen squeezed her hand, sharing the moment with her. His eyes gleamed with tears. Although Penny desperately wanted to be reunited with her son, it was a huge relief to know he was okay.

Maybe this would all work out. Her father would bring the money, and she'd be back in L.A. with Cruz tomorrow afternoon.

Shane seemed annoyed by their display of affection. Obviously, a happy ending wasn't in the cards for him. Penny could identify him by name. Even if he pulled off the exchange and paid his debt, he couldn't just walk away. He'd spend the rest of his life on the run or in prison…assuming he lived.

She looked away, refusing to feel sorry for a man who'd threatened to cut out her tongue and search her body cavities. He'd arranged for Owen to be beaten and almost allowed Dirk to kill him. Shane had made his bed; now he could die in it.

They traveled around the southernmost tip of the

JILL SORENSON 221

Salton Sea and headed north. Again, the shore was
on the driver's side, and miles in the distance. By the
time she spotted a sign that read Bombay Beach, it
was early evening. As Shane turned left and drove
toward the sea, she straightened in her seat, eager to
get a better view.

It wasn't what she expected.

Bombay Beach was a small community of aluminum trailers and ramshackle dwellings. Despite
its name, she saw no Indian influence. If anything,
there was a Dutch theme in the sprinkling of pointed
roofs and windmills. Many of the houses appeared
empty, their windows boarded, surfaces scrawled
with graffiti. Others were occupied, judging by the
dusty vehicles parked outside. She saw several golf
carts milling around.

"Is there a golf course nearby?" she asked.

Shane laughed at the question. "There's nothing
out here."

"They use electric carts because the gas station is
so far away," Owen said.

"Why is it called Bombay?"

"You tell us, Miss Geography."

She had no answer, being only vaguely familiar
with India. They continued over a man-made barrier
that separated the town from an even more devastated
area by the shore. It looked like a postapocalyptic
junkyard. Abandoned structures and vehicles, some
half-buried in sand, littered the landscape. Boats,

buses, trailers, furniture—everything had been ravaged by the elements and left to rot.

"This part of town floods during the rainy season," Owen explained. "It used to be the resort area."

Beyond the graveyard of sunken refuse was the sea. She finally got a full picture of the awe-inspiring expanse. It stretched many miles in every direction. At sunset, golden light gleamed across its flat surface, beckoning swimmers to take a dip—if they could ignore the reek of dead fish and other signs of decay. Murky puddles surrounded the debris, glimmering with colors not seen in nature, and thick with floating algae.

There was something beautiful and horrible about the sight. Never had she witnessed such a devastating display of neglect. The largest body of water in California, sitting in the middle of the desert, gone to waste.

Shane parked the Jeep next to the remains of an old yacht club. He backed the trailer into a space between two crumbling concrete walls, close to the shore. Hopping out, he unhitched it, leaving the boat hidden amongst the rubble.

She wasn't sure why he'd bothered, but his plans were a mystery to her. Maybe the boat was his getaway vehicle.

From there, he drove back into the main part of town and stopped at what appeared to be a deserted motel. Apparently it was open for business. Shane turned off the engine and got out, preparing to rent a room.

"Stay cool," he warned Owen. "I don't want to have to shoot this guy."

She watched him go inside, her stomach roiling. "You think he'd do it?"

"In a heartbeat."

"What about us? Are we safe with him?"

A muscle in Owen's jaw flexed. "He can't collect the ransom if he hurts you."

Owen didn't say *he* would escape Shane's wrath. Brother or no, Owen was still dispensable. Shane didn't care about him. He only cared about the money. If the exchange went wrong, they'd both be dispensable.

Bombay Beach, although sparsely populated, was the kind of place where people looked the other way. Its residents seemed downtrodden and tight-lipped. The faces they'd passed were weathered from sun and age. They'd find no saviors here. Shane could probably drive down the middle of town, shooting his gun in the air, and no one would call the police.

He came out of the office with a key. She doubted he'd had to show ID to get it. He moved the Jeep and parked in front of the hotel room. Exiting the vehicle, he gestured for Owen and Penny to follow. He unlocked the hotel room for them.

The dilapidated interior came as no surprise. A double bed sat in the corner, next to a lamp without a shade. The orange-striped wallpaper hurt her eyes. There was a battered-looking desk with a lumpy armchair.

After a cursory inspection of the bathroom, Shane directed them inside. Penny shuffled forward with Owen, noting that the fixtures were outdated but clean. There was a shower stall, a toilet and a sink. No window to escape through.

Shane grabbed the plastic bag of clothes from the Jeep. After he rifled through the contents, he tossed the bag in the tub. Then he retrieved a few pillows and blankets from the bed. He came back and dumped them on the bathroom floor.

"Nighty-night," he said.

"Are you going to unlock the cuffs?" Owen asked.

"No," Shane said with a smirk. "I'm going to barricade this door, crank up the TV and get drunk. You two have fun."

CHAPTER SIXTEEN

OWEN STAYED QUIET, listening to Shane move furniture around the room.

It sounded as if he'd upended the desk and leaned its corner against the bathroom door, balancing there. Owen didn't want to open the door and get crushed to test the theory. It didn't lock from the inside.

A few seconds later, the television turned on at high volume. There was no one in the motel to complain.

He turned to Penny, apologetic.

She seemed annoyed by their entrapment, but not horrified. The air-conditioning whirred into action, sending cool blasts through the vent. Penny sat down on the closed lid of the toilet and used her free hand to search the bag of clothes. He took a seat across from her, on the edge of the tub.

"Look what I have," she said. "Toothpaste!"

He smiled at her enthusiasm. "Any deodorant?"

"No. There's a toothbrush, a little bottle of shampoo and a square of soap." After setting those items on the sink, she removed a box of bandage strips and a tube of antibiotic ointment. "These will come in handy."

"What else?"

She pulled out an old checkered dress. "These are for you," she said, passing him a bundle of cotton briefs and athletic socks.

He accepted the hand-me-downs, frowning.

"Your dad's?"

"Yes."

She cocked her head to one side, her hair a tangled curtain. "Tell me something good about him."

"I already did."

"You only have one positive memory?"

He shrugged, looking away. Talking about his father made him uncomfortable. Even his pleasant childhood experiences were tainted by dysfunction. Decent people came from decent families, like hers.

"Surely he had his finer points."

"He was loyal," Owen said finally. "He didn't cheat on my mother."

"That's nice," she said, her mouth softening.

"He cheated everyone but her."

She laughed, as if this was a joke. "Maybe you'll take after him and be faithful to one woman forever."

Owen nodded. It was the only way he'd follow his father's footsteps.

"Kids from lasting marriages tend to have those kinds of relationships themselves. Did you know that?"

"No."

She waited for a moment, seeming to expect more from the conversation. He realized he was giving his usual monosyllable answers and "sharing very little." In his defense, the topic was unpleasant. His parents had loved each other, or thought they'd loved each other. But they hadn't stayed together for the right reasons.

The situation was awkward, as well. He and Penny were alone together in a tiny bathroom, without Shane's interference or Cruz acting as a buffer between them. There was no way for him to maintain a polite distance.

"I wish he hadn't been faithful," he said in a hoarse voice.

"Why?"

"If he'd been a horrible person all of the time, instead of most of the time, maybe she could have found the strength to leave him."

"It's not about strength."

"What's it about?"

"Mental health, usually. And self-confidence, which gets chipped away little by little, year by year."

He recognized the truth in this. His mother had suffered long periods of depression, catatonic states. She blamed herself for everything. She would instigate arguments with his father, as if the anticipation of violence was more unbearable than the abuse itself. "I haven't been a good son to her."

"Why?"

"I couldn't help her, so I…retreated."

"Maybe she needed to help herself."

"Maybe she did," he said, considering the possibility. His mother had taken steps to get sober on her own. She hadn't been able to do it until his father was out of the picture, but Owen was still proud of her.

"I've felt the same way," she said. "Like I haven't been a good daughter."

"Why?"

"My parents were crushed when they found out I was pregnant. They wanted me to go to college and be somebody important."

"You did go to college. And you are somebody."

"I'm not the person they hoped I'd be. I don't share their religious beliefs or fit in with their social circle. I'm a disappointment."

"No. They're not disappointed."

"How do you know?"

"I saw it in their faces at your graduation."

"They love me and Cruz," she said, conceding his point. "And I appreciate their support, but it comes at a cost. They expect me to attend political events and date upstanding young men from the country club. I want to make my own decisions and be with whoever I like."

Him. She meant him. Pleasure tingled over his skin, along with a healthy dose of unease. There were no more walls between them, no contracts to hide behind. He didn't know how he was going to keep his hands off her. He was handcuffed *to* her.

"I think I'll shower."

Oh, God.

"I'm hideous," she said, touching her tangled hair. "I can't even look at myself in the mirror."

He studied her for signs of imperfection. She had streaks of dirt on her face and knots in her hair, but she was still gorgeous. Her knees were scraped, which concerned him. While he watched, she took off one of the boots she was wearing, wincing in pain.

"Let me," he said, grasping her ankle. He used his right hand unconsciously, which jerked her left hand along for the ride.

"We're going to have to coordinate movements."

Lifting her foot to his thigh, he peeled away the black dress sock. She had several blisters, flattened and raw. He removed the other boot and sock, finding her left foot in the same condition. "You need Band-Aids."

"After I shower."

"Maybe you should take a bath," he said. A shower would be torture. He'd have to stand outside the beveled glass door with his wrist connected to hers, watching water stream down her naked body. "You can soak your muscles."

"That sounds heavenly, actually."

He let go of her foot and moved out of the way while she inspected the tub. Deeming it acceptable, she turned on the water and plugged the drain. Soon the room thickened with steam. "I should have rinsed off first."

"Why?"

"I'm going to be sitting in filthy water."

"Getting clean before you bathe kind of defeats the purpose, don't you think?"

"Yes, but I've never been this dirty before."

"You can rinse off after."

The tub was already half full, so she didn't argue. He wondered if she was nervous, too. She knelt and dipped her hand into the water, testing its temperature.

"Warm enough?"

"Yes."

"How are we going to do this?"

She studied the cramped space. "You can sit there, next to the tub. I'll get in and let my arm rest on the rim."

He hadn't been thinking that far ahead. His mind was stuck on the prebathing process. What should he do while she took off her clothes? He swallowed hard as she shut off the water. Setting a towel on the sink, she placed the toiletries inside the tub and adjusted the glass doors. Then she raised her hands to undo the tie at her neck. When the bodice of her dress fell away, she clutched it to her chest.

Owen couldn't turn around politely because that would make it more difficult for her to move her arms. Offering to help would just tangle their limbs together, and he wasn't adept with female garments.

He stared at the floor, his throat working in agitation.

Penny abandoned modesty and let go of her dress, reaching behind her back. His right hand followed.

He smothered a moan as his knuckles skimmed her bare skin. She released the clasp of her strapless bra. It didn't fall down, so he figured the lingerie was sort of…molded to her body. Now she needed only to push off the loosened clothing, along with her panties, and climb in the tub.

He clapped his free hand over his eyes, not trusting himself to avoid temptation.

She laughed softly at this action, but maybe it put her at ease, because she finished undressing. When he sensed her weight shift, he shuffled a little closer. The water splashed as she stepped into the stall. She slid the door closed, leaving space for their cuffed wrists. He dropped his hand and opened his eyes, assuming it was safe.

Mistake.

The beveled glass blurred her image like an old oil painting. Even so, the sight of her naked form was highly erotic. He could make out the shape of her beautiful breasts, full and lush with dusky peaks.

Groaning, he looked away.

"Can you see me?" she asked.

"I don't… I can't…"

"You can't what?"

"I can't answer that."

With another low laugh, she sank into the water, forcing him to sit down on the floor. "Oh, my God, this feels good."

Gaze averted, he searched for an accommodating position. He couldn't twist around, so he ended up sitting cross-legged and facing the wall, his right elbow bent and his hand gripping the shower door. The urge to glance sideways, through the narrow opening, was hard to resist. He turned his head and stared at the sink cabinet until his eyeballs burned.

The water sloshed gently as she shifted, making a sound of pleasure. He tried not to think about her bare breasts, wet and round and bobbing above the surface, but it was a lost cause. He pictured her soaping them generously, her mouth a sexy moue, dark nipples visible beneath the frothy bubbles.

Did women even wash their breasts like that, outside of porno movies? He lathered his armpits, not his pecs, but girls were probably more fastidious than guys.

Focus on something else.

"I'm sorry about Shane," he said, clearing his throat. "He's a jerk.

"Has he always been that way?"

"Pretty much."

Penny squeezed his hand and let it go. "I have to wash my hair."

He listened as she slid lower into the tub, soaking her head. Then she came back up, water streaming from her hair. Her wet hands brushed his as she opened the shampoo bottle, pouring the liquid into her palm. A light floral fragrance tickled his nostrils, accompanied by the scrunching sound of bubbles. When she submerged to rinse, her left arm slipped, pulling his hand into the stall.

The awkward angle wrenched his wrist. He aligned his body toward hers with a wince and accidentally pushed the shower door open a little more. She sat up again, giving him an unfettered view of her soap-slick curves.

"Sorry," she gasped, returning her left hand to the rim of the tub.

Incapable of speech, he struggled to move his gaze from her chest. Heat suffused his face and neck, climbing to the roots of his hair. He turned his head and studied the toilet as if it contained the mysteries of the universe.

Penny finished rinsing and stayed still for a few minutes. Her inactivity didn't calm his raging hormones or erase the Playmate-worthy visual she'd just treated him to. It danced inside his skull, sending a rush of blood to his groin.

"How old is your brother's son?" she asked.

"Eleven."

"He's the one you visit in Salton City?"

"Yes."

"You never told me his mother was a...dancer."

It wasn't the sort of information he'd volunteer in passing.

"Have you ever been to a strip club?"

"No."

"You sound strange."

"Strange?"

"Gruff."

He adjusted his straining fly, unsure what to say.

"I'm aroused." Why hide the obvious? His hard-on wasn't going away.

"Does it hurt?"

"Not really."

"It hurts me," she said, shifting her legs.

He froze. "It does?"

"It's like a throbbing ache."

Was she toying with him? Next she'd be complaining about how stiff her nipples were. His cock swelled harder, demanding to give them both satisfaction.

"I want you to touch me…but you never do."

"You think I don't want to?"

"Do you?"

"Yes," he ground out.

"Since when?"

"Forever."

"After the earthquake?"

"Yes." He'd been a sick bastard, even then.

"What's stopping you?"

"I already told you."

"What about before you took the job? That night we danced at Sam's wedding, I practically handed you my panties."

He flinched at the exaggeration. Had she, really? He couldn't believe he'd been so dense. "I had no idea you were interested."

"If you had, would you have acted on it?"

"No."

"Because you think I'm too good for you?"

Now that he'd had a chance to reflect, he understood her annoyance. She didn't appreciate him making decisions for her, like her father always did. And maybe Owen had been hiding behind excuses. "You are, but that's not the only reason."

"What is?"

Shame rose up, threatening to choke him.

"I've seen the way you avoid women. How you react to touch."

He didn't bother to point out that he avoided men also. She was talking about dating and sexual relationships, which intimidated him more than casual male contact.

"Were you that way before prison?"

"No. I was sketchy and cautious, but not like this."

"Did you have girlfriends?"

"Just hookups." Drunk, fumbling encounters with girls as troubled as he was. Shane used to take him to Slab City, a huge parking lot full of squatters and vagrants who flocked to the Salton Sea every winter. "Ass City," he'd called it.

When he didn't offer more information, she finished bathing and sat up. "I should get out before I wrinkle."

"Do you still want to rinse off?"

"No, it's too much of a hassle with these handcuffs on."

He grabbed the towel from the sink and unfolded it, glad he no longer had an embarrassing erection to deal with. They both stood at the same time. He managed to keep his eyes above her neck as she pushed aside the glass door and stepped out of the stall. She couldn't get the towel wrapped around her body, so she just held it to her front.

"I need both arms free to put on the clean dress," she said, frowning. "I didn't think of that until now."

"Here," he said, taking off the T-shirt he'd donned at his mother's house. It dangled on the cuffs between them, inside out. He moved the sleeve up her arm and put the collar over her head. She let go of the towel, slipping her hand through the opposite sleeve. The hem was long enough to cover the important parts.

"Thanks."

"No problem."

Her gaze traveled up his bare chest. "You have blood on your neck."

He glanced at his reflection, spotting the dried rivulet that snaked down into the hollow of his throat. Dark bruises arced over his rib cage, there were cuts on his back, and his knuckles were swollen. His face was all stubble and scrapes and sharp angles.

She wanted this beat-up, tattooed miscreant to touch her?

An ugly voice whispered that his low-class persona was part of the draw: Daddy would *never* approve.

"Maybe I'll brush my teeth before you shower," she said.

"Be my guest."

They stood side by side in front of the sink while she applied a dollop of toothpaste to the small toothbrush. She cleaned her teeth with practiced motions.

His gaze was drawn to her jiggling breasts, soft and round beneath the worn cotton. When she was finished, she leaned forward to rinse her mouth. The hem of the T-shirt rode up in back, revealing the fleshy undersides of her bottom.

"Do you want to?"

Owen jerked his gaze up. "What?"

She straightened and readied the toothbrush for him, leaving it on top of the sink. He used his left hand, glancing sideways at her while he brushed. She watched him spit and rinse, her eyes gleaming.

There must be something wrong with him, to find this sexy. He didn't know if it was the enclosed space or the handcuffs or the charming domesticity of the scene. Maybe it was the way she looked in a man's T-shirt, her long legs bare. Suddenly he was desperate for a taste of her. Like this, with him dirty and her clean. He wanted to give in to every animal instinct, take her in every filthy way he could imagine.

She wanted it, too. She'd said as much, and desire radiated from her. He could see it in her trembling lips and the fluttering pulse at the base of her throat. Rich or not, none of those Ivy League boys made her feel like this. They hadn't fought for her, hadn't killed for her. Right or not, he had, and he would.

Maybe she was excited by the idea of him being rough and uncivilized. He faced her, resting his hip against the edge of the sink.

"You have a little toothpaste," she said, touching the corner of his mouth.

"Did you get it?"

She leaned closer, as if she might lick the spot. He didn't give her a chance. Burying his hand in her damp, tangled hair, he covered her mouth with his. No chaste kiss would satiate the beast inside him. It roared for a deep plunge and total possession. She parted her pretty lips, and he delved inside.

He groaned at the sensation. She was so sweet and hot and fresh, so ripe. Her breasts settled against his chest as his tongue explored the silky depths of her mouth. All of the blood in his body rushed south, swelling him to full arousal in seconds. He tried to reach beneath the hem of the T-shirt, intent on filling his hands with her gorgeous ass, but the cuffs got in the way, tugging on his wrist.

And that was all it took to trigger him.

He broke contact with her mouth, traveling back to that horrible moment. Facedown on the shower floor, his wrists trapped in a cruel grip. Fists pummeling him, smacking his wet flesh. Nose bloody, cheek crushed against the tile, legs forced apart.

Then he snapped out of it, returning to the present. Penny was watching him in concern. "What's wrong?"

"Fuck," he said, stepping away from her. Avoiding her gaze.

"Is it me?"

"No."

She flinched at his sharp tone.

"It's not you," he said, hating himself for snapping at her. "It's definitely not you."

"Is it…something that happened to you in prison?"

He couldn't bring himself to answer. A few seconds ago, he'd been shaking with the need to touch her. Now he was just shaking.

"Have you tried to work through it? With a woman, I mean?"

Dragging his left hand through his dirty hair, which still had flecks of gunk in it, he leaned against the sink. He couldn't avoid this conversation forever. "I went out with one of Janelle's friends once."

Her brows drew together. "When?"

"About a year ago."

"What happened?"

"Not much," he said ruefully.

"Was she pretty?"

"Yes."

"And willing?"

He nodded, flushing at the memory. They'd had a few drinks at the bar to break the ice. She'd been sweet, but not too sweet to take him home. "We went back to her place. One thing led to another, and we… almost had sex."

"What went wrong?"

"I froze up, just like this."

"So you stopped?"

"Of course."

"How did she react?"

"She was pretty nice about it."

"Did you tell her why?"

"No. I think she understood."

"Then what?"

He didn't want to go into specifics.

"Did you try again?"

"Not really."

"Did she touch you?"

"No."

"Did you touch her?"

"No."

"What then?"

"She touched herself while I watched."

Her eyes searched his face, not judging. "And you liked that?"

"Yes."

"Did you see her again?"

"No."

"Why not?"

"I don't know," he said, fumbling for an answer. "I was embarrassed. I didn't want to lead her on. I felt...nothing for her."

She fell silent for a moment. "Is that why you went out with her?"

"Probably."

"Is it the same reason you avoid me?"

He nodded, swallowing hard. "She didn't matter to me. You do. I can't stand the thought of failing with you. Of being weak and helpless in front of you."

"I'd never see you as weak, Owen."

"But that's how I feel when I have a flashback. I can't move. I have no control. I'm powerless."

"Have you ever told anyone what happened?"

"No."

"Talking about it might help."

He knew she was right. The conversation had already sucked all of the sexual energy from the room. If he tried to touch her again, he might have another episode. Either way, no one was getting laid.

Story of his fucking life.

She sat down on the edge of the tub, pulling the plug to drain it. He took a seat opposite her, on the closed toilet lid.

"What do you want to know?"

"Everything, or just a little bit. Whatever you feel like sharing."

"The first few weeks were tough," he said, thinking back. "I'd already spent several months in jail, but I wasn't prepared for prison. I thought no one would notice me if I kept my head down and my mouth shut. I was wrong."

She grasped his hand and held it tight.

"I was only eighteen when I got arrested, and the older guys prey on young men. I was smaller then. Skin and bones, from doing drugs. I couldn't defend myself. During my second week, a group of guys…" He broke off, wiping the sweat from his forehead.

Just say it. Get it out, get it over with.

"It's okay," she said. "You can tell me."

"A group of guys caught me in the shower. The

guard didn't come to help me, so maybe he'd been bribed." He paused for a minute, pressure building behind his eyelids. He couldn't look at Penny, couldn't bear to see her reaction. His heart thudded with panic, like the attack was happening in real time. "I refused to perform oral sex. I don't know if that made any difference. They wanted me to fight. They held me down and…took turns…raping me."

"How many?"

"Three. I sort of blacked out, or just faded away. It was like I was watching from a distance. I woke up in the infirmary."

"Did you tell anyone?"

"They already knew."

"I'm sorry," she said, her voice cracking.

He nodded bleakly. "It happened more than once. I didn't fight as hard the second time. I thought it might hurt less if I cooperated. It didn't."

She made a funny sound, like a strangled sob.

"I went to the Aryan Brotherhood for protection. I didn't give a fuck about racial equality or anything else at that point. I wanted to look as tough and ugly as possible. I'd have put a swastika on my forehead to prevent another attack."

She wept for him, maybe because he couldn't weep for himself. He watched her cry, feeling totally disconnected from his emotions. "I'm not proud of what I did for the gang, but I can't say I was a reluctant participant. I channeled my anger into violence. I felt stronger every time I won a fight. Once I…acted as lookout while they raped someone else. He screamed for help, and I ignored it. As long as it wasn't me, I didn't care."

Her face was red and crumpled, her cheeks wet with tears. He grabbed some toilet paper off the roll and handed it to her.

She dabbed her eyes, taking a deep breath. "I'm glad you told me."

"You don't look glad," he said uncharitably.

"Do you feel better?"

He felt nothing. "I think I'll shower now."

"Don't," she choked.

"Don't what?"

She closed the distance between them. Taking a seat on his thigh, she framed his chin with her right hand and forced him to meet her gaze. "Don't shut me out."

"There's nothing you can say to make it better, Penny."

"It's not your fault."

"I know."

"Do you?"

He stared at her for a moment, pinned by her empathy. Tears he hadn't known he was holding back came rising to the surface. He brushed them away impatiently, pushing her aside. With their wrists cuffed together, he couldn't get away from her. Kicking off his shoes, he stepped into the shower with his pants on, retreating the only way he could. He wondered if he'd ever be clean again. His chest ached like he was drowning.

As he stood under the spray, letting it wash over him, he hung his head and cried.

CHAPTER SEVENTEEN

PENNY'S HEART BROKE for Owen.

She stood by the shower door, her left arm getting wet from the spray as he crouched down with his back to her. He rested his forehead on the shower wall, his body shaking uncontrollably. He hadn't taken off his pants, but they'd needed washing, anyway. The water streaming toward the drain ran reddish-brown from all of the dirt and blood the fabric had accumulated over the past few days.

She couldn't give him the privacy he seemed desperate for. Nor could she fail to offer him comfort while he was hurting. She studied the green clover tattoo on his right shoulder, watching droplets accumulate on his skin. After a moment, she shut off the faucet and stepped inside the stall.

He flinched as she slipped past him, her cuffed hand grasping his. Sitting down in the tub, she wrapped her free arm around him. He didn't push her away, perhaps because the damage was already done. His level of vulnerability couldn't go any higher. So he just gave in. Burying his face in her neck, he let it out. All of the tears he'd kept bottled up inside, all these years. All of the rage and anguish and shame.

She stroked his wet hair, murmuring words of comfort. He cried for a long time, his shoulders shuddering from the force of his sorrow. He'd endured so much, holding in the pain as if releasing it would unleash ugliness on the world.

Finally, his sobs quieted. He seemed embarrassed by the loss of control, even though it had to be cathartic. This wasn't the shower activity she'd fantasized about, either, but she was glad to be here for him.

"Feel better now?" she asked.

"No," he said, sniffling. He sounded stuffed up, the way everyone did after a good cry. "I need a juice box and a nap."

She smiled at his self-deprecating humor, even though there was nothing weak or childish about his display of emotion. On the contrary, it revealed his inner strength. He'd had the guts to tell her about a horrific experience. He might not have wanted to cry in front of her, but he'd accepted her embrace rather than shut her out again.

"Maybe finishing your shower will help."

He lifted his head from her shoulder, staring at the damp fabric. "I got you all wet."

"It's not the first time."

His bleary gaze met hers and narrowed. "Are you trying to be suggestive?"

"Too soon?"

He didn't answer. If he thought his story had cooled her desire for him, he was wrong. Sharing it had brought them closer together.

"What happened doesn't make you less of man."

"That's the way it made me feel."

"Why?"

"Because…men are supposed to be strong."

"You were just a teenager, and outnumbered three to one. Would you blame a woman for her own assault?"

"Of course not."

"Because women are supposed to be weak?"

"They aren't expected to defeat a group of assailants."

"Men are?"

"Yes."

"Says who?"

"Bruce Willis."

She laughed softly, stroking his wet hair. He could still make fun of himself and challenge his own preconceptions. If that wasn't strength, she didn't know what was. He was the bravest person she'd ever met. Not because of the abuse he'd suffered, but because of the actions he'd taken to survive and the hardships he'd overcome.

She rose to her feet with him and stepped out of the stall. He shut the door partway, leaving space for their wrists. Turning the faucet back on, he removed his pants and boxer shorts. From this side of the glass, she could see the blur of his tattoos, a dark shadow of pubic hair and the outline of his penis.

A flush rose to her cheeks, and she looked away, giving him the same courtesy he'd shown her earlier.

The air-conditioning kicked off as the room temperature stabilized. She heard the noisy banter of a news program. In an unprecedented move, her father had stepped down as the GOP nominee. The reporters didn't mention the kidnapping or Cruz.

Penny had seen the article at Owen's mother's house. She still couldn't believe her father had dropped out of the race. His lifetime goal, shattered in one fell swoop. Even though she hadn't wanted him to win, losing this way wasn't fair.

Owen shampooed his hair and washed up quickly, not lingering over the task. When he turned off the water, she passed him a towel. Like her, he couldn't wrap it around his body with one hand, so he held it to his front as he slid the door open. Their eyes met, and her breath caught in her throat.

The view through the beveled glass hadn't done him justice. Even with the towel covering his male parts, he was a delicious combination of sculpted muscles and wet skin. His stomach was flat and tight, his biceps hard and his chest well-defined. Lightly tanned above the waist, his pale hip gleamed like marble.

While she watched, mesmerized, he fumbled with the towel. Her knuckles brushed the narrow strip of hair on his lower abdomen as he secured the fabric around his waist. The terry cloth was thin and damp, leaving little to the imagination. His penis jutted forth, not fully erect, but not soft either.

She was a puddle of womanly longing, eyes half-lidded. Her pulse thundered in her ears, and her mind turned to mush.

"I'm getting out now," he said, giving her a strange look.

She realized she was blocking his exit and moved aside. Although she could happily ogle his lovely physique for the duration of their entrapment, she didn't want to make him feel uncomfortable. She'd already broadcast her desires, loud and clear.

Her cheeks heated at the memory of her brazen behavior. Telling him he got her wet, *como atrevida!*

She searched for something else to occupy her thoughts. And her hands. "I'll bandage your wounds," she offered, picking up the first-aid supplies.

"Let's do yours first."

She perched on the edge of the sink while he took a seat on the lid of the commode, soothing her skinned knees and sore feet with antibiotic ointment.

"Your legs are smooth," he commented.

"I had them waxed before the convention."

His hand stilled on her ankle, his gaze traveling up her thighs. She'd tucked the hem of the T-shirt between her legs. If he'd peeked at her through the shower door, he already knew she wasn't completely bare down there. His neck turned red, and his hand shook as he applied bandages to the raw spots.

When he was done, they switched places, and she returned the favor, dabbing ointment on his various injuries. His knuckles were bruised, his palms blistered from the wheelbarrow. There were cuts all over his back. His elbows were in bad shape. She bandaged the worst of the wounds, wrapping his forearm up tight.

The air conditioner came back on, rattling noisily.

She lifted her gaze to his face. He was leaning against the sink, his left hand gripping the towel at his waist, as if he didn't trust it to stay put. He had a raw-looking scrape on his cheekbone and his lips were chapped. She smoothed ointment on the affected areas, watching his blue eyes darken. "I thought Shane had killed you this morning. I put my arms around Cruz and covered his ears, turning away from the sight. When I heard the blast, I assumed you were dead. I felt like I'd been shot."

He stared back at her, absorbing her words.

"That's the second time I thought he killed you in as many days. I'm afraid he's going to shoot you tomorrow."

"He won't."

"How do you know?"

He didn't, so he fell silent.

She changed the subject to something slightly less disturbing. "Was that girl you went out with a stripper, like Janelle?"

"What difference does it make?"

Penny wasn't sure. Maybe because she'd been raised by staunch Catholics and led a sheltered life, she resented the rules of decorum. The idea of a woman being so free with her body both attracted her and repelled her. "None, I guess."

"I hardly knew her."

"What happened before the flashback?"

"Just kissing, mostly."

"Did you touch her?"

He seemed reluctant to say. "Yes."

"What triggered you?"

"Penetration, maybe. I thought I'd be okay if I touched her and she didn't touch me. It worked at first. But then I put my fingers inside her and...that was it."

She smothered a wave of jealousy as she pictured him with another woman, sliding his long fingers in and out of her body. If he only knew how many times she'd fantasized about him doing the same to her, stroking her with his fingertips, parting her slippery flesh.

"You can do everything else?"

"I don't know."

"Penetration isn't that important."

"For men, it is."

"It was all Tyler wanted," she said.

"He wasn't much on foreplay?"

"No."

"Did he ever...satisfy you?"

"Not even close."

He made a sound of commiseration. "Most teenage boys are clueless."

"Were you?"

"I was drunk *and* clueless."

Tyler didn't have that excuse. He'd been careless,

rather than clueless, taking what he wanted after a token effort to please her.

"Has there been anyone since?"

She shook her head. "I've gone out with a few guys, but none of them held my interest."

"Why not?"

"They don't make me feel the way you do," she said simply. He still didn't seem to believe she really wanted him, despite her blatant come-ons. If only he could see himself through her eyes. "You're brave and smart and *hot*..." She swallowed hard, glancing at his chest. "You have a good heart. You're kind to my son."

"Is that what this is about?"

"No," she said, flattening her belly against his. "It's about us."

He wanted to kiss her. She could feel the tension coiled in his muscles, the heat of his swelling erection. Their linked hands were braced against the edge of the sink. "I might not be able to..."

She tilted her head back. "I don't care."

He slid his free arm around her waist, moving slowly. She felt the cool air on her buttocks as the hem rode up. A moan escaped her lips, drawing him in. He brushed his mouth over hers, just once.

She pressed her breasts to his chest, letting him feel her nipples through the worn cotton. "Is this okay?"

"Unh," he said, licking the corner of her mouth. She parted her lips, encouraging him to come inside.

He touched his tongue to hers, tentative. Instead of delving deeper, he retreated after a shallow taste.

She let out a little huff of frustration, wanting more. More of his tongue, his hands, his throbbing erection. Trying not to push him too far, she threaded her fingers through the short hair at his nape and nibbled on his lower lip, biting gently. He responded with a groan, tracing her open mouth with the tip of his tongue.

"Touch me," she whispered.

He smoothed his palm over the curve of her bottom. "Like this?"

"Yes."

His cuffed hand followed, cupping her other cheek. She bent her left arm behind her back to accommodate him. He held her against his erection, seeming to revel in the sensation. She certainly was. Her breasts felt full and heavy, her skin hot. She'd been aroused for hours, aching for him. Panting, she rubbed her lips back and forth across his.

Penetration was important, she realized. She couldn't wait for him to plunge his tongue into her mouth. She knew he wouldn't be cured by one kiss, one conversation, or even one night of perfect sex, but every little bit helped.

"I want to see you," he said hoarsely.

She raised her arms so he could tug the T-shirt over her head. Instead, he fisted his hands in the fabric and tore it down the middle, making her gasp. He tossed the ruined garment aside and stared at her breasts for a few seconds. His hungry gaze lowered to the apex of her thighs, stroking her like a caress.

"Jesus," he said, shuddering.

"What's wrong?"

"I'm going to come, just looking at you."

She smiled at the flattery, wondering if he was serious. Then his towel fell open, revealing a rampant erection. Passion-flushed, it looked painfully hard and swollen, encircled with veins. He was much bigger than Tyler. She had an overwhelming urge to drop to her knees and soothe the plumlike tip with her tongue, to stroke his shaft and kiss away the discomfort. But when she reached out to touch him, moistening her lips, he caught her hand and held it, preventing her from exploring.

"You first," he rasped. "Please."

She glanced at the closed bathroom door, aware that his brother could remove the barricade and barge in on them at any moment. "Let's go in the shower stall."

His throat worked with agitation. "Okay."

She stepped over the edge of the tub, self-conscious. He followed her inside and closed the beveled glass doors behind them. Instead of standing face-to-face, he turned her around in a dance-style maneuver, with their linked hands crossing the front of her body. His erection nestled against her buttocks, hard and hot. She leaned back into him, her heart racing with excitement. He cupped her breasts and squeezed them together, panting on her neck. Her nipples tingled in the center of his palms. Kissing her shoulder, he brushed his thumbs over the stiff tips, making her stomach quiver.

He didn't linger on her breasts. Urgency seemed to drive his hand down her belly, between her legs. They both groaned as his fingertips found her, wet and swollen. He inhaled a sharp breath, parting the lips of her sex.

"Like this?" he asked, stroking her clitoris.

She jerked in response.

"Too much?"

"No."

"Show me."

She covered his right hand with her left and demonstrated the amount of pressure she liked. He strummed his fingertip over her in slow circles. He was remarkably apt and attuned to her reactions. Her moisture eased his way, and her soft gasps guided him, encouraging him to stroke a little harder, a little faster. The pleasure built inside her, hot and bright. Her focus narrowed to the rhythmic glide of his fingertip.

She exploded, crying out his name.

He seemed surprised by her orgasm and stopped too soon. She gripped his hand, holding it more firmly against her until her tremors subsided. When it was over, she became aware of his ragged breaths on the nape of her neck.

As soon as she released his hand, he whirled her around. Teeth gritted, he lifted her against the wall. Her shoulders met the tile, and he gripped her hips, hooking her right leg over the crook of his arm. He slid his shaft along her slippery sex, up and down. His fingernails dug into her skin as he thrust against her. She held on for the ride, thrilled by the primal display. She imagined him deep inside her, filling her to the hilt.

He came with a low groan, his body jerking against hers. Hot fluid spurted from the head of his penis, splashing her breasts and belly. It jetted across her torso in silky ribbons, dripping from her taut nipples.

After spending a long moment with his face buried in her neck, he lifted his head. Seeming chagrined, he set her down and turned on the water. He washed her off in a hurry, as if his semen had defiled her purity.

Penny moaned as his fingertips brushed her nipples. She felt sexy, not dirty, maybe because she was still aroused. This was the most erotic experience of her life, by far. "Owen," she said, her voice strained.

He shut off the water, curious. "What do you need?"

"More."

His gaze traveled from her quivering breasts to her wet cleft. He lowered himself to his knees and kissed her there. She swallowed hard, her legs trembling as he swirled his tongue over her clitoris, sucking and stroking her. She was so keyed up it only took a few seconds. With a muffled scream, she climaxed again, sagging against his strong shoulders.

When it was over, he stood. Cupping her chin with his free hand, he studied her flushed face. She didn't know what he was looking for. Her eyes felt heavy, her body boneless with satisfaction. Leaning in, he touched his lips to hers. They tasted of her, slick and sweet. He surprised her by plunging his tongue inside her mouth, kissing her fully. She clung to his neck, her pulse pounding.

He ended the kiss and pulled back, as if in awe. She felt the same way, her heart full of emotions she didn't recognize.

They prepared for bed, arranging the pillows and blankets on the floor. He turned off the light and they lay down. She rested her head against his shoulder, closing her eyes as he wrapped his free arm around her.

"*Now* I feel better," he said, sounding pleased with himself.

She smiled, drifting into sleep.

CHAPTER EIGHTEEN

BY QUITTING TIME on Sunday, Janelle was exhausted.

After her last performance, she slumped into the chair at her makeup station and scrolled through her phone messages, searching for a response from Owen. Something weird was going on with his family. He hadn't responded to any of her texts, which was unusual. Apparently his mother had called her mother's house to speak with Jamie, another rarity. Janelle hadn't fostered a relationship with Shane's parents for multiple reasons.

Frowning, she set her phone aside.

"What's up?" Tiffany asked, breezing by her in a black spandex costume that wrapped around her body like electrical tape. "Hot date tonight?"

"I wish," she said, although she just wanted to go home, take a long shower, and sleep. "How about you?"

Tiffany shrugged, sipping her bottled water. Despite her edgy outfit, tousled blond hair and heavy eyeliner, she had a dewy innocence about her that men loved. "I've got no prospects. I'm so tired of dating jerks." She wiggled out of her costume. "Your sweetheart brother-in-law can hit me up anytime, though."

Owen wasn't her brother-in-law, but Janelle knew what she meant. "Did he ever call you again?"

"No," she said, sighing.

Janelle wasn't sure why Tiffany considered Owen a sweetheart if he'd used her once and dropped her. Judging by her wistful expression, she hadn't minded. But Tiffany struggled with emotional issues, and her behavior was often self-destructive.

Speaking of jerks. "Did you see that guy I took to VIP last night? Black T-shirt, big shoulders?"

"Yeah," Tiffany said, her blue eyes lighting up. She pulled on a lacy white thong and turned to study her perfect backside in the mirror. Janelle's had never looked that firm or round. "I'd have done him for free."

"Has he come in before?"

"Not that I know of."

The more Janelle thought about him, the more uneasy she felt. Men became fixated on certain girls and requested private dances all the time. Normally they browsed the merchandise before making their selections, however. This guy had zeroed in on her from the start. His attention had seemed personal.

Maybe this business had jaded her. She didn't suspect every customer of being a psycho predator, but her opinion of the opposite sex slipped a notch lower every year. And it hadn't been high to begin with. She'd learned to be wary of men early in life.

Desiree and Ginger joined them in the back room, sipping fruity alcoholic beverages. They weren't supposed to drink on the clock, but it was last call. Chuck didn't work on Sundays, and Kevin didn't care.

Desiree was the newest dancer at Vixen, and already popular. Janelle had caught her giving a guy a hand job in the VIP room. Although she hadn't reported Desiree, Janelle had warned her against repeating the offense. It was illegal, and it sullied the club's reputation.

Desiree wasn't her given name, of course. It was Dolores. Ginger was really Jennifer. Janelle went by Jezebel on stage. They all teased Tiffany about her alter ego, Tara, saying she'd gotten the two names mixed up.

"Do either of you girls want to earn some extra cash?" Desiree asked.

"How?" Tiffany asked.

"Table ten just invited us to a party at Twin Palms. Two hundred each for an hour of topless, plus tips."

"I'm in," Tiffany said, nodding.

"No way," Janelle said at the same time. "Are you crazy?"

Desiree rolled her eyes. "They only want three girls, so that's fine."

"Is Kevin going?"

"What's it to you?"

"I wouldn't do a private party without a bodyguard."

Desiree's pretty mouth twisted. "Because you're so much better than us?"

"Just older and wiser," Janelle said, tamping down her temper. She knew from experience how dangerous men at parties could be.

"You got the 'older' part right," Desiree said.

Janelle glanced at her reflection and acknowledged the harsh reality. Her makeup was stale, her skin sallow and her eyes dull. She still had a dancer's figure, slim and lithe, but her muscle tone wasn't what it used to be. Her breasts were neither large nor perky. She couldn't compete with Tiffany's fresh beauty or Desiree's surgical enhancements.

She was still the best dancer in the joint, but already washed-up at twenty-eight, her beauty fading.

Kevin poked his head into the dressing room. "Some guy wants a double VIP. Brunettes."

Shit. Janelle and Desiree were the only dark-haired girls on tonight.

"There's no accounting for taste," Desiree said. "Ready?"

Janelle's feet groaned in protest as she rose. She didn't mind doing doubles, a deluxe kind of lap dance that catered to the common girl-on-girl fantasy. Janelle was comfortable with her body and with the other dancers. It was a performance, like any other. Doubles paid well and felt safer because of the two-to-one ratio.

She didn't want to go into the VIP room with Desiree or anyone else, but work was work. Mood didn't matter in this business. If she waited until she felt sexy to take her clothes off, she'd never earn a dollar.

"Break a leg," Tiffany said, sounding envious. She liked doubles.

Their customer was an older man in a suit with square-framed glasses and balding hair. An oil company executive, maybe. He looked harmless. When the music started, Janelle faced Desiree, skimming her hands along the other woman's curves. There was no rule about touching each other or themselves, as long as they didn't engage in sex acts. After a moment of choreographed almost-kissing, their tops came off.

Janelle felt even more disconnected than usual. She stared at the rings on the businessman's soft hands, picturing the man with the tattooed knuckles. He hadn't come in tonight, to her…relief.

She tried to refocus, aware that she was putting on a mediocre show. Turning around, she bent over and wiggled her hips. Desiree raised the ruffled skirt and spanked Janelle's bottom. Her slap was a little too hard to be called playful.

Ignoring the sting, Janelle straightened. Desiree went down on her knees and removed Janelle's skirt with an exaggerated pout. When she sank her teeth into Janelle's thigh, Janelle fisted her hand in Desiree's hair and gave it a sharp tug.

Desiree rose, her dark eyes flashing. Janelle unzipped Desiree's skirt and tossed it aside. They gyrated together in thong bikinis, front to front, and then front to back. For the finale, they were supposed to kneel at the customer's feet, arms entwined. Desiree bumped Janelle's shoulder, perhaps on purpose, and they both fell across his lap.

The customer took advantage of the mistake by grabbing a handful of Janelle's ass. Feeling trapped between two bodies, she panicked. When she shoved at Desiree, her elbow slammed into the man's groin. He roared in pain and let go, cupping his crotch. Janelle went tumbling to the ground with Desiree.

Janelle scrambled to her feet. An apology stuck in her throat. She'd overreacted, but he'd touched her inappropriately.

Kevin came to investigate. "Is there a problem, sir?"

"Yes," the man said, his teeth clenched. "One of your whores punched me in the balls."

"There's no reason to use offensive language," Kevin said.

"Fuck you! I want my money back."

He nodded, signaling at the girls to leave. "Of course."

Desiree and Janelle collected their clothes and retreated, hair disheveled. As soon as they were in the dressing area, the claws came out.

"Nice going," Desiree said.

"It was your fault, bitch."

"I was trying to get us a better tip! All you had to do was giggle and apologize and we'd have an extra fifty to take home instead of jack shit."

Janelle didn't want to argue. "If you ever do that again, I'll punch *you* in the crotch."

"Fine," Desiree said.

Tiffany watched the exchange with worried eyes, nibbling her lush lower lip. Janelle's hands trembled as she wiped off her face and changed into her street clothes. It wasn't the first time a customer had copped a feel or called her a whore. It wouldn't be the last. What upset her more was the confrontation with Desiree. The dancers always had each other's backs. They were a close-knit group. But lately she'd felt like an outsider. Maybe it was because she'd dared to step above her station by pursuing a college degree.

Or maybe she was just getting too old for this crap.

She grabbed her keys, stuffed her costumes into her bag and gave Tiffany a goodbye hug. "Be careful tonight."

"I will."

"You don't have to go to the hotel. We could watch a movie at my mom's house."

Tiffany gave her a distant smile. She didn't like to be alone. When the demons were chasing her, a quiet night with a girlfriend just wouldn't cut it. Already in party mode, she left with the other girls, ponytail bouncing.

Janelle searched for a cigarette on her way out, cursing as she remembered smoking the last one. Maybe she had an extra pack in her glove compartment. She stepped into the parking lot, which had been full when she'd arrived. Now it was dark and dead, with only a half-dozen cars near the entrance. The orange halogen lights gave off a dull, Halloween-like glow that failed to permeate the black night.

She hurried toward her car, gripping her keys like a weapon. Drunk or disgruntled customers were known to harass dancers on their way out. In addition to the recent break-in and Tiffany's attack, there had been other…incidents.

A few years ago, Janelle had found a crude message on her rear windshield. The word *slut* was smeared across the glass with a sticky substance. She'd actually touched the letters and smelled her fingertips before she realized what it was: semen. Some sicko had masturbated on her car and written in his own fluids.

She shuddered at the memory, feeling violated anew. At that time, it hadn't occurred to her to call the police. They probably wouldn't have done anything.

When she reached her vehicle, her heart dropped. There was no message scrawled in jizz, but the covering for her back window was ripped. The plastic edges fluttered in the evening breeze, as if someone had shoved their fist through the opening. Maybe their entire body. She couldn't see inside the cab.

Pulse racing, she glanced around the parking lot. An engine revved in the distance, tires squealing down a deserted road. She took a tentative step forward, trying to peer into the backseat. It looked empty, but she wasn't quite sure. Grasping her keys tight, she inched closer, eyes straining.

"Last chance."

She yelped, almost jumping sky-high. Placing a hand to her hammering heart, she looked over her shoulder. Her coworkers had pulled up in Ginger's noiseless hybrid car. It was a cute little silver bullet, smart and silent.

"You sure you don't need the extra cash?" Desiree asked with a smirk. "Maybe you could use it to fix that window."

"I'm sure."

"Okay, then. Have fun at your trailer in Slab City."

"Salton City," she corrected. Slab City was a wasteland of nomads and homeless freaks. "Have fun sucking cocks."

"We will!"

Ginger stepped on the gas pedal, and they zipped away. Tiffany waved from the backseat, and Desiree whooped like a banshee. Three fast, beautiful girls, hell-bent on self-destruction. Why did she wish she was with them?

She had nothing against sucking cocks. If she could find a decent guy attached to one.

Blinking the tears from her eyes, she unlocked the car door and inspected the interior. It was free of intruders, so she climbed in. Forget them. Forget everything. She had Jamie to take care of. Tomorrow, she'd wake up early and make him breakfast. Those girls might have someone to grab on to tonight, but come morning, they'd be alone again.

She pulled out of the parking lot, sniffling. There

were no cigarettes in the glove compartment. Typical. She always smoked more than she planned and forgot to stash an extra pack.

Time to quit: stripping and smoking.

She switched on the radio to keep her company and settled in for a long drive. She'd have to stay at her mother's house again tonight, which meant getting up at the crack of frickin' dawn to take Jamie to school. Her eyelids grew heavy from lack of sleep. Yawning, she found a piece of sugar-free gum to chew on.

About halfway to Niland, on a lonely portion of the 115, she hit a pothole. Or something. Jerked into a more alert state, she clenched her hands around the wheel. It sounded as if a chunk of asphalt had flown up into her engine.

Another *thunk* followed, louder than the first.

She pulled to the side of the road and idled for a moment. Maybe she'd run over a rabbit or a big lizard. She couldn't afford to drive around with damaged engine parts, possibly a mangled carcass twisted around her fan belt. Groaning, she turned off the ignition and popped the trunk.

Getting out of the car, she released the mechanism under the hood and propped it up with the lever. She didn't have a flashlight—of course—so she used the butane flame of her Bic to inspect the engine. The problem was easy to identify. Her battery had come loose from its mount.

"Damn it," she muttered, trying to shove it back into place.

While she was busy under the hood, a truck passed by, slowing down to rubberneck. During the day, she'd have welcomed help from a stranger. At three o'clock in the morning, she prayed the driver would move on.

He didn't.

The man pulled over and got out. While his car door was open, the interior lights illuminated his face, just for a second. It was the tattooed man from Ace Demolition. She froze, considering the implications of his presence.

This was not a coincidence.

He hadn't come inside for a lap dance, but he'd followed her from the club. He'd *sabotaged her vehicle* and followed her from the club.

Janelle didn't shut her open car door, slam the hood or pause to grab her purse from the passenger seat. She just took off running, her cowboy boots kicking up gravel. She hadn't gone far, maybe twenty feet, when a searing jolt struck the back of her thigh. Her muscles stiffened, and her entire body convulsed.

She collapsed on the asphalt, twitching.

"Sorry," he said, scooping her into his arms. He carried her over his shoulder like a sack of potatoes. After depositing her in the front seat of his truck, he tied her wrists and ankles with the swift ease of a cattle roper. She couldn't move, could only weep. He locked up her car and retrieved her purse before climbing behind the wheel.

She realized he'd shot her with some kind of stun

gun. Her thigh burned from the sting, as if a swarm of wasps had descended on her. When he reached across her body, she flinched, expecting the worst. But he merely locked her door and secured her seat belt. Starting the engine, he drove away.

Janelle had heard somewhere that the majority of abductions turned into murders, not just sexual assaults. She was as good as dead. Her instincts had warned her about this brooding pervert. He was going to rape her and cut her into little pieces.

Thoughts of Jamie filled her head, making her eyes well with fresh tears. She didn't want to leave him.

"My—my son," she stammered.

"What about him?"

"He's all I've got." She'd said that wrong; she'd meant the opposite. Jamie couldn't count on Shane to stay out of prison, let alone take care of him. If this man killed her, her son would have no parents. "I'm all *he's* got."

Maybe it was true both ways.

Her captor offered a nod of acknowledgment, driving on in silence. Her mind must have been playing tricks on her, stretching minutes into hours, because it was still dark when they arrived in Bombay Beach, a coastal ghost town just thirty miles down the highway. After traveling down the dark, empty streets, they passed by what appeared to be an abandoned motel. He circled around the block and parked in a secluded area.

Then he lit up a cigarette and sipped from a mug.

Coffee, she suspected, her nose detecting no alcohol. His body language suggested they weren't leaving soon. She followed his gaze to the motel parking lot. The only occupant was a dusty Jeep.

"What are you going to do with me?" she asked.

"Nothing."

"Are we going inside?"

"No."

This waiting scared her more than any action could have. Her tension and anxiety grew until she felt as if her mind might snap. She was thirteen again, staring at the knob on her bedroom door.

Why did he have to *smoke?*

"Do you—do you want me to blow you?" she asked, remembering his dissatisfaction with the lap dance. If she could please him, maybe he'd go away. It had worked with her stepfather.

He studied her, considering. His gaze traveled along her bare legs, from the tops of her boots to the frayed hem of her jean shorts. "Do you want to blow me?"

"Yes," she said immediately.

He laughed without humor, glancing away.

She smothered a sob of desperation. He didn't like her scared face, was that it? She tried to guess what he preferred, based on his actions the previous night. "I'll do it for free," she said. "You don't have to pay."

He gave her an impatient look. This wasn't a selling point; she was at his mercy.

"It would pass the time," she blurted.

"That it would," he said, making no move to unzip his pants.

Why was she begging to give this guy oral sex? His dick wasn't a cigarette. She squirmed with a mixture of fear, discomfort and embarrassment. The back of her thigh ached where he'd struck her.

"Why don't you tell me what you really want," he said.

"Besides my freedom?"

"Yes."

"I'll take one of your Marlboros."

His brows rose with surprise. Shuffling another smoke from the pack, he lit the end and passed it to her.

She tucked her knees to her chest and bent her elbows, bringing her bound hands closer to her face. Inhaling deeply, she closed her eyes and wallowed in the nicotine's effect. It swam in her head and stirred her blood. "Thank you."

"Don't."

Don't thank him? She found it ironic that he'd laugh at her blow-job offer and take offense to her gratitude, but whatever. This guy was weird. Weird and cold and dangerous. She shrugged and kept smoking, resting her chin on her knee.

CHAPTER NINETEEN

OWEN TIGHTENED HIS ARM around Penny as he woke, disoriented.

They were naked on the bathroom floor, a pile of blankets underneath them and a thin sheet over the top. Penny was asleep on his shoulder, which felt numb from the hard ground. Her eyes were closed, her dark hair spread across his chest. A disturbance outside warned him that Shane was about to come in.

Sure enough, his brother opened the door partway and stuck his head inside. Penny roused at the sound, blinking in confusion. When Shane saw her bare shoulders, he smirked. "Rise and shine, kids."

"Can you unlock these?" Owen asked in a roughened voice, raising their cuffed wrists. "We can't get dressed like this."

Shane took the key out of his pocket and released Penny's cuff, which was closer to him. Owen couldn't stand up without exposing them both, so he stayed on the floor, waiting for Shane to shut the door again.

"Two minutes," Shane said.

Owen kissed Penny's forehead and rose, tugging on underwear. She watched, clutching the sheet to her breasts. Although her gaze wasn't sexual, his body responded to it, unsatisfied by the fleeting pleasure of the previous night.

He grabbed his clothes, which were hanging over the shower door, and pulled them on. Not bothering to zip up his pants, he turned his back to her and lifted the toilet seat. Attempting to piss while half-hard was a familiar chore, made slightly more challenging by the handcuff dangling from his right wrist.

When he was finished, he flushed and washed his hands. She stood up, her body still wrapped in the sheet. With her tangled hair, lush mouth and honeyed skin, she was the most beautiful thing he'd ever seen.

He was so in love with her, he could die.

The realization stunned him, even though it shouldn't have. Something had shifted inside him the first moment he'd seen her. That feeling had grown over the years, but he hadn't recognized it for what it was.

Last night, all of his fears had come true. He'd had a flashback and embarrassed himself. A lifetime's worth of pent-up emotions had flooded out of him, unleashing tears and passion and a soul-deep love for Penny. He'd held it inside, buried with everything else.

Shane popped back in before Owen had a chance to say anything. He wasn't ready to declare his affections, anyway. If the exchange went well, he could tell her afterward. If it didn't...the less said, the better.

"Cuff your free hand," Shane said. "Let's go."

Owen snapped it into place and followed his

brother out the door, giving Penny some privacy. Shane had several snack items from their mother's pantry on the bed. He sat down, tossing Owen a small bag of chips. Owen ripped open the bag and took a seat in the armchair across from Shane.

"What's the plan?"

"We need another boat for Sandoval," Shane said. "I know a guy who'll rent me one."

"You want to do the exchange on the water?"

"Yeah."

It was smart. The Salton Sea was forty miles wide and offered infinite escape routes. "What was the original location?"

"Red Mountain Mine. I was going to grab the cash, enter the mine shaft, and get to the Jeep waiting on the side."

Owen wasn't sure why he'd decided against the mine idea. His crew was gone, and he hadn't called for reinforcements. Maybe he didn't want whoever was in charge to know how much of a disaster this kidnapping had become. But they'd find out soon enough and make Shane pay the ultimate price for his mistakes.

"Who's your contact with the AB?" Owen asked.

"Don't worry about it. He's just a middleman."

"Does he know I was in the gang?"

"No."

"They'll kill you after you deliver the money." Shane didn't argue that.

"Why don't you run now, while you have a chance?"

"I already told you. They'll go after Jamie."

"Since when do you care about Jamie?"

"Fuck you," Shane said tiredly. Grabbing the empty bottle of whiskey by his pillow, he chucked it at the trash can—and missed. "I've always cared."

Owen ate a handful of chips, skeptical.

"You think you're some kind of role model father, is that it? Getting a tattoo of a kid's name because you want a piece of the mother's ass doesn't make you a parent, dude."

Owen's temper flared. "I never said it did."

"Then who are you to criticize?"

"I've been there for Jamie, more than you have. I've seen him more often. You weren't even in his life before you went to prison."

Shane rubbed his jaw, mouth twisting.

"You didn't call or send letters from the joint, either."

"Janelle wouldn't take my calls."

"For good reason." Shane had been verbally abusive throughout their relationship. They'd argued constantly.

"I sent letters. Birthday cards, too."

"He never got any."

"I sent them," he repeated.

Owen was surprised to hear this. Maybe Janelle had kept the cards or thrown them away in an attempt to protect Jamie from Shane's negative influence. "You put him in danger when you agreed to this plot."

"You put everyone in danger by playing hero," he said, his voice rising. Typical Shane. He'd never taken responsibility for his actions when he was younger, either.

"Did you really expect me to go along with it?"

"Yes! You could have pretended to go along with it, like you did in prison. Instead you took on a group like Rambo."

"What were you planning to do if I didn't cooperate?"

"Not this," he said.

"Obviously."

"You were going to let Dirk kill me."

"No. I said I'd do it myself, but I wouldn't have. I didn't care if you ratted on me. I'd planned on making a run for the border anyway."

Owen massaged his eye sockets, saddened by his brother's life choices. Shane was better off behind bars, where he couldn't hurt anyone, including himself. He wouldn't be able to stay out of trouble in Mexico.

"I should have known it would end up like this," Shane said, bitter. "You're such a fucking White Knight."

"What's that supposed to mean?"

"You're the good one, the smart one, the noble one. Mom's favorite. Dad's favorite."

"*Dad's* favorite? Are you high?"

"He was proud of you."

"For what, getting sent to prison?"

"For playing the hero during the earthquake, and again at that nature park."

"I don't believe you."

"He was excited for you. The last time we spoke on the phone, he kept blabbing about how you were going to be a firefighter and save people."

Owen shook his head, unable to fathom it. He couldn't remember a single compliment his father had given him, other than a pat on the back after he'd rebuilt that Chevy. But the insults still rang in Owen's ears. "He called me a faggot every day of my childhood. And a pussy."

Shane laughed under his breath. "Guess he was wrong on both counts."

"You were the strong one. He liked you."

"He liked to hit me," Shane corrected. "You got yelled at. I got beat up."

"You made him mad on purpose."

His brother fell silent, neither agreeing nor disagreeing.

"Why did you do that?" Owen asked.

"Why do you think?"

Owen had never questioned his brother's motives for violence before. Shane just reacted, often without thinking. He was argumentative and impulsive. It hadn't occurred to him that Shane might have provoked their father for altruistic reasons.

"You couldn't handle the beatings," Shane said.

"You were too sensitive. So I took most of them for you."

"No," Owen said, his stomach clenching.

"When I was big enough, I stepped in for Mom, too. And when I was big enough to win, he stopped beating all of us."

That was the truth. After Shane busted their father's lip in an epic, bloody battle, the abuse had ended. Until both brothers went to prison. With them out of the way, Christian had picked up where he'd left off, and their mother had used drugs to escape.

Owen finished his bag of chips, disturbed by the revelation. Shane might have protected him from some of their father's abuse, but he'd also bullied Owen relentlessly. Their boyish scuffles hadn't felt like abuse, though. They were just kids.

Shane passed Owen a soda, which he accepted with gratitude. Penny stayed in the bathroom, maybe brushing her teeth or trying to untangle her hair.

"How was she?" Shane asked.

"Shut up," Owen said, flushing.

"I don't know what a girl that good-looking sees in you."

"I don't, either."

"Looks like you've been working out," Shane said. "If you wear a bag over your head she might keep you around."

Owen didn't laugh at the lame joke. Pressure built behind his eyes, and he had to will the tears away. His brother hadn't kidded around with him like this in almost a decade. Owen had a bad feeling that they wouldn't do it again for ten more years.

Maybe never.

Penny came out of the bathroom a moment later, carrying his shoes. His mother's faded dress looked nice on her. She'd tied her hair back with a strip of cloth. With a nervous glance at Shane, she handed Owen his shoes. Fresh socks were tucked inside.

"Thanks," he said, wanting to kiss her. A real kiss, like he'd done last night.

"Have some breakfast," Shane said.

She selected a snack bag and sat at the edge of the bed. Although she must have been starving, she nibbled slowly, as if each bite of junk food was a spoonful of medicine she had to force down.

"Your chef doesn't serve chili-cheese chips, princess?"

"They're stale."

"Let me see." Shane grabbed the chips away from her and shoved a few into his mouth. Grimacing, he reached for another bag. "Try these."

She seemed to find the second snack edible.

"Did you sleep well?"

"Knock it off," Owen said.

"I'm just making conversation."

"You're trying to embarrass her."

His brows rose with mock surprise. "Does she have something to be embarrassed about?"

"I slept fine," Penny said, ignoring Shane's innuendo. "Knowing Cruz was safe helped. Thank you for that."

Shane scowled at her polite response. After she finished the snack, they left the motel room. Owen took the passenger seat while Penny sat behind him in the back of the Jeep. They headed a few miles north, to the Salton Sea State Recreation Area. The maintained shoreline was a little cleaner and less bizarre looking than the ruins of Bombay Beach, but it was no crown jewel. Oxygen-deprived fish and diseased birds died here, just like everywhere else.

Shane met an old man at the boat launch facility, paying him a couple of twenties for the use of a small powerboat. As soon as the owner drove away, Shane left one of the walkie-talkies on the nearest the picnic table and called Sandoval.

"Tell him to come here alone with the money," he ordered Penny.

She spoke into the receiver, giving the terse instructions. Shane hung up and flung the phone far out into the sea before turning to Owen. "Find a hiding place down the shore," he said, handing him another walkie-talkie. "Watch him from a distance and make sure he follows my instructions."

"Then what?"

"Then run like hell to Bombay Beach. How long will it take you?"

Owen figured it was about two miles as the crow flies. "Ten minutes."

"We'll be waiting for you."

Owen didn't want to leave Penny with Shane, but he had no choice. Shane unlocked the handcuffs, aware that he could control Owen through Penny. Owen shoved the radio into his pocket, glancing over his shoulder at her. She looked scared.

"Why don't you kiss your girl goodbye?"

Owen tore his gaze away, his heart pounding. He refused to put on a show for his brother's entertainment. "If you hurt her I'll fucking kill you."

Shane inclined his head, accepting those terms.

There was nothing he could say to change Shane's mind. Owen felt powerless over the situation. With each second that ticked by, he became more convinced that everything would fall apart. He couldn't stop the impending disaster. Shane was going to shoot someone or get shot. This plan had been doomed from the start.

With a sound of frustration, Owen opened the passenger door and exited the vehicle.

"Owen!"

He stared at Penny, his brother's prisoner. She didn't deserve to be traumatized this way. No woman did.

"Be careful," she said, her eyes swimming with tears.

His throat closed up, so he just nodded. Shane stepped on the gas, leaving a cloud of pulverized fish bones in his wake. Owen had to walk down the shore for half a mile, searching for cover. Tilapia skulls from recent die-offs crunched beneath his shoes with every step. There were a few lonely palm trees along this stretch of the Salton Sea, but nothing else. No convenient hills or boulders to duck behind. The water was blue, and the shore was bleached white. Everything flat and still, as far as the eye could see.

The hiding place he found was just a dip in the ground, like a natural fort. Unfortunately, there was a murky orange puddle on the other side. Scientists said the color of the water reflected algae, not chemical pollution or human waste, but it looked nasty. He lowered himself into the lukewarm cesspool, watched the picnic table and waited.

His thoughts turned to Penny, to the night they'd shared. After his painful confession and humiliating crying jag, he'd felt pretty low. He'd wanted to stay strong for her, to protect her and comfort her. He'd let his guard down instead, sobbing like a baby, and she hadn't seemed fazed. Upset and saddened, but not disgusted.

She'd still found him attractive. She'd kissed him and rubbed against him and begged him to touch her.

He'd studied her for signs of sincerity, wondering if she was throwing him a pity bone. The desire in her eyes seemed genuine, and her physical responses… God. She couldn't fake being wet. He didn't think she'd exaggerated the moans and gasps of pleasure. If anything, she'd been trying to stay quiet. Owen couldn't believe how easy it had been to get her off, or how satisfied he'd felt after pleasing her. Twice.

He'd brought her to climax *twice*.

The fact that he'd come all over her from less than a minute of stimulation was a little embarrassing, but she hadn't seemed to mind that, either. Maybe next time—if there was a next time—he could do her right. He wanted to kiss her for hours and get inside her, with his fingers and tongue and cock.

The stirrings of arousal made it difficult for him to concentrate on surveillance, so he focused on the present. This was no place for sexual fantasies. He was lying on his belly in a puddle of foul-smelling muck.

He'd be lucky to get out of this situation alive. There would be a media shit storm no matter what happened. Penny might not want to continue their relationship. He could face criminal charges.

Taking shallow breaths, he stared at the powerboat in the distance. It was docked and ready to go. The sun beat down with relentless heat, burning the back of his neck, his hairline, the tips of his ears.

Finally Jorge Sandoval arrived in his modified SUV. The windows were tinted, the body bulletproof. There could be six FBI agents crouched in the back.

"He's here," Owen said into the radio.

"Is he alone?"

Owen couldn't tell. Sandoval got out of the driver's seat, hefting a large duffel bag. "Looks like it."

With cautious steps, Sandoval approached the picnic table. He found the walkie-talkie Shane had left there and lifted it. "Hello?"

"Do you have the money?" Shane asked.

"Yes."

"How much?"

"Two million, unmarked. Just like you said."

"Take off your clothes and put them on the table. Leave everything there. Your keys, wallet, phone, clothes."

Even from far away, Owen could read Sandoval's reluctance. He was a former governor, for Christ's sake. He didn't want to strip naked in public. But he mumbled an affirmation and set the radio aside. With efficient motions, he kicked off his shiny shoes, unbuttoned his shirt and removed his expensive trousers. When he was standing in socks and boxer shorts, he picked up the radio again. "Now what?"

"Did he do it?" Shane asked Owen.

"Yes."

"Get in the boat and go south. Bring the money and the radio. I'll give you the exact coordinates in a minute."

Sandoval climbed into the powerboat with the duffel bag. The keys were in the ignition. He started it and drove away from the launch area, as instructed. Owen stared at the SUV on the shore, detecting no movement. Maybe Sandoval really *had* come alone. Maybe he hadn't contacted the authorities at all.

It seemed impossible. More likely, there was an entire task force nearby, and they were a lot better at hiding than he was.

Owen got up and started running, heedless of being followed. If police officers or members of Sandoval's security team were in the SUV, they might see him, but they couldn't catch him. He was fast.

Shane was waiting for him with Penny at the ruins of the yacht club, where he'd hidden their dad's boat. They'd ducked behind the crumbling concrete wall. Penny's mouth was tense, her face pinched with fear.

"Did you see any cops?" Shane asked.

"No," Owen said. "Where's the Jeep?"

Shane ignored the question. "Help me with the trailer."

Together, they pushed it into the water. Then Shane pulled the gun from his waistband. Not pointing it at him, just holding it. "Give me the walkie-talkie."

Owen gave it to him.

He tossed it into the boat. "Now cuff yourself to the trailer."

Owen glanced down, noting that one of the handcuffs was already attached to the front end. The other hung loose, ready for him to snap it on his wrist. Shane wanted to make him stay here on the shore. "No."

Shane grabbed Penny by the crook of the arm and jammed the barrel against her ribs. "Do it."

"You're not going to shoot her before the exchange."

"I won't kill her," Shane countered.

"You said you wouldn't hurt her."

"No, I said you could kill me if I did. I'd rather not, but the choice is yours. Do you want to fight me now and risk her safety? Or do you want to shut the fuck up and wait here while I deliver her to her father?"

Clenching his jaw, Owen put the cuff on.

"That's what I thought," Shane said.

Penny tried to jerk her arm from Shane's grasp. When he held tight, she cursed him in Spanish.

"Speak English," he reminded her.

"Fuck you."

He laughed in approval and let her go. With a strangled sob, she threw her arms around Owen's neck and pressed her lips to his, kissing him desperately. Not caring that Shane had orchestrated this scene, Owen kissed her back with the same fervor, dipping his tongue into her mouth.

"Break it up," Shane said, clearing his throat. "Jesus, you two are like a couple of teenagers."

Penny released Owen with reluctance, returning to Shane's side. He holstered the gun and secured her arms behind her back with duct tape. Then he lifted her into the boat, climbed inside, and pushed away from the shore. The ignition started the first try.

"Do me a favor," he shouted above the roar of the engine. "Say goodbye to Mom and Jamie for me. Tell them…tell them I love them."

Owen sank to a sitting position on the shore, devastated.

"Will you do it?"

"No," he yelled back in a hoarse voice, but it was a lie. He held Penny's gaze until she disappeared into the blue.

CHAPTER TWENTY

JANELLE WOKE WITH A START.

She lifted her head, disoriented. Her wrists were still bound, her right shoulder stiff from leaning on it. Sometime during the long, terrifying night, she'd fallen asleep in the passenger seat of the stranger's pickup. He'd given her a balled-up sweatshirt to use as a pillow. The fabric smelled of motor oil, Marlboros and male deodorant. She straightened, glancing around. The stranger wasn't in the cab.

Janelle reached for the door handle with numb fingers. When it didn't work, she remembered the door was locked. She scooted across the seat and tried the driver's side door, her mind sluggish from sleep. It swung open, and she tumbled out, falling on her hands and knees in the dusty gravel.

"Going somewhere?"

The stranger was standing nearby, facing a concrete wall. Before turning toward her, he made a shaking motion and zipped up his pants.

Heart racing, she searched for an escape route. It was early morning. They were in Bombay Beach, a local ghost town. Other than the run-down motel and a bunch of condemned buildings, there was nothing out here.

She had nowhere to run. And she couldn't actually get up. "I'll scream," she said in a tremulous voice.

He shrugged, crossing his arms over his chest.

Tears welled in her eyes, and blood trickled down her shin. She didn't make a sound. When he stepped forward to help her to her feet, she said, "I have to pee."

"Go ahead."

She unbuttoned her shorts with trembling hands. He averted his gaze, as if he hadn't already seen the goods, while she squatted down. After she was done, she stood, pulling her shorts and panties up.

He lifted her back into the cab and pushed her across the seat. Climbing behind the wheel, he slammed the door and shook two cigarettes out of the pack, giving her one. She put the end in her mouth and leaned toward the flame of his lighter to spark it.

The stranger didn't want sex. That much was clear. He'd made no attempt to touch her, harm her, or humiliate her. Maybe he would keep her as his domestic slave, or get her hooked on drugs and turn her into a prostitute.

Whatever his intentions, he was a sick fuck. She could tell by the way he just sat there, smoking. And by the way he twisted off the cap from a bottle of water before offering her a sip. Only a deeply disturbed individual could remain so calm and polite, as if he wasn't planning to hack her up with a chain saw.

He stared at the Jeep in the parking lot, saying nothing.

It occurred to her, somewhat belatedly, that he knew the person inside the motel room. The stranger might have stolen her to fulfill another man's perverse appetites. What were they waiting for? Why didn't he hand over the goods?

She watched the motel door with increasing anxiety. Finally, a man came out. "Shane," she breathed, recognizing him on sight. He had the same bad-boy swagger, with bigger muscles and longer hair.

This was all about Shane, she realized. The stranger was after him, not her.

Leaving the door open, Shane grabbed a bag from the back of the Jeep. Then he walked back inside the motel room.

"Does he owe you money?" she asked.

The stranger didn't answer.

"If you think you can get revenge on him by hurting me, you're wrong. He doesn't care about me."

"Is there someone else he cares about?"

Her stomach dropped. Did he mean Jamie? "No."

"I know where your son is," he said. "I followed you Saturday night, too. You went to your mother's house."

"Don't you dare touch my son," she growled, ready to claw his eyes out. "I will rip your goddamned face off."

He smiled at this warning, a bit sadly.

The fact that he hadn't kidnapped her for deviant

sexual purposes didn't ease her fears. Shane wouldn't bail her out. He wasn't capable of unselfish actions. She could have endured another rape, or survived years locked in a dungeon. But counting on *Shane* to save her? That was laughable.

"You want something from Shane," she said, "and you're holding me hostage until you get it."

"Yes."

"Does he know what you want?"

"Of course."

"Are you sure he has it?"

"He doesn't have it yet. That's why we're waiting."

"What if he can't get it?"

"Then he'd better hope the police find him before I do."

"What if he gets it but doesn't give it to you?"

"He dies."

A chill traveled up her spine, because she believed him. She was afraid to ask what he'd do to her in that case. If this man was going to kill her, he wouldn't tell her about it. And she wouldn't believe him if he said otherwise.

Janelle wasn't interested in the details of whatever deal Shane had made with this devil. She only knew that her ex wasn't dependable. He was cocky and charming, fairly good in bed, but useless in all other things. He wouldn't hold up his end of the bargain. So she had to negotiate a release on her own terms.

Or at least give herself some…wiggle room.

She studied the stranger once again. He was attractive in a rough-edged way, his skin coarsely tanned. She pegged him as a former drug user as well as an ex-con, though he looked strong and clear-eyed now. He'd probably grown up poor in this area or a similar community. Janelle knew a desert rat when she saw one.

Beneath the harsh exterior, he seemed hollow. But he hadn't been disrespectful in the VIP room, and he hadn't forced himself on her. She was almost certain he'd declined her offer for a blow job because he didn't believe she *wanted to.*

Maybe if she was more convincing, he'd weaken. She had no other tools at her disposal, no weapons but sex.

"Why did you come into the club?" she asked.

"Why not?"

"You already knew who I was."

"I wanted to make sure."

"And you needed a lap dance to identify me?"

"No," he said. "I identified you while we were discussing your…price. Then it seemed rude to walk away."

She shook her head, feigning insult. "Wow."

"What?"

"I've never had a pity customer."

"I didn't feel sorry for you, honey. You're hot, and I was curious. Pity doesn't make a man's dick hard."

Biting her lower lip, she let her gaze slide down to his crotch.

He looked from her mouth to the motel room door and back again. "Do you think I'm stupid?"

Her eyes widened. "What do you mean?"

"Just spare me the stripper bullshit. You're a lot more appealing as yourself."

She'd been too obvious. Cheeks heating with shame, she looked away. Fake-horny was the only card she knew how to play, and now she was out of ideas. She should have asked him about himself, warmed him up a little. It wasn't like she'd never worked a mark before. Fear had made her clumsy.

He *wasn't* stupid.

After a tense silence, the motel room door opened again. A dark-haired young woman Janelle recognized as Penny Sandoval stepped out. Owen followed, his hands cuffed in front. Shane didn't seem to catch sight of the black truck in the distance. It was disguised among palm trees and piles of rubble.

"Who's that, his brother?"

Janelle didn't answer.

"Doesn't look like he's in on it."

In on what? she wondered. "He wouldn't be involved in anything illegal."

"How do you know?"

"I just do. I know him."

He squinted at her. "How well?"

"Well enough."

"Are you sleeping with him?"

She gave him a dirty look. "He's my son's uncle."

"He's not *your* uncle."

"I'm not sleeping with him."

"And he's a straight arrow, you say?"

"Yes."

He made a noncommittal sound.

"What?"

"Looks like you picked the wrong brother to have a kid with."

True or not, the observation stung. She regretted getting mixed up with a loser and becoming a teen mother, but she loved Jamie to pieces. Her son was perfect and innocent. Without Shane, she wouldn't have Jamie. "Don't talk about my son."

The stranger followed Shane's vehicle away from the motel, keeping several deserted city blocks between them. They entered the Salton Sea State Recreation Area. Shane left Owen there and headed back to Bombay Beach, parking the Jeep among the ruins of an old playground. He got out and walked across the bone-scattered beach with Penny, a gun tucked into the waistband of his jeans.

"She's his prisoner," Janelle guessed. She'd never met Penny Sandoval, but she'd watched the recent television interview with interest. Penny was beautiful and smart and rich. She wouldn't go anywhere with Shane by choice. "He's ransoming her to her father."

"Do you know her?"

"No."

The stranger parked behind a ripped canvas billboard, close enough to keep an eye on the Jeep without being noticed.

"Now what?" Janelle asked.

"We wait."

PENNY SAT ON the aluminum bench in the middle of the boat, her heart pounding.

Owen knelt in the crushed bones on the beach and watched them speed away. She held his gaze as long as possible, terrified she'd never see him again.

Shane puttered around the Salton Sea until he found the right spot to do the money exchange. Then he looked up the coordinates on his GPS radio and gave them to her father. They settled in, waiting for him to arrive.

Penny felt Shane watching her. She didn't want to look at him or speak to him. She wanted to close her eyes and think of Owen, to touch her fingertips to her lips and replay their goodbye kiss.

Last night, she'd been so full of unfamiliar feelings. The intimate contact had caused something to shift inside her, revealing a hidden bud she hadn't known was there. This morning, it had blossomed, spreading throughout her chest.

She was in love with Owen.

She was in love with him.

She loved him.

Penny wasn't sure if she'd felt this way all along, and their frantic groping had broken down her inhibitions, or if the connection they'd always shared had deepened little by little, growing exponentially in the past few days.

How unfair it was to realize this now, after they'd parted. She should have known earlier, whispered it to him in the shower. She hoped that Shane wouldn't cause some terrible tragedy before she had the chance to tell Owen.

Tears blurred her vision as she studied their surroundings. The Salton Sea wasn't ugly up close, and it only smelled bad on the shore. Out in the middle, its surface was like a blue mirror, shimmering with hidden depths.

"My brother's in love with you," Shane said.

She turned her gaze to him, surprised. "Did he tell you that?"

"He didn't have to."

Her pulse jumped, and she glanced away, uncomfortable. Shane bore an uncanny resemblance to Owen, only his good looks hid a black interior. She assumed his reason for starting this conversation was to needle her, and she resented being pushed around by him, physically and emotionally.

"Are you toying with him?" Shane asked.

"No."

"Some rich girls like to go slumming."

"I'm not slumming."

"Yes, you are."

"Then we disagree on the definition. Slumming is hanging out with someone from a lower social class just for kicks."

"I think it means dating a guy you wouldn't introduce to daddy."

"My father already knows Owen."

"Does he know you're fucking him?"

She fell silent, refusing to answer. Then she said, "You're breaking his heart, you know. He can't help but love you."

Shane paused for a moment, weighing her words. "He might love me, but he doesn't expect anything from me. I'm a worthless bastard. You're his dream girl. He got a taste of you, and now he's done for. He's so whipped on you, he thinks your pussy's the pathway to heaven. You'll crush him."

She flushed at his crude language. "He doesn't believe he's good enough for me."

"He's wrong," Shane said, staring across the sea. "I got all the bad in the family. He's as good as gold, always has been."

Penny didn't like Shane, but she could appreciate his sincerity. "Let's make a deal. I won't hurt him if you won't."

He studied her face, seeming to be conflicted. Although he didn't agree to uphold his end of the bargain, she got the impression that he wanted to. Maybe he didn't trust himself to follow through on any promises.

The sound of a powerboat alerted them to her father's presence. He slowed down and drifted closer, his body language tense. His state of undress made him look unbearably vulnerable. Penny wasn't used to seeing him shirtless, scared or alone. Her eyes filled with tears, and she pictured Cruz. There was nothing worse than being afraid for your child. She couldn't wait to be reunited with her son.

Shane held up a hand in greeting. "I'm going to throw you this bag," he said, showing him a canvas knapsack. "Transfer the money into it slowly."

Her father looked at her. "Are you okay, *mija?*"

"I'm fine, Daddy."

Shane didn't ask Jorge to speak English, but he seemed annoyed as he tossed the bag into the powerboat. Her father unzipped his black duffel bag and took out fat green stacks of bills, shoving them into the knapsack. Shane watched closely, as if he suspected the money of being marked or bugged. He kept glancing up at the sky.

When her father was finished with the task, he cinched the knapsack closed. "Do you want me to hand it to you?"

"No," Shane said. "Leave it there. Throw the empty bag into the water."

Jorge did as he was told. The duffel bag floated on the flat surface like a black stingray, handles outstretched.

"How's Cruz?" Penny asked.

"He's safe," her father answered. "Worried about you."

She nodded, blinking her tears away.

"Thank you for sending my grandson home early,"

her father said to Shane. "And for not harming my daughter. I am forever in your debt."

Shane grunted a response, unimpressed by the lip service. "You're paying good money for something I stole from you, so cut the crap. I'm not going to be impressed by the fancy manners you learned here in America."

Her father didn't even flinch at the insult. "Very well."

"What do you think of your daughter and my brother?"

His brows rose. Racially charged remarks, he expected. This, he did not. "Your brother?"

"Don't pretend not to know what I mean."

"Owen Jackson, of my security team," her father said, nodding. "He helped Penny during the San Diego earthquake. He's earned my gratitude and my respect."

"How about your daughter? Has he earned the right to touch her?"

Her father wore a bland expression. "My daughter makes her own decisions," he said, lying with casual diplomacy.

"Tell him how you feel about Owen," Shane ordered Penny.

She didn't know what to say. She'd only just realized how she felt. Her love for Owen was too new to share with anyone. She wanted to savor it, hold it inside, and declare it to Owen—when she was ready.

The pressure was too much. She resented Shane's

manipulations, as well as her father's. Trapped between two opposing forces, she had no room to breathe. She was tired of being told what to do and who to date.

"That's what I figured," Shane said, drawing his gun.

"No," her father shouted. "Please!"

"Quiet down, padre," he said, breaking his English-only rule. He grabbed Penny by the arm and yanked her to her feet.

She just stared at him, her heart in her throat.

"Maybe my brother's too good for *you*." He was so close she could see the individual whiskers above his lip, short and spiky. He crushed his mouth over hers cruelly, stealing the sweet kiss Owen had given her.

Then he pushed her overboard.

She screamed as she hit the water, her legs flailing. Her cry was swallowed by the sea as she sank below the surface. Bubbles flurried from her nostrils and salt burned her eyes, as if she'd been submerged in lukewarm brine. Gagging on the brackish taste, she struggled to free her hands, to no avail.

Above her, the muffled sound of gunshots rang out. Bullets tore through the bottom of the boat, whizzing past her like submarine missiles.

Her last thought was *Cruz*.

CHAPTER TWENTY-ONE

OWEN COULDN'T BUDGE the trailer.

It took every ounce of strength he possessed to lift one end out of the water and drag it a couple of feet. He couldn't go anywhere with a large metal object attached to his arm. If he wanted to get free, he had to break the handcuffs.

He searched the beach for members of his security team and law enforcement officers, but the shoreline was deserted. There was nothing out here, not even a stray dog. Although yelling might bring help, he stayed quiet. Penny and her father would be safer if the exchange wasn't interrupted. Shane's motto was live fast, die young. He'd welcome a shoot-out with the authorities. Cop killers were heroes behind bars.

Owen found a chunk of concrete among the shells and bones on the beach. He gripped the edge of the trailer with his cuffed hand, pulling the steel chain taut over the metal bar. Then he struck the chain, trying to bust it. The concrete broke apart instead, scraping the skin on the inside of his wrist.

Making a sound of frustration, he tossed the crumbled pieces aside. He needed something stronger than steel to damage the handcuff chain. He looked around, as if that kind of material would be washed up on the beach. The trailer offered one option. The hoist hook was made of hard chrome, a metal alloy. It could damage steel.

He slid the handcuff down the metal bar until his free hand reached the hoist. It was bolted down, but the nuts hadn't been tightened in years. One side was loose. He freed the hook from the mount and felt its weight in his hand. Inside a sock, it would make a powerful bludgeoning tool.

Holding the hook by its hinged end, he repositioned the handcuff chain over the edge of the metal trailer bar. Then he struck it again and again, hammering away like a blacksmith. After an extended effort and lots of sweat, the chain fell apart.

Victory.

The cuff still encircled his wrist, but his hands were free. Smiling grimly, he shoved the hook into his pocket. Now what? He couldn't steal a boat and go after them. The Salton Sea was the largest lake in California, with a surface area of almost four hundred square miles. His chances of finding them were slim and none. He trudged along the shore, reluctant to seek assistance from locals or make contact with the police. The exchange should only take a few minutes. Where were they?

Filled with anxiety, he went in search of the Jeep. As soon as Shane got the money, he'd dump the powerboat on the shore and take off. Owen could intercept him there and make sure the exchange had occurred safely.

He found the Jeep parked behind a particleboard shack near an old playground. Metal poles for swings stood empty. A rusted metal slide was half-buried in the sand. There were stray chairs and pieces of recreation equipment, some impossible to identify. While he crouched by the slide and waited for Shane to show, a sound caught his attention.

It was a sharp cry, quickly muffled.

He gazed into the distance, zeroing in on a black truck that was almost completely concealed by a ripped canvas billboard advertising Lots For Sale. A faded image of Salton Sea's heyday, more than thirty years ago, peeled away at one corner. It depicted women in colorful bikinis, men fishing and children frolicking. Owen had never seen that brief period of prosperity, which had come and gone like the desert wind.

A newer-model truck didn't belong here. Tourists visited Bombay Beach to bird-watch or gawk at the devastation, but Owen didn't think the vehicle belonged to a day-tripper from L.A. The truck was hidden near the Jeep on purpose. He'd bet the inhabitant was doing the same thing he was: waiting for Shane.

Owen ducked down a little more, wondering if the person in the truck had seen *him*. Then two faint thumps rang out across the sea, like the banging of a drum. His stomach roiled as he realized it was Shane's 9 mm. Although his brother must have been miles away, the conditions here were unusual. There was almost no breeze today. The water was flat and calm, free of other boats and noise disturbances.

Disregarding the black truck for now, he stood and ran toward the shore, pulse pounding. Shane couldn't have shot Penny. He refused to believe that his brother was so evil and emotionally detached that he'd kill an innocent, defenseless woman.

When the powerboat came into view, Owen's stomach dropped. Shane was behind the wheel. He drove it right into the beach, almost flipping the boat over in a spectacular crash. He hopped out with a military-style canvas rucksack and hit the ground running.

Owen took the hoist hook out of his pocket and held it in his fist as his brother approached.

Shane slowed to a stop. He looked more surprised than guilty. "You crafty son of a bitch. I should have known you'd get out of the cuffs."

Owen's vision went dark with fury. "Did you kill them?"

"No," Shane said, recoiling at the accusation. "Hell, no."

"I heard the shots."

"I shot through the bottom of Dad's boat," he said, impatient. "As long as they can swim, they'll be fine."

Owen grabbed Shane by the front of the shirt with his free hand. He gripped the hook until his knuckles went white, tempted to smash his brother's face in. "You left them out there, miles from shore, in a sinking boat?"

"Calm the fuck down," he said. "They have life jackets."

He tore his gaze away from Shane and examined the crashed powerboat, his blood pumping with adrenaline. There was no way he could get it back in the water, but the walkie-talkie might give him their location. The Salton Sea was warm and buoyant and flat. Easy to float in, even without life preservers.

"I have to get out of here," Shane said, jerking free of his grasp. "The cops are going to swarm in any minute."

"Somebody's waiting for you by the Jeep."

"Who?"

"I don't know. They were in a black truck."

"Thanks for the heads-up." Shane took a gun out of his waistband and released the safety before tucking it in again. With grim determination, he continued walking.

"Is it an enforcer for the AB?"

Shane didn't answer.

"He'll shoot you on sight."

"Not if I shoot him first."

"Leave the money with me and run," Owen said. "It's your only hope."

"Leave the money with you, after what I just went through to get it? Fuck that, brother. Fuck that all the way to Mexico."

"Just take your cut, Shane. Take what you can easily carry."

"No," he said, his eyes hard. "I killed a good friend for this. I risked going back to prison. Now I have to live the rest of my life on the wrong side of the border with a measly fifty grand to my name?"

"What about Jamie?"

His mouth tightened with regret. "He's better off without me."

"You said they'd go after him, you asshole!"

"Then it's up to you to keep him safe while I'm gone."

Owen wanted to howl in frustration. He hated Shane at that moment, more than he'd ever hated his father. More than he hated the men who'd assaulted him in prison. Driven by the pain of a thousand wrongs, he drew back his fist to strike.

Shane jerked sideways at the last second. The blow glanced off his bottom lip instead of his cheekbone, splitting it wide. Blood rushed down his chin. Evading the next swing, Shane dumped his rucksack on the beach and put up his dukes, spitting on the sand. "You want to go, motherfucker?"

"Yeah," Owen said, "I want to go."

Nostrils flared, Shane lowered his shoulder and charged, tackling Owen around the waist. They fell over the old playground slide, arms and legs tangled. When Owen tried to punch Shane in the ear, his brother trapped his wrist and banged his closed fist against the metal ladder. Several of Owen's knuckles cracked before he dropped the hook, writhing in agony.

"You had enough?" Shane asked, his grin red.

"Not yet," Owen said, head-butting him.

Shane slumped down the slide, clapping a hand over his brow. "Bastard," he yelled, blood dripping into his eye.

Owen jumped on him, straddling his waist. Making a fist with his left hand, he punched his brother over and over again, battering his blood-streaked face. When Owen slowed down, taking a ragged breath, Shane picked up the hook he'd dropped. Owen lifted his arm to block the counterattack, but exhaustion made him clumsy. The weighted punch hit him almost full force, knocking him sideways.

He cupped his aching jaw, seeing stars.

Shane declared the fight over. He seemed to consider himself the victor, despite his mangled mug. Gathering the rucksack, he hovered close to Owen, his blue eyes wild and mean. So much like their father's.

"I kissed your bitch," he said, spitting again.

Owen couldn't clear the spots from his vision. "What?"

"She wouldn't admit to being your girlfriend in front of her father, so I kissed her and pushed her off the boat. She tasted the same as every other Mexican whore I've had. I'd move on if I were you."

"Fuck you," Owen groaned, nauseous.

"She doesn't love you."

"I don't care."

"What do you mean, you don't care?"

"You'll never know what I mean, you scumbag. Because you're incapable of loving someone unconditionally."

Shane went silent for a moment as these words sank in. Maybe they hurt. Maybe he was too detached to feel anything.

The black smudges in his vision faded, and Owen stared up at his brother, his chest constricted with sorrow. Even if Shane wasn't capable of love or any selfless emotions, Owen believed what Shane had said about protecting him from their father. Shane had become this monster by choice, saving Owen from the same fate.

"You're wrong," Shane choked out, drawing the gun from his waistband. "I can love. I love you, you little shit. I always have."

Owen swallowed back tears, unable to respond.

Shane lifted the 9 mm and pointed it at Owen. "Goodbye."

JANELLE GNAWED AT THE KNOT on her wrists, trying to loosen it.

The stranger noticed this and didn't seem to care, which suggested that he was confident in his rope skills. But she didn't have anything else to do, so she continued. She was hungry and bored and tired. It felt like an oven inside the cab of the truck, even with the windows cracked. She missed Jamie.

"Can I call my son?"

"No."

"My knee hurts."

"Don't make me gag you."

"I have some gum in my purse."

"Will that keep you quiet?"

She nodded.

He reached into the back and grabbed her purse, rifling through the contents. The first thing he found was a pair of black-lace panties. Setting them aside, he located her sugar-free bubble gum. He gave her a stick and helped himself to one.

"Can I get a tissue for my knee?" she asked, pressing her luck.

He took out the baby wipes she used to remove makeup and scrub man-germs from her skin after lap dances. "This?"

"Yes."

After he handed her a couple of moist wipes, she braced her boots on the dashboard and cleaned the pebbles from the scrape, wincing in discomfort. He replaced her panties in her purse and tossed it in the backseat. She blotted the fresh beads of blood, aware of his eyes on her. Wondering if he felt bad about her injury, she glanced at him. He appeared to be staring at her upper thighs, not her knee.

"You have more blood," he said.

"Where?"

He made a vague gesture. "The back of your leg."

The stun gun he'd used had shot out some sort of

electric barb. He'd removed it when he picked her up off the gravel. Her thigh still felt tender there, but she couldn't reach the spot with her wrists and calves bound so tightly.

After watching her struggle, he grabbed one of the wipes and did the honors himself. Resting his right hand above her knee, he used his left to scrub the blood away. His touch was rough and quick, as if he wanted to get it over with. When she winced, he lifted his gaze to hers. For that single, unguarded moment, she saw something behind it.

Not empty, after all.

Then he looked down and finished cleaning her thigh, a muscle in his jaw taut. Up close, she could smell the same scent from his sweatshirt. Motor oil and male deodorant and cigarettes, mixed with the aspartame of her bubble gum. The hand on her leg felt strong, his palm callused. His tattooed knuckles said *S-L-A-B*.

When he discarded the used wipe, she saw the word on his other hand: *C-I-T-Y*.

"You're from the Slabs?" she asked.

He straightened and made two fists, frowning at his own knuckles as if he'd forgotten what they said. "No one is from the Slabs."

"You live there?"

"I've lived there."

"What's it like?"

"You've never been?"

"Just once," she said, thinking back. When she'd

first started dancing, she'd been as wild and careless as Tiffany. She'd gone to Slab City with another girl to entertain a group of bikers at a bonfire. Compared to those guys, the stranger was a gentleman. "I was hired to dance at a motorcycle party. It didn't go well."

"Why not?"

"They didn't want to pay."

"Which motorcycle club was it?"

"I don't know."

"The Slabs are a freak show," he said, squinting into the distance. "Lots of drugs and trash and mental problems. Old people, young people, life's rejects. Bike gangs. Not a good place for an unprotected woman."

"What is?"

He shrugged. "Beverly Hills?"

"I'll just move there, then. Live like a movie star."

They exchanged a wry smile at the joke. Then he reached into the glove compartment and took out a handgun, cold as ice. She followed his gaze to the playground, where Owen was standing on the other side of a pile of rubble.

She drew a breath to scream.

The stranger clapped his left hand over her mouth as she cried out. He gave her head a threatening shake, but it was too late. The sound caught Owen's attention. He glanced toward the weathered billboard they were parked behind.

"Goddamn it," the stranger said, his fingers digging into her cheek.

Janelle couldn't open her jaw to bite his palm. His grip was too strong. So she thrashed around in an attempt to dislodge him, growling like an animal and pummeling her bound fists against his forearm. It didn't work.

Instead of coming forward to investigate the black truck, Owen turned and walked in the opposite direction, as if he hadn't seen them. The stranger let her go, cursing. Transferring the gun to his left hand, he turned on the ignition.

"What are you doing?" she asked.

"I'm following him! He's going to tip off his brother and screw up everything."

"Leave him alone," she said, her voice raw.

Ignoring her, he stepped on the gas and pulled forward, preparing to drive closer to the playground. He had to make a wide turn and double back. When he skirted close to a gravel slope on the passenger side, she grabbed the wheel with both hands and cranked it to the right. They tumbled down the embankment. Her body flew up, and the top of her head hit the vehicle's frame as it rolled over.

The truck came to rest on its driver's side. Gravity plastered her against the stranger, whose chest was heaving with fury. She felt dizzy and confused, her thoughts scattered. She'd just wrecked his truck. Would he kill her?

Janelle's hands were bound, literally. She couldn't fight this man. She couldn't stop him from following Owen. The only thing she could do was distract him and buy herself some time. Spitting out her gum, she hooked her arms around his neck and kissed his hard mouth. He tried to resist her advances, but he couldn't move. When she flicked her tongue over his closed lips, he made a strangled sound in the back of his throat. She applied more pressure, urging his mouth open and sliding her tongue inside.

He tasted like gum and cigarettes, like her but different. Clean and hot and male. Although he didn't fight, he wasn't passive, either. Taking control of the kiss, he fisted his hand in her hair and thrust his tongue into *her* mouth. She squirmed against him for effect. And because he was a good kisser.

He ended the contact, panting against her parted lips. "Get off me."

"I can't."

Jaw clenched, he released her hair and fumbled behind his back, maybe tucking the gun into his jeans. With both hands free, he disentangled himself from her embrace. She stayed where she was, her body flush against his. He pressed a button on the console to open the passenger window. Turning her around, he gave her butt a hard shove.

She didn't cooperate with his efforts. Why should she? As soon as they got outside, the stranger would find Owen and hurt him. She slumped forward like a slug, not attempting to crawl through the window.

"Move your ass," he said, gripping the seat of her shorts. His thumb slipped under the denim and thrust between her cheeks, perhaps by accident. The rude prodding made her face hot. With nothing but a flimsy strip of fabric to prevent him from pushing inside her body, she felt intensely vulnerable.

Troubled by the reminder of how easily a man could hurt a woman, she inched toward the window and stuck her head out. He adjusted his grip to her hips and forced her through the opening, letting her tumble across the hood. When he climbed after her, his features were twisted into an angry grimace.

His truck wasn't totaled, but it had sustained considerable damage. He couldn't use it for a quick, reliable getaway.

"Fuck," he yelled, raking a hand through his hair.

Fearing for her life, she tried to scramble up the gravel embankment. Men were funny about their trucks. This one might have killed for lesser offenses.

Instead of shooting her, he picked her up and flung her over his shoulder, facedown. She didn't cry out for fear that Owen would come to her aid, and she was too disoriented to struggle. Her belly lurched with every step as the stranger walked toward the playground at a brisk pace. By the time they arrived, Owen was gone.

The stranger approached the Jeep, giving it a cursory inspection. He took her inside the nearby shack and set her down.

She tried not to faint as the blood rushed back to her head. Before she could regain her equilibrium, he lifted her up again. With her arms raised over her head, he hung her from a lag bolt that was attached to the wooden frame of the structure. She dangled there, a few inches above the ground.

Instead of retreating, he kept his lower half pressed against hers. He seemed torn between wanting to punish her and wanting to go after Owen. His big hands spanned her rib cage. Their hips were aligned, his crotch snug in the cradle of her thighs. Maybe he was more interested in payback than punishment.

Pleasure, even.

His gaze dragged up from her torso, settling on her mouth. "I should have gagged you," he said hoarsely.

She moistened her lips. "With what?"

Groaning, he buried his face in her throat. His breath was hot and heavy on her neck as he skimmed his hands down her sides. Fisting them in her tank top, he inched it over her bare breasts. Her nipples were tightly puckered, her chest rising and falling with trepidation. Despite her fear, she was aroused.

After taking a long look, he unbuttoned her jean shorts and lowered the zipper. He stripped her shorts and panties down to her knees, exposing her completely.

His nostrils flared as if he could smell her. "This was what I wanted to see at the club."

She closed her eyes and turned her head to the side. Waiting. For him to just do it, for her body to respond, for her mind to drift.

But when she opened her eyes, he was gone.

CHAPTER TWENTY-TWO

OWEN WASN'T GOING to fight Shane.

The anger left his body the instant his brother pulled the gun. With the sun at his back, Shane loomed over Owen like a dark shadow. A negative space, devoid of humanity. Owen would never forgive his brother for threatening to kill him—and Penny. Shane had been willing to sacrifice Owen for personal gain. He'd put Cruz in danger and disregarded Jamie's safety. He'd only been thinking of himself.

If his idiot brother wanted to get in a shoot-out with the guy in the black truck, so be it. Owen loved Shane, and he believed that Shane loved him back, in his own way. But Owen couldn't save Shane from himself.

"It's your funeral," Owen said.

The words had barely left his mouth when shots rang out across the playground. Shane's shoulder jerked, and he squeezed the trigger, as if on reflex. A bullet sank into the sand near Owen's head, narrowly missing him.

Shane staggered sideways, dazed. He dropped the gun and the rucksack. Then he fell flat on his back.

What the fuck?

Owen scrambled upright, searching the area from a crouched position. He couldn't see the gunman, but there was a pile of concrete debris between the shack where the Jeep was parked and the playground by the beach. It made a protective fort.

He knelt by Shane, his gut churning. His brother's face was pale, his eyes dark with pain. There were two small holes in the front of his shirt. One of the bullets appeared to have gone through his shoulder. The other had pierced his upper chest.

"Owen," he choked, blood seeping from his lips.

He grasped his brother's right hand. "I'm here," Owen said, smothering a sob. "I'm here, Shane."

"Am I shot?"

"Yeah."

"Is it bad?"

Owen couldn't find the words to comfort him. The bullet must have damaged his heart or lungs, because the end was incredibly, unfairly quick. He gripped Shane's hand tighter, as if he could hold him in this world a moment longer by force of will and determination. It didn't work. His brother exhaled a final breath, his eyes glazing over.

"No," Owen said, clutching the front of his shirt. Sorrow welled up within him, clogging his throat and nose. "Don't die," he ground out, tears sliding down his cheeks. He shook his brother's slack form, trying to wake him.

Shane's head listed to the side, lifeless.

Suddenly, Owen was enraged. "I told you to run,

you stupid bastard! I told you to leave the money! Why didn't you listen to me?"

He released the collar of Shane's shirt, wiping the tears from his eyes. His breath hitched as he realized what he should have said at the end: "I love you, too."

But now the words fell on deaf ears. Dead ears.

A man in jeans and a gray T-shirt crept across the playground, armed with a Colt 1911. This was the owner of the black truck. He was also a crack shot. Only an expert could have taken Shane down with two bullets at a hundred yards.

Owen picked up Shane's 9 mm and stood over his brother's body.

The man edged closer, holding up a hand to communicate calm. Owen figured he wasn't going to fire again unless he was fired at. A cop or an undercover agent would show his credentials. When the guy didn't do that, Owen had a tough decision to make: trade shots with a dangerous criminal who was better armed and a better marksman than he was, or let him waltz away with two million dollars.

"I don't want to shoot you," the man said.

"Then get the fuck out of here."

"I'm taking the money."

"You killed my brother," Owen said darkly.

"I saved you," the man replied. "Now step aside."

Owen considered this explanation. To an outsider, it might have looked like Shane was preparing to execute him. Even so, this man hadn't done Owen any favors. He'd acted in his own best interests, not out of concern for others. He was a paid thug for the Aryan Brotherhood or the Freedom Party, and probably a racist psychopath. The world would be a safer place without a piece of shit like him in it.

A dull banging sound echoed from the shack beyond the playground, like someone trying to kick through a door.

Owen froze, remembering the scream he'd heard minutes before. "Who's that?"

"It's Janelle," the man said, his expression inscrutable.

"Did you hurt her?"

After a pause, he said, "She's fine. I'll take the money and leave. No one will bother you or anyone in your brother's family."

The implied threat, of course, was that harm would come to Jamie and Janelle if he didn't cooperate. Owen ejected the clip from the 9 mm and removed the bullet from the chamber before tossing it aside.

"I need his keys," the man said.

Owen knelt to search Shane's pockets. When he found the keys to the Jeep, he threw them near the rucksack. The man edged forward, picking up the keys. Grabbing the bag with one hand, he started to drag it away.

Numb with grief, Owen studied the man's appearance. He was white, with blue eyes and black hair, early thirties, around six-two. The tattooed knuckles and spiderweb elbow looked jailhouse. His scarred boots, bulky shoulders and weathered skin suggested that he worked hard labor, maybe at an oil rig or at a local construction site.

The banging inside the shack stopped. Then the front wall of the structure fell apart, bringing Janelle along for the ride. She cried out, her body slamming against the sheet of loose plywood. Owen expected the whole building to collapse on top of her, but somehow the rest of the shack stayed upright.

His blood went cold as he noticed her state of undress. Her top was pushed up, her shorts around her knees. She was bound with rope.

The roughneck swore under his breath, flushing.

Owen had lost his mind a little when he'd watched Dirk strike Cruz across the face. He couldn't have stopped himself from retaliating then, and he had no control over his actions now. "Motherfucker," he growled, charging Janelle's attacker with his shoulder lowered and tackling him to the ground.

On some level, he was aware that his opponent held all of the advantages. Owen had a set of broken knuckles, a bruised body and a wrecked soul. This thug had twenty extra pounds of muscle and a semi-automatic.

The other man didn't shoot him. He didn't have to. Dropping the gun and the rucksack, he fought Owen with his bare hands.

And he won. Easily.

Although Owen managed to land a few punches, one that would result in a black eye, the bigger man was the clear victor. He pummeled Owen's torso,

socked him in the mouth and bloodied his upper lip.
By the time he was done, Owen felt as if he'd gone
bull riding and hadn't lasted eight seconds.

"Do you know what happened to Roach?" the man
asked, his fist hovering.

"Roach?"

"Tall guy, dark hair."

An ugly, vindictive part of Owen hoped the two
men were related. "I killed him," he said, still reel-
ing from the blows.

"You killed him," he repeated in disbelief.

"Did I stutter?"

"Where?"

"On the trail by Five Palms."

The man hesitated before rising, as if he wanted
to make sure Owen stayed down. An ominous click
sounded behind him.

"Stand up," Janelle said, pointing the Colt at his
head.

Hands lifted high, he stood.

"Take your damned money and go," she said,
her teeth clenched. She'd adjusted her clothing and
worked her bindings loose. The remains of the rope
she'd been tied with hung from her wrists.

The man picked up the rucksack, putting it on his
back.

"The debt's paid, right?" Janelle asked.

Clearing his throat, he nodded. "I'm sorry."

"Just get the hell out of here," she snarled, her trigger finger trembling. "If you ever come near my son, I'll shoot you."

A helicopter hovered at the edge of the horizon, not quite close enough to see them.

After a long look at Janelle, the man jogged toward the Jeep, climbed in and drove away. The dust cloud he left dispersed within seconds.

She lowered the gun, her eyes swimming with tears.

"Are you okay?" Owen asked.

"Yeah," she said, sniffing. "He didn't touch me."

Owen was glad Janelle hadn't been raped, but troubled by the evidence that she'd been tied up and stripped against her will. He cared about her and Jamie. She'd been mistreated too often, by too many men.

"Is Shane dead?" she asked.

"Yes."

Her face crumpled with sorrow. "I don't even know why I'm sad."

When she knelt down beside Owen, he put his arms around her. Shane had been a destructive force in both of their lives. Together, they mourned the passing of a man they were better off without, but whom they'd loved nonetheless.

Moments later, an explosion in the distance startled them.

Owen released Janelle and struggled to his feet. Together, they made their way toward the shack, which offered a better vantage point. The black truck

was resting on its side at the bottom of an embankment, enveloped in flames. Shane's killer must have
set the fire on his way out to destroy evidence.

"My purse," Janelle said, approaching the truck.
There was a ripped, faux-leather shoulder bag sit-
ting next to a pack of cigarettes about ten feet away.
She picked up both, glancing at the burning vehicle.
The helicopter loomed closer, fanning the flames and
whipping her hair around her head.

Owen held up his hands in surrender.

Janelle ignored the police presence, lighting one of
the cigarettes. "Do you know what Shane's cut was
supposed to be?"

"Fifty grand."

"How much was the truck worth?"

"Half that."

A trio of squad cars appeared at the end of the
dirt road, sirens blaring. They'd missed the Jeep by
two minutes.

"I hate cops," she said, taking a nervous drag.

"You don't have to talk to them."

She cupped her palm over his scraped cheek.
"Thank you for what you did. Tackling him. That
was brave."

"It was stupid."

"Yes," she agreed, teary-eyed.

He didn't get a chance to say the same to her, because a group of officers exited their vehicles, guns
drawn. Owen cooperated with every instruction.

Janelle wasn't as quick to follow orders, but they seemed to consider her a victim, rather than a suspect.

While Owen got down on the ground, she was led away by two detectives. She glanced over her shoulder, as if reluctant to lose sight of him. He winced as the officer wrenched his arms behind his back.

Cuffed—again.

"Is Penny okay?" he asked.

Instead of answering, the cop read him his rights.

PENNY'S FATHER GRABBED her by the hair and shoved a forearm under her chin, yanking her toward the surface.

She broke through with a sputtering gasp, her eyes burning. As her father struggled to free her hands from the duct tape, she slipped under again, her mouth filling with water. It was so salty she gagged.

Her father left her wrists bound and swam toward the boat with her, grabbing an orange safety vest. He put it around her neck to keep her afloat while he peeled off the duct tape. When her wrists separated, she brought her arms forward, sobbing with relief. Her shoulder muscles felt strained from the uncomfortable position.

Jorge treaded water next to her, concerned. He looked angry, but unharmed.

"Are you hurt?" she asked.

"No. Are you?"

"I'm fine."

"He shot through the boat."

The fishing vessel was still there. Shane had taken the powerboat and driven away, leaving them to sink or swim. There was another life jacket floating on the surface. Her father donned it and put his arms around her, stroking her wet hair.

Her eyes filled with tears, which helped to ease the sting of the sea. She was alive. Cruz and her father were alive. But the ordeal wasn't over yet. They were miles from shore with a useless boat. She wouldn't feel safe until she was on land, with Owen.

"Where's Owen?" her father asked.

"Shane left him handcuffed on the shore."

"He wasn't…an accomplice?"

"No," she said, offended on his behalf. Owen had saved her life repeatedly. He'd almost died for her and Cruz. "He helped us escape."

Her father swore in Spanish. "Did they hurt you?"

"No." She gave him a brief summary of the kidnapping. Although she emphasized Owen's efforts to protect her, she didn't discuss her feelings for him.

"He'll be well compensated."

Penny doubted Owen wanted anything from her father. "How's Cruz?"

"He's fine. His cheek is bruised, but I don't think he really understands what happened. He's been asking for you, of course, and he had a nightmare last night. He told me stories about trains and trestles."

"It was an adventure for him," she said. "He didn't see the killings."

"That's good."

"Are the police coming?"

"I hope so," he said, glancing up at the sky.

"They know you're here?"

"On the sea, yes. Where on the sea, no. They were following me, and trying to keep a low profile."

"What should we do?"

He inspected the boat for damage. "It will sink faster if we get in."

Swimming next to her father, she peered inside the craft. Water was seeping through the holes in the bottom, filling the hull. "Can we swim to shore?"

"If we have to."

She looked around, wondering which way to go. There was nothing but flat blue sea in every direction. And the water was so toxic. Saltier than the Pacific Ocean, saltier than Baja California's Mar de Cortez.

"They picked up Owen's mother at LAX."

"Oh?"

"She was very cooperative."

"You met her?"

"Yes. She said she'd voted for me in the primary."

Penny could only imagine the disappointment her father felt at being forced to end his candidacy. Shane and his crew hadn't just stolen his money and peace of mind. They'd taken away his lifetime dream. He'd been so close to the White House, he could taste it.

"Can you reenter the election?"

"No," he said, staring across the sea. "I wouldn't risk it anyway, but candidates aren't allowed to drop out and reenter at any point. No one has ever withdrawn *after* receiving the party nomination. I made history."

Not the way he'd planned. "I'm sorry."

"Así es la vida," he said with a shrug. *That's life.*

"Who will replace you?"

"Wendell," he said, naming the GOP runner-up, rather than his VP pick.

"The Freedom Party favorite."

"Yes."

"Owen thinks they're behind this."

"The FBI might agree with him."

Penny fell silent. She'd had mixed feelings about the campaign, but this fight wasn't fair. If the Freedom Party had ties to the Aryan Brotherhood, the whole thing had ugly racial undertones. She hadn't wanted her father to lose because his skin was brown, or because he'd refused to bow down to extremists.

Bastards.

A helicopter flew overhead, causing the water to ripple, and the sinking boat to sway. They both waved their arms at the pilot, who waved back. Penny almost expected a ladder to drop from the sky, but an air rescue wasn't necessary. Within minutes, a boat from the San Diego Department of Fish and Wildlife came to collect them.

Penny asked about Owen as she climbed the ladder, but the men aboard didn't have any information. It was a quick ride to the shore, where a team of security guards and law enforcement personnel waited.

As soon as she stepped on land, a pair of special

agents introduced themselves. They separated Penny from Jorge and proceeded to interrogate her as if she'd masterminded her own kidnapping. Apparently, they'd found security camera footage of her kissing Owen backstage. Both agents seemed to have developed a negative opinion of him, based on his criminal history and family connections.

"Just tell me if he's alive," she said, exhausted by their questions. "Please."

"He's alive. He's being treated at the hospital in El Centro."

"For what?"

"A broken hand."

She almost wept with relief. Owen was okay. As soon as they checked out her story, he'd be cleared of wrongdoing.

Wouldn't he?

Before this experience, she'd had faith in the system. She'd believed in justice and fairness and the American Dream. But, if the bad guys could fix an election, they could also frame an innocent man.

Especially one who didn't look so innocent, on record.

OWEN ASKED ABOUT PENNY again on the way to the station, his tension rising.

Hours passed before he got an answer, a hot meal and a thorough medical exam. Penny and her father were fine. Owen had broken one of the bones in his right hand. When he made a fist, the outermost knuckle disappeared.

At El Centro Medical Center, a technician X-rayed his hand, confirming the break. A doctor reset the bone and taped the knuckle to its neighbor. Owen wouldn't regain full use of his right hand for several weeks.

He considered himself lucky to have sustained only minor injuries. His knuckles throbbed, his jaw hurt like hell and his face was pulverized, but he'd be all right. Compared to Shane, he was in good shape. When Owen was finally allowed a phone call, he dialed his mother to deliver the bad news.

She'd wept silently on the other end, devastated. "Do you want me to come get you?"

"I don't think I'm free to go, Mom."

"Why not?"

Because there was a uniformed officer sitting in a chair outside, guarding the door of his hospital room. "They have some more questions to ask me," he said. Promising to call her back in a few hours, he hung up.

Moments later, Jorge Sandoval paid him a visit. He was alone, wearing the wrinkled clothes he'd removed earlier. His face seemed to have aged four years in the past four days. Even before the kidnapping, stress from the campaign had worn him down.

"How are you?" he asked Owen, his dark eyes watchful.

"How's Penny?"

"Alive, thanks to you. She went home to Cruz."

"Good."

"I'm sorry for your loss."

Owen nodded, already uneasy with this sentiment. Sandoval made him uncomfortable. Penny's father had never treated him like an equal. Why should he? Owen was a convicted felon with an unfortunate history and an uncertain future. There was no need to pretend they were on the same level. But the way Sandoval looked at him now was different. He seemed to respect Owen as a significant threat.

"The police are investigating to see if your story checks out."

"I told the truth, so it should."

"We still have a problem."

"What's that?"

"The details of the case will be kept confidential, for your protection. But the media will publish some of your personal information, including your mug shot."

Owen should have figured as much. He didn't think he had to worry about the Aryan Brotherhood coming after him, though. Even if someone recognized his name and photo, he wasn't going to be working for Sandoval anymore.

The campaign was over.

"The story is too big to bury. There will be widespread speculation about you and Penny, especially if you're seen in public together. They'll say she has Stockholm syndrome."

Owen clenched his jaw. "I'm not a kidnapper."

"You have a criminal record."

"You knew that when you hired me."

Mouth twisting, Sandoval continued, "It's no secret that my daughter has become fond of you. You're a hero to her, climbing out of the rubble after the San Diego earthquake, rescuing her and Cruz from... scum. You're either very brave, or very stupid."

Although Owen had said the same thing to Janelle earlier today, he didn't like hearing it as an insult.

"It would be foolish to read too much into anything Penny has done or said over the course of this ordeal. She's a victim, having a natural response to a terrifying situation. Her emotions are running high."

Owen didn't bother to dispute him.

"Do you really think you're the best she can do?"

"It's *her* decision."

"And she needs time to sort things out. Keep your distance and I'll give you that letter of recommendation you asked for."

"The letter you already promised?"

"It was conditional. I'm assuming you violated the physical-contact stipulation, but I'm willing to let that slide."

Owen resented Sandoval's attempts to keep him and Penny apart. Before the kidnapping, he hadn't felt worthy of her. Now he was willing to fight anyone for her—even her father. He'd rather walk away without the letter of recommendation than walk away from her. He didn't need Sandoval's approval; he only wanted Penny's heart.

"In return for your discretion, I'll sing your praises to the authorities," Sandoval said. "I'll make sure they treat you and your mother well."

"My mother?"

"She's an accessory to the kidnapping. Instead of calling the police, she put my grandson in a taxicab."

He flushed with anger. "My brother was responsible for that, not her."

"I don't think it will be necessary to press charges."

"As long as I cooperate," Owen said flatly.

"Shall we shake on it?"

He hesitated before extending his left hand. "How long do I have to stay away from her?"

"A month."

"After that, if she's still interested, you'll back off?"

"Of course."

Damned snake-oil salesman. Owen shook his hand.

CHAPTER TWENTY-THREE

One week later

"Drop us off down the block, will you?"

Keshawn murmured an affirmative, circling around the funeral parlor in Brawley rather than parking out front. He'd apologized profusely for "failing Penny" during the kidnapping. She'd squeezed his shoulder and waved off his concerns. Owen hadn't been able to prevent the attack, either.

The perpetrators were dead. It was done.

Although the investigation was ongoing, suspicions against Owen had eased. Law enforcement officers had found the two surviving crew members, Jerome Gardener and Brett Peters, in Mexico. Both men had corroborated Owen's story. Brett's gunshot wound was convincing evidence to Owen's lack of cooperation with the kidnappers. Penny's statements, as well as those from Shane's ex-girlfriend, had helped exonerate him.

Her father's money hadn't been recovered. The man who'd killed Shane had disappeared without a trace. Police had lifted a partial set of fingerprints from the handgun he'd left behind, but they were unable to find a match. The burnt-out vehicle offered few clues, having been registered under a fake name.

The FBI was still looking into connections between the Aryan Brotherhood and the Freedom Party. The current GOP candidate, Wendell, had been exonerated, but he was falling way behind in the polls.

Thanks to leaked information about the case, the American public was more fascinated with the Sandoval family than ever. Owen's mug shot had been widely circulated. The media had painted him as an unlikely hero, a reformed criminal who'd changed his ways.

Her father came out smelling like a rose, as well. His forced withdrawal was labeled a Grand Injustice, the antithesis of the American Dream. Even Democrats were outraged, and as quick as always to suspect racism within the Republican Party. Her father's supporters had been chanting his name at Wendell's rallies. The new candidate had called last night and invited her father to be his running mate.

He'd accepted.

Penny didn't know if her father's involvement would make a difference in the long run, but she'd be glad to see his name on the ticket.

She climbed out of the limo with Cruz, holding his hand. It had been a long drive, and he was restless. Maybe he was too young to understand death or attend the ceremony, but he'd begged to come along. He hadn't seen Owen since the kidnapping.

Neither had Penny.

She also couldn't bear to part with Cruz for the entire day. When she'd returned from the Salton Sea, she'd hugged him close, weeping. He'd started kindergarten last week. She was feeling a touch of separation anxiety.

Keshawn stayed with the car while Penny walked down the sidewalk, her heels clicking with each step. She'd taken pains with her appearance despite the weather. She hoped her silk blouse and linen skirt wouldn't wilt in the heat.

A woman drove by in a car with what appeared to be a garbage bag taped over the window. She glanced at Penny and the limo before turning into the funeral home parking lot. So much for her incognito entrance. None of the other attendees lived a life of luxury, and Penny hadn't wanted to rub her wealth in their faces. She'd have driven herself, but her father had insisted that someone accompany her for safety reasons. It was either Keshawn or a bodyguard. She'd picked Keshawn.

The woman with the broken window entered the funeral home at the same time as Penny and Cruz. She had a lanky, sullen boy with her. He had a mop of brown hair and familiar blue eyes. He was wearing a short-sleeved shirt, ill-fitting trousers and a crooked tie. His mother was only a few inches taller than him.

"You must be Jamie," Penny said.

The boy looked from her to Cruz. "Who are you?"

"I'm Penny and this is Cruz."

"Janelle," his mother said, extending her slim hand.

She was pretty and petite, with dark hair and freckles. Big sunglasses hid half her face.

"I'm sorry for your loss," Penny said.

With a curt nod, Janelle ushered Jamie inside. Her black minidress and wedge sandals showed off a slender figure. There was a tattoo on her left ankle.

Penny followed her inside, where she waited to sign the guest book. Owen was standing with his mother nearby, greeting people. He was wearing a gray suit with a striped tie. There was a faded bruise on his jaw, and his right hand was taped.

Cruz wiggled away from Penny and went running to Owen. It was rude, but Owen didn't seem to mind. He lifted Cruz up and hugged him.

"Do you want to sign?" Janelle asked her son.

Jamie tore his gaze away from Owen and Cruz. While he scrawled his name, Penny stepped out of line to retrieve Cruz.

"Sorry," she said.

"It's okay."

"My father sends his regards."

Owen set Cruz back down without comment, his eyes traveling up her body. He looked tall and stoic and breathtakingly handsome. They'd spoken on the phone a few times this week, but their stilted conversations had left her feeling melancholy. He'd been staying at his mother's house, handling the funeral arrangements. She was torn between wanting to comfort him and giving him time to grieve.

This wasn't the place to discuss their relationship,

so she kissed his taut cheek, murmured hello to his mother and tugged Cruz into the main parlor.

To her relief, the casket was closed. A childhood photograph of Owen and Shane had been blown up and put on display. The boys were about six and nine, grinning at the camera. They were both suntanned and towheaded, wearing shorts on the Salton Sea beach. Shane held up a large fish on a line.

Penny studied it for a moment, not recognizing this boy in the troubled man who'd pushed her off a boat.

The ceremony was brief, full of vague praise and empty platitudes. Like the photograph, it didn't fit. She sympathized with Owen's mother, wondering if she held the opposite perspective. Perhaps she was mourning the smiling boy on the beach, not the hardened criminal her son had become.

After the service, they went to the cemetery for the burial. Penny offered Sally and Owen a ride in her limo. When they accepted, she extended the invitation to Janelle. It seemed appropriate to include her and Jamie.

At Brawley Cemetery, they stood by the plot to watch the casket get lowered. Owen's mother put some flowers on top. Owen added a shovelful of dirt. Janelle used her hand, letting the soft dirt fall through her fingertips. Then she dusted off her palms in an unconscious "good riddance" gesture.

For his turn, Jamie picked up a hard clod and pitched it at the casket like a baseball. The angry, frustrated action brought tears to Penny's eyes. Jamie looked around with a rebellious expression, as if expecting to be chastised.

No one said a word.

The crowd milled about the cemetery for another thirty minutes while Owen's mother accepted condolences. Cruz ran around, climbing trees and letting off steam. He seemed to want to play with Jamie, who ignored him.

Penny walked toward a family vault, sensing a human presence. Janelle was crouched down behind it, cigarette in hand.

"Who are you hiding from?"

"The law."

"I think it's still legal to smoke outdoors in California."

"Is it?" She squinted one eye as she lit up. "I can't keep track."

Penny could see Cruz playing with one of his action figures in the shade of an oak tree. About ten feet away, Jamie picked up an old bouquet from a grave site and drop-kicked it. The arrangement flew high into the air.

"Your son is very...athletic."

Janelle followed her gaze. "He's angry with me. He didn't know Shane had been released from prison. I'd refused to let him visit."

"Seems like that was a good decision."

"Yeah, well. He doesn't agree."

"I'm sorry."

Janelle shrugged, taking another drag of her cigarette.

Penny wanted to ask her how she was coping, not just with her son's feelings, but with her own response to the traumatic experience. The topic seemed too intrusive for complete strangers, however.

"Where's your entourage?" Janelle asked.

"Entourage?"

"Paparazzi, bodyguards…"

"I have Keshawn," Penny said, gesturing toward the limo driver. "Photographers don't usually follow me around. They just show up for big public events. This is a private ceremony, and it's a long drive from L.A."

Janelle blew out a puff of smoke. "Are you and Owen dating?"

"Did he tell you that?"

"No."

"We're sort of on hold," Penny admitted.

"What are you waiting for?"

"He lost his brother. He's distraught."

"So, comfort him."

Penny glanced across the grounds, where Owen was standing with his mother. After the kidnapping, she'd made a vow to start living for herself. To tell Owen how she felt. But the idea of taking the next step scared her, even after everything they'd been through. He was so guarded. If she declared her love to him, he might bolt.

"Seduce him," Janelle said, being more specific.

Penny perked up at this suggestion. She could do that. "Okay."

Janelle laughed, shaking her head.

"What?"

"Nothing. You two are cute. Clueless, but cute."

Her cheeks heated at the mild criticism. Penny might be sheltered and inexperienced, but she wasn't a complete innocent. She knew Owen wanted her as much as she wanted him. His desire would be easy to stoke. They didn't have to *talk*.

Janelle stubbed out her cigarette. "Just don't let him get away. Guys like Owen are one in a million. Believe me, I know."

OWEN WATCHED PENNY APPROACH, his heart racing.

He'd known her for years, but he was still knocked out by her beauty. Surprised by it, as if she didn't always look good. Today she looked especially good, with her pinned-up hair and body-hugging skirt.

He couldn't help staring, even at his brother's funeral. His mother noticed and squeezed his arm before she walked away.

Penny flashed a nervous smile, her eyes wandering across the breadth of his shoulders. "You clean up nice."

He smoothed his tie, self-conscious. "So do you."

"How's your hand?"

"Better," he said, glancing at his taped knuckles. For the first few days, he couldn't even close his fist.

"When are you coming back to L.A.?"

"Tomorrow."

"Can I see you?"

An image of their bodies entwined in the shower sprang to mind. "Sure," he said, her father's warning buried under a barrage of hot memories. He couldn't say no to Penny. With a flutter of her eyelashes or a nervous lip-nibble, she turned him into mush.

"I'll come over to your place," she said. "Unless you want to meet somewhere."

Meet somewhere, for the love of God, or you'll be on top of her the second she walks through the door. "My place is fine."

"Great," she said, tucking a stray lock of hair behind her ear. "We can talk."

Talking was a good idea. He should probably tell her about her father's latest scheme. Now that a week had gone by, he wasn't as worried about the arrest threats. He still needed the letter of recommendation, but not if it meant giving up Penny.

One of his weird uncles interrupted them, so she said goodbye and walked away. When Owen unglued his eyes from the back of her skirt, he caught sight of Janelle in the distance. She gave him a suggestive okay sign, indicating that Penny was prime stuff. Neck warming, he tried to focus on his uncle's condolences.

"Thanks for coming," Owen said, patting the man's shoulder.

He'd promised Janelle he would talk to Jamie, so he headed in the boy's direction. Cruz was playing under a tree while Jamie threw rocks at grave markers. He had a damned good arm. When Cruz saw Owen, he ran toward him, his shirttails flapping.

Smiling, Owen ruffled the little boy's hair.

"I'm sorry about your brother," Cruz said.

"Thanks, bud."

"Are you sad?"

"Yes."

"Like when your dad died?"

Owen nodded, although this situation was far more difficult. His father's death had been a relief in many ways. His brother's was not. Shane had only been twenty-nine, and he'd left behind a son who deserved better.

Jamie continued to throw rocks, his mouth tense. Cruz followed his gaze. "Is that boy sad?"

"I'm sure he is."

"Was your brother a good dad?"

"No, he wasn't."

Cruz turned back to Owen, solemn.

"How's kindergarten?"

"I like it."

"Is your teacher nice?"

"Uh-huh," Cruz said. Then his eyes lit up with an idea. "There's a boy in my class who has two dads."

Owen studied his eager little face. Cruz seemed to expect Owen to celebrate this news. "Two dads?"

"His stepdad came to pick him up from school yesterday. He's just like a real dad."

"Ah."

Cruz had to spell it out for him. "You could be my stepdad."

"I'd have to marry your mom to be your stepdad."

His brow furrowed, as if he hadn't figured on this complication. "Well, you like her, and she likes you. You can marry her."

"I should probably ask her first."

"All right."

"I'll work on that," Owen promised. "But no matter what happens with your mom, you'll always be my little man, okay?"

"Okay."

He ruffled Cruz's hair again and walked away, his chest tight. He had to pace himself, emotionally. The conversation with Jamie was sure to be gut-wrenching.

His nephew waited for him to approach, a rock clenched in his fist. He was acting out for attention, disrespecting headstones because he felt cheated by death. Owen understood and didn't blame him.

"How's it going?" Owen asked.

"Fine."

"You look angry."

Jamie let the rock fall from his fist, sullen. "He tried to call when he got out of prison. My mom wouldn't let him talk to me."

"She was protecting you."

"From what?"

"Getting hurt by him."

Jamie didn't reply to this. His body language conveyed pure misery. He'd gotten hurt anyway.

"It's okay to be sad," Owen said.

"I'm not sad," Jamie insisted. "He was a fucking loser."

Owen stuck his hands in his pockets, contemplative. He couldn't dispute the second statement, though he doubted the first. If Jamie felt nothing for Shane, he wouldn't be so angry with his mother for keeping them apart.

"I'm never going to be like him."

"I saw your soccer game yesterday," Owen said, changing the subject.

"You did?"

He hadn't stayed to say hello because he'd been too choked up. Overwhelmed by childhood memories, he'd walked away from the bleachers in anguish. "You're a forward. Shane was, too."

Jamie frowned at this information. "What about you?"

"I played defense, but not very well. I wasn't aggressive enough. Shane was a little too aggressive. But you…you're just right."

The boy stared at the grave markers he'd been using for target practice, his blue eyes filling with tears. He strongly resembled Shane, whether he liked it or not. His looks, his speed, his physical presence on the field. "Will you come again next weekend?"

Owen said he would.

CHAPTER TWENTY-FOUR

HE CLEANED HIS APARTMENT in anticipation of Penny's visit.

His injured hand made things difficult, but he wrestled with new sheets, washed the laundry and put away the dishes. Cooking a romantic meal was beyond his capabilities. Instead, he showered and pulled on casual clothes, his nerves on edge.

What would he say to her?

The doorbell rang before he was ready. He went to let her in, his heart tripping at the sight of her. She was wearing a short, flower-print dress with buttons down the front. Her hair was in a sweet ponytail. Even her sandals were sexy. She looked good enough to eat. He shut the door behind her, trying not to stare.

She'd never been here before. He'd called her cell with the address.

"So," she said, crossing her arms over her chest. "This is your place."

It wasn't much, he knew. The space was cramped. He'd forgotten to put the mail away, and there was a pile of newspapers on the coffee table. He didn't offer to give her a tour, because the kitchen was in full view of the living room, and showing her his bedroom seemed suggestive. "Do you want to go out to dinner?"

"No," she said. "Unless you're hungry."

Not for food. He shook his head.

She sat down on the couch, bouncing to test its comfort. The half-buttoned bodice of her dress gaped open, revealing more of her breasts than usual. He moved his gaze to her legs, but that area wasn't safe, either. The skirt rode high on her thighs.

He took a seat next to her, determined to keep his eyes on her face. Unfortunately, her mouth was right there. Tempting him.

She moistened her lips, nervous. "The service was nice."

"It was a joke." The funeral director had spoken of Shane in glowing terms, as if he'd been a swell guy.

"Your mother appreciated it."

He couldn't argue that.

"Did you invite any of the earthquake survivors?"

"No. They didn't know him."

"They know you."

He shrugged, looking away. Funerals were awkward and unpleasant. His friends should thank him for the non-invite. It was a long drive to pay respects to a stranger.

Penny made a sympathetic noise and lifted her hand to his neck, massaging the tense muscle there. It was tense because she was touching him, but he didn't ask her to stop. Her breasts plumped against his triceps, drawing his attention. Blood pooled to his groin as he realized what she was doing.

"Janelle said I should comfort you," she murmured, slipping her other arm around his shoulder.

He turned his head toward her. "How?"

"Like this," she said, brushing her lips over his.

He wanted to kiss her and touch her, to bury his tongue in her mouth and slide between her thighs. She might let him. If he didn't have a flashback, they'd have a good time. Even if he did, they could start over, try again. The fear of failure didn't paralyze him as much as it used to. He already knew he could make her come. It was deliciously easy.

She kissed his bruised jaw and the tattoo scar on his neck. "We don't have to…you know. I can do the same thing that other girl did."

"What?"

"I can touch myself," she said in his ear.

He groaned at the thought.

Taking that as a yes, she fumbled with the buttons on her dress. It fell open, exposing a dark pink bra with a lacy border. He could see her nipples through the sheer fabric. His mouth watered to taste her.

"Wait," he said, stilling her hands.

"What's wrong?"

"I have to tell you something."

"Am I being too slutty?"

He couldn't help but laugh. "No. I love it."

She closed the edges of her dress, uncertain.

"Everything you do turns me on, Penny. You're

incredibly sexy. I'd give a year of my life to watch you touch yourself."

"Don't say that."

"Your father told me to stay away from you."

Her mouth dropped open. "You aren't his employee anymore."

That was true. He'd been released from service. His savings and severance pay were enough to get by on for a while. Owen summarized his conversation with her father at the hospital, not mentioning the threat against his mother.

"Are they going to bring you up on charges?" she asked.

"I don't think so."

"Forget my father," she said, dismissive.

"I gave him my word."

"But he broke his by withholding the recommendation letter."

"I broke the contract by touching you."

She thought about that for a minute. "What we did is none of his business."

Owen conceded her point, smiling.

She let go of her dress and wrapped her arms around his neck again. "If the letter means that much to you, we won't tell him we're together for another month."

"You don't mind sneaking around?"

"It's better than waiting."

He agreed, settling in to kiss her. Although he could have waited much longer—he'd already been

waiting five years—he didn't feel obligated to keep
his promise to her father. In the past, Sandoval's insults and intimidation tactics might have worked. His
assurance that Penny could do better would have reso-
nated deeper. But this experience had changed Owen
fundamentally, just as going to prison had.

He wasn't the same man he'd been when he came
out.

Shane had been right about their childhood. Owen
was more sensitive to their father's violent outbursts.
Christian Jackson had tried to beat all the kindness
out of him, but he couldn't. Owen hadn't turned out
like his brother, hardened and cold. The tender side
of him, the one that his father considered cowardly,
had stayed true.

Until he went to prison.

There, he'd transformed. Doing time had scrubbed
every hint of softness from him. He couldn't rely on
Shane to protect him anymore, so he was forced to go
on the offensive. After the attack in the shower, he'd
built a wall of hate around himself. He'd become as
tough and masculine as possible, because predators
attacked vulnerability. They'd seen him as weak and
called him pretty.

During his incarceration, he'd made some friends.
He'd had good days. But overall it was a hell he'd endured by selling his soul to the Aryan Brotherhood.
His only bright spot had been Penny. The moment
he'd seen her after the earthquake, he'd been floored

by her beauty. Even heavily pregnant, she'd been like a ray of light.

Her gentle friendship had chipped away at his protective shell. Her desire for him had boosted his self-confidence. Her unconditional acceptance had eased his shame and pain so much he hardly felt it anymore. And now he had a new shower memory, a damned good one, to help wash away the horror.

It wasn't just Penny, either. His mother's sobriety had held strong through the past week. She'd given him hope for the future. Jamie and Janelle had shown him that he could form meaningful relationships. He'd made a difference in their lives.

And Cruz. That little boy wanted Owen to be his dad. If Owen was worthy of this honor, he was worthy of anything.

Sandoval would never accept Owen into his family, and that was okay. The people Owen cared about knew he was a good guy, Janelle included. He valued an exotic dancer's opinion more than a shady politician's.

He wasn't sure how to tell Penny any of these things. Maybe it was too soon to say he loved her. So he just showed her.

The first kiss was tentative, a brief meeting of lips. He liked the shape of her mouth, lush and full under his. He liked the warmth of her breasts against his chest, the tug of her hands in his hair. Wrapping his arm around her waist, he urged her closer. She slid her thigh across his lap, close to his swelling erection.

Their tongues met and tangled. Her mouth was deliciously sweet and receptive, inviting him to sink deeper. But he broke the contact, unsure of himself. A hint of anxiety wavered at the edge of his mind. Not unbearable, not insurmountable. The mild, pleasurable ache behind his fly seemed more pressing.

"We can just kiss for a while," Penny murmured, her lips brushing the corner of his mouth. "I could lick you…."

His cock jumped to the conclusion that she meant licking him there, swirling her tongue around the swollen tip. The idea was so erotic, he felt lightheaded. He'd probably explode before she even started.

He kissed her again, harder. Not holding back this time, he thrust his tongue into her mouth in a conscious parody of sex. She moaned and rubbed her breasts against him, not put off by his crudeness. She wanted this. She wanted *him*.

Although he intended to take her to his bedroom and attempt any sexual acts she would agree to, he ended the kiss in hopes of hearing more of her suggestions. "What else?"

Her eyes were half-lidded, smoky with arousal. "I liked what you did in the shower."

He didn't know which part she meant, but he'd do whatever she wanted. He'd taste every inch of her. Returning his mouth to hers, he smoothed his palm up her thigh. The bandage over his knuckles impeded him, but only a little. Her skin was like silk, her mouth wet and hungry, her body straining toward his.

She shifted in his lap, straddling him. Groaning, he slid his hands beneath her skirt, cupping her mostly bare bottom. The panties she was wearing felt very brief. He wanted to see her from behind, to study the fabric between her cheeks. She rubbed herself along his fly, driving him crazy with lust.

Jesus. He wasn't going to last.

"Wait," he said again, panting against her neck. When she wiggled her ass, he squeezed it once more and let go.

"Should we slow down?"

"Unh," he replied, caveman-style. His cock was rock-hard, and she was sitting on it. Coherent speech was beyond him.

She unfastened the remaining buttons on her dress, letting it fall open. Owen stared at her dusky nipples and luscious breasts, her sleek stomach and curvy hips. Her dark pink panties matched her bra. The sheer fabric clung damply to the lips of her sex.

"Oh, God," he said, closing his eyes.

"What's wrong?"

He gritted his teeth. Moving slowly, so he didn't explode, he lifted her off his lap. "I don't want to go too fast."

"Can you do it more than once?"

"Yeah."

"How many times?"

He shrugged. "Five."

"Five, really?"

That was his teenage record, but he felt massively horny right now. He might be able to break it.

"Two is the most for me," she said.

"By yourself?"

She shook her head. "With you."

"You've never gotten off twice in a row on your own?"

"No," she said, smiling. "I didn't know I could."

The casual admission was incredibly hot. He swallowed hard, his balls throbbing with the need to climax.

"It doesn't matter if you come fast," she said, leaning back against the couch cushions and slipping her hand between her legs, finding the wet spot. "Let's both do it now and get it out of the way."

He was tempted. He'd fantasized about watching her strip naked and touch herself while he stroked his cock. But this wasn't the shower stall. He'd finish ten minutes before her. That didn't seem gentlemanly.

"No," he said, adjusting his fly.

Her hand stilled. "No?"

"I want to be the one to touch you. I want to try to get inside you first."

"You do?"

"Yeah."

She seemed in favor of his idea. Cheeks flushed, she rose to her feet with him. He led her to his room, turning on the lamp by the bed. While he was there, he took the box of condoms from the drawer in the nightstand. He'd bought them for this occasion.

Climbing across his navy blue comforter on her hands and knees, she picked up the box. "Twelve," she said, lying down on her back. Her dark hair spread across his pillow. "Is that enough?"

"I can go out for more."

"I hope they're not too small for you."

The regular size fit him fine. "You're flattering me."

"Do you like it?"

"Yes," he said, tossing the box aside and stretching out on top of her. She lifted her lips to his for a deep, penetrative kiss. They were getting good at kissing. He didn't hesitate to plunge his tongue into her mouth, again and again.

When she slipped her hands underneath his shirt, he tensed for a fraction of a second. Then he focused on the feel of her fingertips gliding across his torso, exploring his muscles as if she found them exciting. She tugged his shirt over his head and pushed him on to his back, trailing kisses across his chest.

Her lips paused at the Cruz tribute. "When are you going to get a tattoo of my name?"

He hadn't planned on having more ink done, but the idea appealed to him. "Where do you want it?"

She smiled, as if she thought he was kidding. "I like this place," she said, tracing the underside of his arm.

"By my armpit?"

"Your armpits are sexy."

"If you say so."

"Or here." She splayed her hand over his rib cage. "In cursive, written sideways."

Rib tattoos hurt like hell, but he'd do it for her.

She kissed his clenched stomach, which was already occupied. "This is nice," she said, licking his hip bone. His dick throbbed for the same attention. She gave it to him, pressing her lips to the erection straining the front of his jeans.

"There, too?"

"No," she said, laughing. "I like that the way it is."

So did he. Threading his hand through her hair, he pulled her back up to his mouth, kissing her curved lips. "I love you, Penny," he said, unable to keep it inside another moment. "I've loved you for so long."

She stared at him in wonder. Her eyes filled with tears, and he held his breath, worried that he'd blown it. "I love you, too."

He couldn't believe his ears. "What?"

"I love you, too," she said, sniffling. "I don't know how long it's been. I've wanted you for years, but I didn't realize I was in love with you until Shane separated us. When he demanded that I tell him how I felt about you, I choked."

"It's okay," he said, hugging her closer. "You didn't do anything wrong."

"Maybe it would have turned out different…."

"No. Don't blame yourself." He kissed the tears from her eyes, amazed by the revelation. She was in love with him? Penny Sandoval, the most beautiful woman in the world, was in love with him, Owen Jackson?

Un-fucking-believable.

Instead of questioning it too much, he sought to make himself useful. Maybe if he knocked her socks off with his performance, she'd keep loving him. It couldn't hurt.

He wanted to be on top, but his injured hand impeded him, so he brought her to the edge of the bed. Unbuttoning his fly, he knelt on the carpet before her and kissed her shoulder. Her bra strap fell down her slender arm.

"Do you want me to take it off?" she asked.

"Not yet," he said, cupping her breasts. They filled his hands, and he had big hands. Her brown nipples thrust against the sheer pink nylon. He put his open mouth to her, sucking her through the fabric. When she moaned, twisting her fingers in his hair, he sucked her other nipple, aroused by the sight of the damp cloth on her skin. She was wet between her legs, too. He pushed her sleek thighs wider to look.

She squirmed at his intimate perusal, her chest rising and falling with rapid breaths. Stimulating her nipples through the fabric had worked. He kissed her quivering inner thigh, inhaling her womanly scent. The pretty, swollen lips of her sex were parted. He kissed her gently, swirling his tongue around her clitoris.

Gasping, she tilted her hips toward him, as if seeking firmer contact. He licked harder, pressing down with his tongue. She threw her head back with a groan, bracing her hands on the mattress behind her.

He didn't rush. He loved the little sounds she was making, the way she pressed herself against his mouth. The erotic challenge of holding her at the edge of orgasm appealed to him. But he also wanted a deeper taste. Sliding his hand up her thigh, he tugged aside the damp fabric covering her sex. If he stroked the nub of her clit, she'd come.

"Finger yourself," he said, his voice hoarse.

She took off her bra first, freeing her gorgeous breasts. Then she pushed his hands away and stood, stripping those sweet panties down her hips. Resuming the position, she splayed her perfect thighs for him and slid one finger inside.

This was the kind of penetration that had triggered a flashback. Watching her, he felt only lust and anticipation. When she removed her finger, he brought it to his mouth and sucked, holding her gaze.

"I want you inside me," she said, her expression pained.

He felt the same ache to come, the driving need to become one with her. Heart racing, he replaced her finger with his, testing her snug heat. "Jesus," he said, shuddering as he withdrew. "You're so wet."

She grabbed the condoms and tore open a package with her teeth. Doing the honors, she rolled it down his stiff erection. Her mouth formed a sexy moue as she squeezed him, murmuring her approval.

He placed the blunt tip against her, dizzy from exhilaration. With a kiss for luck, he slid forward, inch by inch.

She panted against his mouth, clinging to him. "Okay?"

A jerk of his hips answered the question for him. He thrust into her with no finesse, no tenderness. "Sorry," he groaned, lost in sensation. "You feel so good."

She wrapped her legs around his waist. "Yes."

"Yes?"

"More."

He withdrew a little, his teeth clenched. The surface of the condom was shiny and slick from her. She was so hot, so slippery and swollen. He plunged in again, hearing her moisture, imagining it against his bare skin.

Owen forgot about her pleasure and took his. Gripping her bottom, he pounded into her, slamming hard and deep, pumping away like a maniac. Her breasts bounced with each thrust, which mesmerized him utterly. She made a sexy little fuck-me sound every time his pelvis bumped into hers.

It was over in the blink of an eye. Two minutes, tops. He tried to last, but she felt like heaven, and he was too far gone. With a hoarse cry, he plunged to the hilt, his shoulders quaking from the power of his release.

When he returned to reality, he became aware of the tension in her body. Her fingernails bit into his nape, and her breath huffed against his neck. Her spine was slightly arched, seeking the satisfaction he'd denied her.

"You didn't…?"

"No," she said, her breasts lifting.

"Sorry," he said, chagrined. "That wasn't the plan at all."

"Don't apologize. Just touch me."

Still buried inside her, he cupped her lovely breasts, sweeping his thumbs over her puckered nipples. Her inner muscles fluttered around his cock, which hadn't softened much. He looked down at where their bodies were joined, curious. Placing his thumb over her clitoris, he moved in slow circles. "Like this?"

"Yes."

After a minute, he realized that his mindless banging had used up some of her moisture. He licked the pad of his thumb and repeated the same motion, with better results. She moaned, rocking her hips. He studied her face, enthralled by the sight of her sensual abandon. When she came apart, he felt it. Her thighs quivered, and her sheath gripped him like a silky fist. She cried out his name, bucking against him. He groaned at the sweet pulse of her flesh as his cock hardened inside her, ready for more.

When the tremors subsided, Penny opened her eyes. Aware of his renewed arousal, she glanced down. "Again?"

"If you want," he said, hopeful. "I can do better."

She laughed, hugging his neck. "You were perfect."

It had been the best sex of his life, so he didn't argue. "I should probably...get a new condom."

"Good idea."

He closed his hand around the base of his penis and pulled out. After disposing of the used condom, he came back to bed and donned another.

"Where were we?" she asked.

"Right here," he murmured, sliding back into her.

He lasted longer this time, and moved slower, discovering new ways to make her moan. He learned every inch of her body, and she explored his. They experimented with taste and touch and different positions. When she climbed on top, he felt a mild panic, which she eased with a lingering kiss. "I love you, Owen."

For those words, he'd brave anything. Face any obstacle, fight any demon.

"I love you, too," he said, his throat tight. Pushing aside the pain and trauma of his past, he focused on the present. There was only pleasure, only Penny. He took the solace she offered and gave his entire self in return.

He was hers, body and soul, forever.

CHAPTER TWENTY-FIVE

"WHAT WILL YOU DO if my father doesn't write you that letter?"

Owen rolled on to his stomach, mumbling his response into the pillow. He'd made good on his vow to do better, so good that Penny finally had to shove him away in exhaustion, overstimulated but happy.

He loved her; she loved him. They both loved Cruz. This was going to work out.

"Seriously," she said, nudging his shoulder.

"I'll get by."

"How?"

He lifted his head, resting his weight on his elbows. "Well, I won't have a chance with the LAFD. It's too competitive. I have some firefighter contacts in San Diego, but that's also a tough market."

"Where else could you go?"

"I'd have to be open to travel anywhere in California. Even then I might not get an offer. They don't want convicted felons in public safety jobs."

"They hired you at Sierra National Park."

"I could go back there. I like rescue work."

Penny frowned at this answer. She didn't want

Owen to leave L.A. The Sierras were rugged and iso-lated. "What about private security?"

"Iffy, without references. And I don't really like it."

"You're good at it."

He shrugged. "Worst-case scenario, I can get a job welding or in auto mechanics. I know how to fix things. I'm handy."

She stretched out on her back, contemplative. It troubled her to think of Owen living in the sticks or taking odd jobs for low pay. His calm acceptance of the situation only served to emphasize the dif-ferences between them. He expected hardships, and met them with equanimity. She expected fairness and smooth sailing.

He kissed her cheek. "Don't worry. I'll take care of you."

She sighed, clutching the sheets to her chest. He was so handsome, with his disheveled hair and sleepy blue eyes. He'd overcome so much. She be-lieved him capable of anything. "Should I get a tat-too, you think?"

"No."

"Why not?"

"Your skin is flawless."

She compared her arm to his, noting the different shades. "You don't want your name on my body?"

His gaze traveled south, studying her curves. "There is one place...."

"Where?"

To her surprise, he grasped her hand and brought it to his lips, kissing her ring finger. "Here."

She flushed at the romantic gesture. Before she could form a response, he stripped away the sheet and marked a few other choice locations. She dissolved into giggles, her tummy quivering from his kisses.

When he was done tormenting her, he drew her into his arms and fell asleep, his face buried in her hair. She longed to drift off with him, but she couldn't stay. Her sister was babysitting Cruz, and they both had school in the morning. Easing out of the bed, she pulled her clothes on. Before she reached for the bed-side lamp, she took a long look at Owen, her chest swelling with love for him. He was lying on his stomach, one knee bent, his arms tucked under the pillow. The clover on his well-muscled back proclaimed him lucky. He'd certainly been blessed with a strong body, a quick mind and a pure heart.

Switching off the light, she slipped out of the room. Her purse was sitting on the coffee table next to a stack of mail. When she picked it up, she accidentally knocked a few letters off the edge. As she knelt to replace them, she saw a letter from her father. His return address was scrawled on the corner of the envelope. Maybe he'd had an attack of conscience and sent the recommendation early.

She tore it open, her pulse racing. This correspondence *was* her business. Owen had saved her life and promised to take care of her. She felt obligated to protect him, in return. He needed an ally against her father.

The letter inside wasn't a recommendation to the LAFD. It was an employment offer from Chief Pritchard of the Mendocino County Fire Department in Northern California. Mendocino County was hundreds of miles from here, farther away than Sierra National Park. There was a check attached to the offer, with a brief note from her father:

> An opportunity and a bonus, per our last conversation. I'm deeply sorry for your loss. Thank you for all you've done for Penny.
> JS

"Son of a bitch," she said, dropping the contents on the table. The check offered a generous sum, too sizable to ignore. Without waking up Owen, she walked out the front door, locking it behind her. The drive home took less than ten minutes.

She seethed the whole time, her hands clenched around the steering wheel.

How could her father do this to her? And *why?*

As soon as she parked in their huge garage, she got out and stormed into the house, her heels clicking on the granite flooring. Her parents had a dinner party scheduled this evening. Penny entered the dining room, interrupting dessert.

"I need to speak with you," she told her father in Spanish.

Her mother stared at her with dismay. Penny realized how she must look: hair mussed, dress hastily buttoned. She probably appeared to have been doing exactly what she'd been doing. Her mother apologized to the guests—John Wendell among them—while her father rose from the table, tossing down his napkin. "Excuse me."

Playing the doting father, he led her to the study. He was wearing an elegant three-piece suit, his tie loosened, shirt slightly wrinkled from a long day. When she was a little girl, she'd thought him the most handsome man in the world. Now he looked older and less princelike. "What is it?"

As if he didn't know. "Is Owen going to face charges?"

"No," he said, after a pause. "His statements match up with yours and the accomplices. The evidence supports his story."

"Then why did you threaten him and warn him away from me?"

"I only want the best for you, *mija.*"

"What makes you so sure he's not it?"

"He's so…damaged."

"And that makes him unworthy?"

"It makes him unpredictable."

"Bullshit," she said, crossing her arms over her chest.

"There are two types of heroes," he said sadly. "Any military leader will tell you this. There are men who take risks because they're brave and self-sacrificing. And there are men who do it because they have psychological issues."

Her eyes narrowed. "Psychological issues?"

"Personality disorders are common after traumatic experiences."

"He doesn't have a personality disorder, but I'm starting to wonder if you do."

"He's unstable."

She shook her head, annoyed. "You don't know him like I do."

"Every infatuated girl says that."

"I'm not a girl, Dad. I'm twenty-three years old, and I'm a mother."

"You're a caretaker. You want to save him."

"He saved *me,*" she said, her fist to her heart.

"And you're mistaking gratitude for deeper feelings."

"Don't tell me how I feel!"

His brows rose at her outburst. "I've worked very hard to get where I am, to build a better life for my family. I've given you the best of everything. Of course I don't want to see you throw yourself away on a man of such little consequence."

His words were so insulting, her jaw dropped open. "How dare you judge him like that? Being poor isn't a personality disorder or an indication of faulty character. You also came from nothing, remember?"

"I didn't rob a liquor store or shoot a handful of people."

"That's not fair and you know it. Owen had a tough

childhood, and he got in trouble as a teenager, but he's a good person. He's strong. He's that first type of hero."

"He's a convicted felon. It's an embarrassment."

"Like my pregnancy?"

He dragged a hand down his face, not answering.

Penny realized that she'd encouraged her father's overzealous behavior, to some extent. She'd been too dependent on him, too accepting of his interference. She'd brought shame upon their family by having a child out of wedlock. When her father welcomed her return with open arms, she'd been relieved. He *had* given her everything.

But now it was time for her to stand on her own. Next to Owen.

"What happened to accountability and rugged individualism and pulling yourself up by your bootstraps?" she asked, throwing his own words back at him. "Owen has come a long way, and he's going to make something of himself. He epitomizes the American ideals you emphasize, but you give him a handout to get rid of him?"

He stared at her for a moment. "I didn't know you listened to my speeches."

"I listen. I just don't agree with you."

"At least you understand well enough to form an opinion. Raven disagrees with me just to be contrary. And Leslie agrees to be…agreeable."

Penny nodded, knowing this was true.

"The check is a token of my appreciation, not a

handout. It's also an apology of sorts. I regret what I said about bringing charges against his mother."

"You threatened his mother," she said, stunned.

"He didn't tell you that?"

"No. I can't believe you'd stoop so low."

"I went too far," he admitted. "Will he accept my offer?"

"I have no idea. I opened your letter while he was asleep and came right here."

He examined her disheveled appearance, aware that she'd been in bed with Owen. She didn't care if he thought her behavior was loose or immoral. "Why don't you consider this a test? If he cashes the check and leaves, it wasn't meant to be between the two of you."

She pointed her finger at him. "If it's a test, then you're the one who failed. Owen deserves better, but I think he'll take your shady deal. And when he moves to Mendocino, I'll go with him."

His mouth went slack. Clearly he hadn't realized how serious she was about their relationship.

"Cruz and I will go with him."

"You can't."

"Watch me."

"Why are you so determined to ruin your life?"

"Why are you so determined to control it?"

"Because you're exceptional, Penny. You have that spark. Everyone sees it. When your face is on the television screen, people stop to look. They *listen* to you, and they believe you. You remind me of myself at your age."

"I have to live my own life, Dad."

"You want to be a firefighter's wife, living paycheck to paycheck?"

She was frustrated with him for assuming that Owen would drag her down, and for suggesting that she was wasting herself if she didn't marry someone rich and important. "You don't get it. I love him, and that's what really matters."

He grasped her upper arm. "Please."

She shook loose. "I don't need your support or your approval. If you can't wish me well, stand aside."

"I wish you the moon and the stars."

The words brought tears to her eyes. He used to say that when he'd tucked her in at night. But she wasn't his little girl anymore.

"Don't go," he said. "I love you and Cruz."

She glanced back at him, weakening. "You're one of the reasons Owen fought so hard against the kidnappers, you know."

"What do you mean?"

"He thought they might attempt to assassinate you during the money exchange."

Her father took a moment to absorb this information.

"I'm sorry about the campaign," she said with sincerity. "But you can't blame Owen for what his brother did. He risked his life to protect our family."

He met her gaze. "You've really got your heart set on him?"

"Yes. I don't care how much money he makes. I love him, and he's wonderful with Cruz. We'll be happy."

His struggle to come to terms with this—another loss—was plain to see.

She put her arms around him, resting her head on his shoulder. "I'm an adult now. I need you to let me make my own decisions."

"Will you stay in L.A.?"

"Not if Owen leaves."

"He was an exemplary employee," her father said begrudgingly.

"I know."

"I'll give him a letter of reference. I'm sure he can get an entry-level firefighter position here in the city."

She smiled up at him, pleased. "Thank you."

He patted her head. "Let's not mention this to your mother."

CHAPTER TWENTY-SIX

OWEN WOKE TO SILENCE.

He knew Penny wasn't beside him before he opened his eyes. Lifting his head, he stretched out his arm anyway, grabbing the extra pillow. He brought it to his face and inhaled, trying to detect the scent of her hair. She'd turned off the light before she left, perhaps just minutes ago. It was still early.

Rising, he pulled on his jeans. His apartment felt empty without her, unnaturally quiet. The opened letter on the coffee table snagged his attention. Curious, he sat down on the couch and studied its contents.

Mendocino County Fire Department? Wow.

It was a good opportunity. He'd done firefighter training in that area during the last year of his prison sentence. The small, low-security facility he'd been transferred to after the earthquake—thanks to Sandoval—had a work-release program. Owen had completed two semesters of college classes there, also.

The employment offer boasted a generous starting wage and excellent benefits. He couldn't accept it now, of course. He wasn't supposed to leave L.A. until the investigation wrapped. Even after that, moving away from everyone he loved would be difficult. It was an eight-hour drive to Mendocino. If he lived that far north, he couldn't attend Jamie's soccer games or spend weekends with Penny.

With a frown, he read the accompanying note and found the check. He swore under his breath, aware that Penny had seen this.

She thought he was accepting a bribe from her father.

Folding the papers, he stood and shoved them into his back pocket. He put on a shirt and shoes in a hurry, grabbing his phone and keys on this way out the door.

There was a text from Janelle: How was it, stud? ;)

Ignoring the playful message, he climbed behind the wheel and tried to call Penny. She didn't answer. His anxiety built as he drove from his low-end Torrance neighborhood to her father's sprawling mansion in Rancho Palos Verdes. The security code had been changed, so he waited outside for someone to buzz him in.

When the gates opened, he drove forward, parking between a Rolls Royce and a Jaguar. Her parents had guests over. Christ.

Penny's mother let him in. She was an attractive woman with pale skin and a cloud of fluffy brown hair. Her cool reserve never wavered. She was wearing a simple black evening gown with a strand of pearls.

"How are you?" she asked.

"Getting along," he said.

"I'm very sorry about your brother."

"Thank you."

"Thank *you,* for bringing Penny and Cruz back to us safely."

"Just doing my job."

She smiled at his answer. "Penny's in the study with her father, and I left guests in the dining room. Do you mind waiting here?"

"Not at all."

As he watched her glide across the room, he felt a pang of guilt over the scene he was about to make. Penny's mother probably didn't know what her husband was up to. Before she reached the door to the study, Penny came out with her father. She looked as if she'd been crying. Sandoval wore a slightly guilty expression.

With shaking hands, Owen removed the letter from his pocket. He ripped up the check, the note and the employment offer, letting the pieces flutter to the floor. Penny's mother stared at the mess he'd made, clutching her pearls. Sandoval appeared impatient, as if he didn't have time for such theatrics.

Penny clapped a hand over her mouth.

"I don't want anything from your father," Owen said, determined to say his piece. "I just want you, Penny."

She came forward with a little cry. He met her halfway, feeling a rush of pleasure as she threw her arms around his neck. Maybe her faith in him had never wavered.

When he released her, Owen noticed their audience. He'd embraced Penny outside of the open dining room doors. John Wendell, the current GOP candidate, was among her parents' guests. His views were even more conservative than Sandoval's. The reactions around the table ranged from titillated to disapproving.

Penny's mother gave them a helpless glance.

"Why don't you two take this outside?" Sandoval suggested. "We're in the middle of dessert."

Penny nodded, grasping Owen's hand. "Have a wonderful evening."

"You too, dear," her mother said.

Penny led him out the door and into the lighted garden, where they could talk privately.

Owen wasn't sure what was going on. He hadn't expected her parents to be so calm. He'd interrupted their dinner party, thrown trash on the floor and practically groped their daughter in front of esteemed guests.

"You didn't have to tear up the check," she said. "It would have served him right if you'd cashed it."

"I was so worried," he said, awestruck. "I thought you'd left angry."

"Not with you."

Although he was curious about her conversation with her father, he wanted to get a few things off his chest before he chickened out. He'd come here to win her back by baring his soul to her, laying his heart on the line. The scene hadn't gone the way he'd planned it, but she deserved to know how he felt. "I reflected on what you said. About what I have to offer you, and what you can offer me."

She smiled, cocking her head to one side. "You did?"

"Yes."

"What did you come up with?"

He faltered, unsure where to start. "Before I went to prison, I considered myself weak. But now I see that I was just…caring. My father couldn't beat that out of me, but getting locked up did. It made me hard, inside and out. I was in survival mode for years. I did a lot of things I'm not proud of."

She squeezed his hand, encouraging him.

"When I first saw you…this feeling of hope awoke inside me. My entire existence had been like the dark cavern we were trapped in. You were the crack of light in the corner, that tempting glimpse of freedom."

Her eyes filled with tears.

"I lost myself, for a long time. You brought me back. When I looked at you, I remembered the good in the world, the beauty and the sweetness. I remembered the decent person I'd once been."

"Owen," she whispered, biting her lip.

"It hurts to feel, after you've grown numb. It's easier to disconnect, to not care. That's one of the reasons I stayed away. Being with you…hurt."

"Does it still hurt?"

"No." He experienced moments of discomfort, and he might always have flashbacks, but he'd grown accustomed to human contact. Loving her had transformed him. Touching her had boosted his confidence. Through her, he'd rediscovered the best parts of himself. "I'm not numb anymore. You revived me."

"So that's what I have to offer you? Yourself?"

"Is that...enough?"

She cupped her hands around his face. "It's everything."

He swallowed hard, aware that he'd just thrown away a solid job opportunity. "I'll find work in L.A...."

With a soft laugh, she dropped her hands.

"What?"

"I interrupted my father's dinner party to tell him that Cruz and I were moving to Mendocino with you."

"You didn't."

"I did."

"What did he say?"

"He said he'd give you a reference letter for the LAFD."

"Really?"

She nodded. "The police aren't going to bring charges against you or your mother. I'm so sorry he threatened you with that. I think the stress of the kidnapping and the campaign brought out the worst in him."

Owen understood. Her father had always been controlling and overprotective. He couldn't blame Sandoval for trying to keep a tattooed ex-con out of his family. Owen might never win her father's approval, but he vowed to make Penny happy.

"I told him to back off," she continued, twining her arms around his neck. "He won't bother you anymore."

"You're amazing."

"Yes."

"I'll treat you right."

"I know."

"I love you, Penny."

"I love you, too."

"I want to marry you someday."

"When?" she asked in a teasing voice.

"Whenever you like."

"Let's get jobs first, and maybe live together for a while."

"Okay."

"That check you tore up would pay for a pretty lavish wedding."

He chuckled at her mischievous expression. She was so smart and beautiful and bright. His heart ached at the sight of her.

"Kiss me," she said.

Owen knew a good thing when he had it. Without a second's hesitation, he lowered his mouth to hers, kissing her soundly. As if he was made for her, and they were meant to be. Always and forever.

* * * * *

Don't miss Jill Sorenson's
next romantic suspense
in the AFTERSHOCK *series,*

BACKWOODS
Coming June 2014 only from
Harlequin HQN Books!

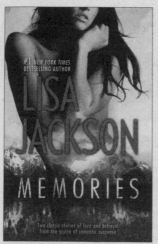

Three sizzling tales from
New York Times **bestselling author**

LORI FOSTER

USA TODAY **bestselling author**

CHRISTIE RIDGWAY

and *USA TODAY* **bestselling author**

VICTORIA DAHL

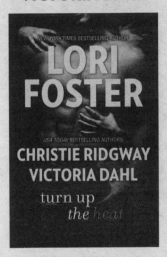

Available now, wherever books are sold!

Be sure to connect with us at:

Harlequin.com/Newsletters

Facebook.com/HarlequinBooks

Twitter.com/HarlequinBooks

www.Harlequin.com

REQUEST YOUR FREE BOOKS!

2 FREE NOVELS
FROM THE SUSPENSE COLLECTION
PLUS 2 FREE GIFTS!

YES! Please send me 2 FREE novels from the Suspense Collection and my 2 FREE gifts (gifts are worth about $10). After receiving them, if I don't wish to receive any more books, I can return the shipping statement marked "cancel." If I don't cancel, I will receive 4 brand-new novels every month and be billed just $6.24 per book in the U.S. or $6.74 per book in Canada. That's a savings of at least 22% off the cover price. It's quite a bargain! Shipping and handling is just 50¢ per book in the U.S. and 75¢ per book in Canada.* I understand that accepting the 2 free books and gifts places me under no obligation to buy anything. I can always return a shipment and cancel at any time. Even if I never buy another book, the two free books and gifts are mine to keep forever.

191/391 MDN F4XN

Name	(PLEASE PRINT)	

Address		Apt. #

City	State/Prov.	Zip/Postal Code

Signature (if under 18, a parent or guardian must sign)

Mail to the Harlequin® Reader Service:
IN U.S.A.: P.O. Box 1867, Buffalo, NY 14240-1867
IN CANADA: P.O. Box 609, Fort Erie, Ontario L2A 5X3

Want to try two free books from another line?
Call 1-800-873-8635 or visit www.ReaderService.com.

* Terms and prices subject to change without notice. Prices do not include applicable taxes. Sales tax applicable in N.Y. Canadian residents will be charged applicable taxes. Offer not valid in Quebec. This offer is limited to one order per household. Not valid for current subscribers to the Suspense Collection or the Romance/Suspense Collection. All orders subject to credit approval. Credit or debit balances in a customer's account(s) may be offset by any other outstanding balance owed by or to the customer. Please allow 4 to 6 weeks for delivery. Offer available while quantities last.

Your Privacy—The Harlequin® Reader Service is committed to protecting your privacy. Our Privacy Policy is available online at www.ReaderService.com or upon request from the Harlequin Reader Service.

We make a portion of our mailing list available to reputable third parties that offer products we believe may interest you. If you prefer that we not exchange your name with third parties, or if you wish to clarify or modify your communication preferences, please visit us at www.ReaderService.com/consumerchoice or write to us at Harlequin Reader Service Preference Service, P.O. Box 9062, Buffalo, NY 14269. Include your complete name and address.